Lavender Girl

Lavender Girl

Ann Cliff

ROBERT HALE · LONDON

ISBN 978-0-7090-8714-4

Robert Hale Limited
Clerkenwell House
Clerkenwell Green
London EC1R 0HT

www.halebooks.com

2 4 6 8 10 9 7 5 3

Typeset in 11½/14½pt Janson
by Derek Doyle & Associates, Shaw Heath
Printed and bound in Great Britain
by the MPG Books Group, Bodmin and King's Lynn

ONE

Masham, Yorkshire 1895

'Greenwood! Where have you been? I had thought you would be here earlier. I am so pleased you have deigned to come at last; my daughter is extremely ill and my nerves are quite gone to pieces; I really need a nurse, but you will have to do; I expected you to come at once.'

Alice suppressed a sigh and smoothed her print dress. She had been warned that this could be difficult. 'I am sorry, Mrs Grey, I came as soon as I could.' Better not explain that she had been helping to round up somebody's stray sheep; that would not sound professional.

'What can you do, Greenwood? Have you been properly trained? You were recommended by Dr Dent as a qualified lady's-maid, but at times he can be too charitable, I feel. Not critical enough.' Mrs Grey's aristocratic nose elevated slightly; she would obviously have to make up for the lack of criticism. 'We have had such a difficult time ever since we came back from India, and we do so miss our Indian servants. The people of Masham do not know the meaning of deference.' The accent was clipped and the voice was loud and hard.

'I worked as a lady's-maid, Mrs Grey, and I was trained in service up at the castle.' That should impress the old trout. 'Since my husband died I have taken temporary work.' Better not mention that she'd studied herbs, and grew them herself. And better, too, to speak quietly, in the modified Yorkshire she had learned to use with the employing classes.

'I suppose you'll have to do.' Mrs Grey looked her up and down and Alice stood still to be inspected, keeping her face straight with difficulty. Her soft dark hair was neatly tied back under a little cap and she wore quiet shoes; that should get her past the inspection. Since Tom died five years ago, she had worked in a variety of houses and found great differences in the way she was treated, but a family from India was a new experience. If it was deference they wanted, she would see what she could do, but her sense of the ridiculous would have to be held down.

'You may have to bite your tongue a little,' Dr Dent had warned her with a smile. 'Indian army families are used to command.' It was only for a few days; surely she could put up with the woman for a day or two. Alice followed Mrs Grey up the wide oak staircase to the sickroom. Birchwood Hall was imposing; through the long windows she could see the carefully raked gravel drive, backed by tall hedges that hid the old sandstone house from the rest of the world. You would hardly guess that the busy little town of Masham was just beyond those hedges.

On the landing Mrs Grey paused for breath, her enormous bosom heaving; it wouldn't do to think how her bulk must have suffered from the heat in India. Alice drew in her own breath sharply, as she came face to face with a tiger. Of course, she had known there would be tiger skin rugs with evil yellow eyes, strange eastern paintings and ivory ornaments, and here they were, just as the old doctor had described. He had also said that Colonel Grey and his wife were opposites. 'She's loquacious and he's laconic, if you know what that means.' Alice had looked up the words, so as to be prepared. Laconic just about described her strong and silent brother-in-law, Gabriel Turner, and loquacious spoke for itself.

'I am not strong, you see, and all this is too much for me, I really do not know what we shall do, the dear child is supposed to be recovered from influenza, but she gets worse every day instead of better and I give her all the care I can. I spend positively all my time with Laura, no thought for anything else.' Mrs Grey opened the bedroom door.

The woman was deafening. And here was the young lady, lying still and straight in the big bed with her eyes closed. The mother must be got out of the way first, before anything could be done. Politely, Alice took Mrs Grey by the elbow and steered her out of the room in a firm grip. 'Come along, madam, let me take you downstairs and ask someone to make you a cup of tea. You must be worn out! Your daughter is safe with me for a while.'

Surprisingly, Mrs Grey allowed herself to be led away, talking as she went. 'You must understand that the child is only eighteen and very delicate; we are so worried that the change of climate has affected the lungs, you know, but Dr Dent seemed to think that she is recovered, whether he really knows—'

Back in the room, it seemed very quiet once Mrs Grey had gone. A pair of large blue eyes peered out from the bedclothes. 'I know you. You're the lavender girl!' Laura's voice was high and plaintive.

'Yes, miss.' There was no point in denying it. Some people in town thought it was disreputable to sell herbs, but it was a fact of Alice's life, and she actually liked it.

'You're just a hawker! You sell on a common market stall, I've seen you, you are not a lady's maid at all. I was promised a proper lady's maid! What are you doing here? Get out of my room!' The voice rose to a crescendo.

This little bully was in need of care, and she seemed young for her age. The bedclothes were rumpled, the fire was smoking into the room and the air was stale. 'Now, Miss Grey, I can make you more comfortable. Just let me try,' Alice said quietly.

The patient's eyelashes fluttered. 'Bring me a glass of water, Greenwood.' There was a glass of water on a table, out of Laura's reach, with a film of dust on the surface. It was easy to find a bathroom with huge brass taps, wash the glass and fill it again. How long was Laura going to need a personal maid? A week would be too long in this place. Surely they would only expect Alice to stay until they could find someone who suited them better.

'That took you a long time, Greenwood. You'll have to move faster, if you want to work here.' Miss Grey flopped back on the bed, not realizing how close she was to getting a glass of cold water in her face.

Bite your tongue, get on with the work and thank goodness this is not a permanent position. Alice opened the window, made up the fire and smoothed the sheets. There were clothes lying across a chair and she brushed them gently and put them away; some hems were torn and there was a general look of neglect about Miss Grey's wardrobe. She was certainly in need of a maid.

When the room was set to rights, Alice looked at the tousled young lady. 'Would you like me to brush your hair? It might make you feel better.' Miss Grey's long blonde hair was brushed and her rather hot face and hands sponged, all in silence. Alice sat down by the bed. This was a pretty young woman, a storybook princess with big blue eyes and a rosebud mouth, but flushed and not very happy. There were several watercolours on the walls and a stack of bright flower paintings beside an easel. Perhaps the young lady dabbled in art. 'Did you paint the flowers? They're very pretty.'

Alice's remark was ignored. 'Servants don't sit down, Greenwood. Whoever trained you?' The beautiful eyes had a hard stare.

Alice folded her arms and tried not to laugh. 'I am sure you have been quite ill, Miss Grey. I have been asked to look after you, and you may call me Alice. Now . . . would you like some soup?' It was well past lunchtime, but there was no sign of a meal. Let's hope the cook had some soup.

Laura Grey smiled faintly. 'Mama says we must be firm with

the servants . . . yes, I will take a little soup.' She stared again. 'Why do you sell lavender?'

'I grow herbs, for part of my living.' Alice stopped at the door, on her way to fetch the food. 'I am a widow, you see, Miss Grey.' But Laura had lost interest; her head was turned away.

By the end of the day, Alice had persuaded Mrs Grey that she was much too ill to look after her daughter. There were maids to bring the patient what she needed and Alice would come back the next morning, sheep permitting, although she kept that bit to herself; no need to say that her sister was married to a farmer, and that Alice liked to help them when she could. She looked at the paintings again and tried to get Laura to talk about them, but the girl's eyes remained closed. Laura would not now respond to anyone. It was as though she wanted to be ill.

At the end of a week, apart from being cooler and cleaner, Miss Grey was just as before. The fever had retreated but she still lay in bed, making no effort to do anything for herself. Even lying down, she managed to look down her nose at Alice, but the temporary maid showed amazing patience, even surprising herself. This brat needed a quick slap, but maids never slapped.

'See if you can get her to talk,' suggested the doctor, speaking to Alice on the landing.

'But Mama says we don't talk to the servants,' Alice said demurely.

Dr Dent grinned. 'But doctor says we must be firm with the patients. She's not a happy lass, is she? She should be out of bed and running about by now, you know. If she doesn't move soon, I know of a good laxative that will do the trick.' He dived into his bag and produced a bottle. 'Only as a last resort, mind.'

Alice went back into Laura's room and decided to be bracing. 'Now, Miss Grey, we've done all we can to make you comfortable. It's for you to decide that you want to get up and be well again. Lying in bed is not good for you! And the weather is warm, it's nearly summer.' How anybody could stay indoors when there were spring blossoms everywhere, she couldn't ima-

9

gine. Laura's big windows should have tempted her out to the hall gardens and beyond, where the Grey's estate sloped away from the town, down towards the river.

Alice had thought of going back into service as a maid to some lady, but she loved independence: being outdoors in the herb garden was so much more appealing than working all day in overheated rooms. If she could tempt this girl outside, it would be good for both of them.

'Why bother?' The long lashes were down on the girl's cheeks.

'You look much better with your eyes open; they're a nice blue. Well then, if you're really ill, you have to swallow some of this drastic medicine from the doctor!' Alice towered over the bed, suddenly fearsome. The bottle she held was black and menacing.

Laura gave a shriek and disappeared under the sheet. Then she peeped out and glared at Alice. 'My old nanny in India never treated me like this! Till the day she died, she never said a cross word! Are you trying to kill me?'

'Of course,' the maid said cheerfully. 'Then you can go to heaven and join that wonderful old nanny.'

The girl burst into tears and sobbed pitifully. Alice thought it might do her good. After a few minutes, she patted Laura on the shoulder. 'Well, miss, what's the problem? Why are you so downhearted? Surely a pretty young lady like you has nothing to worry about?'

Laura looked at Alice as thought she saw her for the first time. 'I'm so unhappy! Alice, what shall I do?' This was the real person at last.

Mrs Grey bustled in on a wave of perfume and Laura sank down the bed again. 'Young woman, it is time you pulled yourself together and made an effort. Mr Paterson . . . Bradley is here to see you and I will give you half an hour to get dressed and come downstairs, we have had enough of this nonsense, the influenza is quite gone away and there is no reason why you should not behave in a civilized fashion, especially with your future husband waiting. He is in the study with your father now, discussing the marriage settlement . . . you should not keep your fiancé waiting; when I was a young girl we knew how to behave, we knew what was good for us and we knew a good marriage was essential, how my poor nerves will stand all this—'

'Excuse me, Mrs Grey.' Alice knew that she should never interrupt, and only speak when she was spoken to, but rules were made to be broken. 'Miss Grey is too ill at present to go downstairs.' Laura gave a realistic groan. 'She needs absolute peace and quiet; Dr Dent's orders.'

The doctor's name convinced her, and Mama retreated, still scolding. There was a blessed silence. It was strange how you could feel protective of your lady, so soon.

After a few minutes Laura opened her eyes. 'Thank you,' she said faintly.

Alice laughed and shook her head. 'You're not that sick, are you? I can see the problem now. Why don't you want to marry Mr Paterson?'

There was no reply. A maid came in with an offering of red roses, but Laura would not look at them.

It was a day or two before Alice was able to ask the question again. Dr Dent had established that Miss Grey was low in spirits and needed a companion, for at least one day a week; someone to accompany her on walks, someone sensible like Mrs Greenwood, the lady's maid. Mrs Grey was far too 'delicate' to walk with her daughter. So Alice was given the job, and a quiet routine was established. Alice was thankful that they had managed to get the lass out of bed at last. She wouldn't look at her paints and pencils; she showed no interest in anything, but she was out of bed.

Eventually, on one of their walks Laura admitted her trouble. Swallowing hard, she whispered as though afraid her mother might hear. 'Mr P. is so old, Alice! He's old enough to be my father; he's been married before and his wife died. I don't want to be an old man's plaything . . . and I feel, sort of, repelled. I don't know what it is. I hate him to touch me.'

Alice considered this as they walked slowly along a field path by the river. 'Well, Miss, age doesn't matter too much, you know. He seems a pleasant man – kind and thoughtful, from what I've heard of him. Everybody in Masham speaks well of Mr Paterson.' And patient, too, she thought. He's been waiting to see Laura for at least three weeks. But she was only eighteen . . . and young for her age, as far as could be judged. 'They say he has a beautiful old house, more like a mansion—'

Laura was not listening; she was looking at a horse and rider in the distance. 'That's my father's new estate manager. I do like the green of England, so different . . . India was dry and dusty. I missed India, but I could bear it until they said I had to marry Mr Paterson—' the high voice tailed away. 'Adam Burns is the manager, he came down from Scotland to work here.'

Alice looked at her keenly and thought that there was a flicker of interest in the blue eyes. 'Do you like him, then, Miss?'

Laura turned away. 'I've never actually met him. Father sees him at the farm office, but he's never invited to our house. He's not quite socially acceptable, you know, to be invited to dinner.'

Looking after Laura was a strain; it was good to cross the cobbles of the marketplace after a day at the Hall and to go home down the lane, to the tiny cottage and the peace of the herb garden. In the days after Tom had been lost at sea, sister Ruby had come to the rescue. She had never reproached Alice for going off and marrying a sailor. The marriage had been short; when Tom was drowned, there was no money left. Alice had refused to live in the farmhouse with Ruby, Gabriel and their little son, but she was desperate. Their cottage in Whitby had been rented, and with no income to pay the rent, she was homeless. Then her quiet brother-in-law, Gabriel, had found a solution. 'We've a right little shepherd's cottage on back lane, with a big garth. We could fettle it for you, lass.'

'Fettling' the old stone house had consisted of relaying the floors, plastering some of the walls and painting the doors and windows. Freshly whitewashed, the little house suited Alice very well. There was just room for her furniture, she made a few rag rugs for the stone floors and, best of all, she was able to replant her precious herbs, kept in pots since she moved from her old home.

Herbs had always been a part of her life, but now they were essential, to help her to earn a living. Since coming back to Masham she had taken a market stall and sold as many as she could. It helped to believe in what you sold, and it was good to know that the plants you grew had many uses. As a lady's maid, Alice had made creams and lotions and knew the remedy for a sore throat or the toothache. In Laura's case, she had sprinkled lavender water in the room, and a few drops of lavender oil had eased the girl's aching head. But there was no herb that could make her happy with the future she could not escape, and Laura was not happy.

'Good evening. I believe you are Miss Grey's maid. She is in good hands, I know. And how is the dear girl today?' Alice found her way down the drive blocked one evening by a large and handsome man. She remembered seeing Bradley Paterson about the town; he owned half the moor, folks said, and was good to his farm tenants. And this was Laura's suitor, the lucky girl!

'Not well enough for visitors yet, Dr Dent says!' Alice lied firmly. Laura was improving and they had walked by the river, through the gardens and down to the ornamental lake, but she would not see Mr Paterson, and Alice couldn't talk her into it.

The tall man shrugged. 'Next week, perhaps? I should be in Masham again then.' Seen in classic profile, Mr Paterson looked like a girl's dream husband: dark and vital, glowing with health and, so they said, with a healthy fortune, too. He pulled on his driving gloves and then turned to Alice again. 'This illness – she is taking too long to recover—' he stopped short and turned away. There was nothing that Alice could say.

It was a surprise to see Mr Paterson again a few minutes later, when Alice passed her sister's house on the way to the cottage. Ruby and Gabriel were both deep in talk with the landowner, so she waved to them and passed on.

After her evening meal Alice went into the herb garden. Evening was quite a good time to pick herbs for sale, after the heat of the day. She was busy with bunches of rosemary when the gate clicked and Ruby came up the flagged path, her face alight with news. 'Guess what, Alice! No, you can't guess. Gabriel might be going to buy some more land! Mr Paterson offered Ellershaw to him at a decent price, and of course Gabriel's uncle left him that money, last year. And Mr Paterson had heard that we were looking round ... he's such a pleasant gentleman. Talked to us like equals.'

Alice carefully tied raffia round a bunch of rosemary. It was Tuesday night; there would be a market tomorrow and she had a lot to get through. 'What would you do with another farm, Ruby? It sounds like more work for you both.'

Ruby smiled and looked down at her hands. 'Well, we're not after more work. I make as much butter and cheese as I can, already.' Ruby's dairy supplied most of the town; she was small and thin, a hard worker and on the wrong side of forty. 'Nay, Alice, I reckon we'd be best to let the farm to a good tenant. Money's safer in land, Gabriel always says, but it's three mile off, too far away to run with our land. I came over to see if you'd like to go with us tomorrow, to have a look round.'

It wasn't often that Alice had an afternoon off, a break from the work that took up most of the time. 'If I can sell the herbs early, I'll come,' she promised. 'A ride out to Ellershaw would be grand, if it doesn't rain.'

The next morning there was a heavy dew and the spiders' webs in Alice's garden hung like jewelled necklaces, sparkling in the sun. She took a deep breath as a light breeze brought her the scent of apple blossom. A little bit of the joy of life was coming back with the approaching summer, a joy that had been missing since she had lived a widow's life.

On the market stall, the baskets of herbs soon sold and so did a few early radishes and carrots, made up into bunches. Alice often advised people to eat fresh produce from the garden, but most of her customers were sceptical. 'Garden stuff is nowt but water; you need a good suet pudding to build you up,' one woman argued. By noon everything was gone, even the pots of salve, and Alice took her empty baskets home with money in her pocket.

A warm day in May was perfect for an outing and Alice felt light-hearted as she stepped up into Gabriel's trap that afternoon, although as they passed the Hall the thought of young Laura lounging indoors was depressing. They clopped up the moor road out of Masham and little Bobby wriggled with excitement, watching the road carefully. 'Can I drive, father?' he asked wistfully, but at six, he had no hope of taking the reins.

'Wait till you're a bit older, son.'

The retiring tenant of Ellershaw, Joe Bainbridge, was in his seventies, bowed from years of heavy work, but still cheerful. Alice thought that he'd looked after the place well, remembering sagging barns and ruined walls on some of the moorland farms.

'Well, Mr Paterson's a grand landlord,' Bainbridge explained. 'He allus found me some timber to mend fences and he put a new roof on yon old barn. Better nor most landlords, he was. You could do worse than buy Ellershaw, lad.'

There, Laura – a testimonial to your suitor. Would she be impressed?

Gabriel was grave as ever behind his beard, but Alice sensed that a lot of calculations were going on. 'Could do with a bit of drainage,' he said quietly to the women.

Alice looked away across the slopes to the high intake, a piece of land claimed from the moor, with its wide views, and down to the well-watered meadows in the bottom land. A skylark went up into the blue, soaring and singing as if carried up by the song. Suddenly she heard voices and saw two men on horses coming towards them.

Bradley Paterson jumped off his big black horse. 'Glad to see you wasted no time in looking it over,' he said to Gabriel. 'We're taking a short cut over to one of my other farms . . . this is Mr Adam Burns. He's the colonel's estate manager, of course, but I have borrowed him for consultations.' So this was the young man that Laura had pointed out on their walk. Alice looked at Gabriel, who had been known to question the wisdom of hiring farm and estate managers with a lot of book learning and no common sense, especially when they came from far off.

The young man had also dismounted. His coppery hair shone in the sunshine and his blue eyes were merry. 'I'm very pleased to meet you all.' He shook hands gravely with Bobby, who was delighted to be noticed. Adam Burns had a pleasant voice with a slight Scottish accent, and a friendly manner.

Alice had by now got used to her frequent changes of status; when she was with Ruby and Gabriel they were of the yeoman farmer class, but on her own she was a domestic servant and inclined to be overlooked. And a stallholder on the market was even lower on the social scale. People talked to each other in front of Alice's stall as though she wasn't there; she was invisible.

Gabriel was soon talking easily to the stranger, who was clever enough to ask his opinion on a number of local farming matters. Gabriel had picked up the habit of reading and was quite well informed and Ruby was behind him, very ambitious and wanting them to succeed.

Paterson stood and listened with a slight smile. Soon he led the way to the shade of an oak tree, then drew Gabriel away to show him the boundaries of the farm. 'Stay there in the shade; we won't be long,' he suggested. Alice and Ruby sat on the grass and Adam Burns flopped down beside them after tying up the horses.

'I've only been here for a few weeks,' Adam admitted in answer to a question from Ruby, who liked to think she knew everybody for miles around. 'Yes, I'm enjoying the job. It's good that the colonel gives me a free hand.'

So this was the socially unacceptable young man that Laura had mentioned; what a nice lad he seemed. Alice pointed out various landmarks that could be seen from this high pasture. The white towers of York Minster gleamed in the sun across the Vale of York; and to the east they could see the blue line of moors in the East Riding that lay between them and the North Sea.

Adam said eventually, 'You work for the colonel too, I believe. I have seen you with Miss Grey.' His sky-blue eyes were very direct. 'She seems . . . very sad. I sometimes wonder how young ladies manage their time, with no life's work to get interested in – until they marry, ye ken.'

Alice thought of mentioning that Laura was almost engaged to be married, but her training had taught her discretion. The less said the better about your employers' business. And Laura wasn't formally engaged, not yet.

TWO

'She's not improving, Doctor. Miss Grey is very low in spirits.'

Alice had crossed the square to the surgery the next week after another day spent with a listless Laura, who could not be roused to do anything. She was not sure whether the girl was physically unwell, or whether the problem was in her mind. Either way, the doctor should know what to do.

'Try to get her to eat liver, or black pudding – something with iron in it. She may be anaemic,' suggested Dr Dent briskly. 'And do you grow dill? You could give her dill water, for the digestion.'

'Yes, I used to make dill water for my ladies when I was in service. It sells well on the stall, for babies. Gripe water, they ask for. 'But' – better not laugh – 'I don't think Miss Grey will try black pudding, it's too . . . common. What about the low spirits? She cries a lot.' Anybody would cry with that mother, but what could you do?

The doctor shook his head. 'We can't alter her circumstances, can we?'

In the time after Tom died, there had been comfort in a little black cat, a stray that seemed even more unfortunate than Alice herself. It had made the cottage its home and Sooty was still there, a small presence, keeping her company. 'How about a little cat or a dog, Doctor?'

This was not medicine, but the doctor seemed to think it was a good idea. 'Jacob knows somebody who breeds little dogs,' he said thoughtfully. 'Go and have a talk to him. A dog might give Miss Grey something else to think about.'

After a startled glance at the doctor, Alice ventured into the stable yard. Folks did not tangle lightly with Jacob Fowler, the doctor's right-hand man; in fact, they often wondered why poor Dr Dent put up with such a surly brute. But the horses liked him, folks said, so that was probably the reason. Jacob was grooming a horse and talking to it softly when she looked into the stable. As she hesitated, the doctor crossed the yard. 'Go in, he won't bite you!' he encouraged.

'I'm not so sure about that,' Alice called back and then bit her lip as she realized that Jacob had heard her.

'Go away, woman. I don't need your herbs and I don't want your company.' Jacob turned back to the horse and the silly creature nuzzled him as though he were a normal, friendly groom.

It was wise to ignore his rudeness, but she made sure that she was between Jacob and the door for a swift escape if need be; you never knew what he might do. He'd thrown a bucket of oats at a travelling salesman last year. Alice had heard all about it on the marketplace, the great information exchange centre of the town, as she stood behind her stall.

'Well, and what sort of herbs do you use with horses? I suppose you'll have some recipes.' She had never needed to speak to the man before, but he evidently knew who she was. Everybody in Masham knew Alice as the herb woman, or the lavender girl.

Jacob didn't look at her, but the brushing stopped and he seemed to be thinking. He was a lean man, weatherbeaten, with a cap pulled down to hide his eyes. The firm mouth and chin were fixed in a grim expression. 'Aye, there's plenty. Comfrey, for one – the boss got some salve off your stall last year and it healed up this young fella's cuts, right enough. But it was too sticky.' He ran his fingers over some slight scars on the horse's dappled grey chest.

Coming from Jacob, this was high praise. 'That's good. I

always like to hear success stories. What about – have you ever used comfrey for broken wind?' Alice tried a slight smile.

The groom shook his head. 'Nay, but I've heard tell of a horse over Thorpe way that could hardlins walk about, broken winded, it was. It seems they fed it comfrey and they managed to heal up the lungs, somehow. Do you – have you got the leaves, if ever we was to need 'em?'

This was developing more like a normal conversation. 'In the summer, I have fresh leaves, but they die down in winter. It's a bit too early yet, another few weeks. I save the dried leaves though, and you could sprinkle them on the feed.'

Jacob resumed the grooming. 'Aye, well, I've no use for owt of the sort right now. Good day.' He turned his back on Alice.

It was time to come to the point. 'Dr Dent said you might know of a litter of puppies that's for sale. What breed are they? I know a young lady who – well, I think she'd like a small dog, but not a large breed.'

This time, Jacob took off his cap with an irritable movement, revealing a much younger and fresher face than suited his gloomy expression. He was far too young to be so sour, only a year or two older than Alice. His eyes were grey and thoughtful, but not evil, as she had half expected. 'Boss said that, did he? Expects me to go traipsing all over country looking for daft dogs for stuck-up young women? As if I've nowt better to do.' He settled the cap back on his head.

Alice turned to go; she would ask someone else about the litter of puppies. 'Never mind, sorry I asked. I would hate to make you even more bad-tempered than you are already.'

To her surprise, Jacob smiled and the grim expression vanished just for a moment, before he frowned again. 'Forward hussy, you are.' Then he growled, 'I'll see what can be done.'

Two days later, Alice was crossing the square when Jacob appeared, leading a small dog on a string. 'I've got that dog you wanted, unless you've changed your mind. Women often change their minds.' Jacob handed over the string to her with a bad grace, not looking at Alice. 'I want nowt to do with brass, pay for it yourself And you make sure it's looked after right, or it'll be the worse for you,' he threatened. The groom picked up the tiny pup and held it by the scruff of the neck, dangling in the air.

'Don't, that's cruel!' The puppy dared to lick his face; animals seemed to have no sense of danger. Alice took the little white scrap gently; it felt soft and warm.

'Rubbish, woman, that's all you know. Bitches carry their pups like that, they don't mind a bit. Now get on, I've got work to do, even if you haven't.'

The happy, bouncing little pup was one of a litter that had been weaned on to solid food and were ready to make their own way in the world. A shop in Silver Street had a dog collar and lead; luckily, Laura was due for a visit that afternoon. At the Hall, the dog was shut in an empty stable and then it was time to persuade Laura to come out for a walk.

By now it was May and shearing time at the Hall farm, taking advantage of the good weather. They could hear bleating from the sheep pens, as the farm men moved the ewes up to the shearing stand. Laura reluctantly came out under a pink parasol, saying she didn't want to go far. Her pretty muslin dress contrasted with Alice's simple grey cotton, but over Laura there hung a dark cloud that you could almost touch. 'My kid shoes are dirty, Alice,' she said petulantly, kicking at a stone. 'Why didn't you clean them?'

'I will clean them with milk, Miss Grey, after your walk,' Alice said firmly. There was no point in cleaning them twice. 'Lady's-maiding', as her sister called it, could be a very demanding job.

Down at the stables, the puppy was beginning to squeak for attention. Laura looked over the stable door. 'Oh, a dog.' Her tone was flat, lifeless. This was not promising.

Alice went in and picked up the wriggling little scrap and it seemed to laugh at her. 'What a sweet little dog! Let's take him for a walk!' she enthused, and watched as a faint smile flitted over Laura's face.

The puppy was bright enough for all with them; it was irresistible. After a while, Laura picked it up, and remarked that it didn't smell. Alice led the walk at a smart pace; at least Laura would be tired after her walk, even though she might not be cheerful. She made sure that they kept well clear of the sheep, because manure stains would be almost impossible to remove from skirts and shoes.

By the end of the afternoon, Laura had walked for several miles and had fallen in love with the puppy, which she had carried herself when it was tired. She had also met Adam Burns. When they came back from the lake, the puppy ran ahead and clambered all over the copper-haired young man, who was supervizing the end of the shearing. Burns smiled, picked up the dog and returned it to Laura. 'Is he yours, Miss Grey? Better keep him on the lead; the men might throw him in the sheep dip!'

Laura, with more animation than Alice had ever seen, laughed. 'I want to keep it. Is there a kennel available? Would you, Mr Burns? – I believe you are our new farm manager; how do you do – be able to arrange it? I will have to ask Papa, of course.'

'I commend your taste, Miss Grey. You've chosen a Scottish breed.' Adam agreed that it would be no trouble to find a kennel, or have one made. It was all most polite, and so very unlike Laura at her childish worst.

Whether it was the Scottish dog or the Scottish gentleman, Alice couldn't be sure, but Miss Grey improved in health and temper after this. Laura visited the puppy's home, paid for him and inspected his parents. The dog's owners, a retired couple, told Alice afterwards about the visit: what a lovely young girl she was, so sweet and so polite. Of course, she had to consult Mr Burns about the dog's diet and general management, and he was happy to oblige. He lent her a book about dogs and how to train them. They agreed that Hamish would be a good name for the little fellow, who seemed to be equally devoted to Miss Grey and Mr Burns, and very fond of Alice.

Adam's comment, that day at Ellershaw, had hit the mark; Laura's biggest problem was boredom. But what could she do? The girl had no friends, having been brought here from India. She was not allowed to mix with local people, of course, but was expected to marry soon and join Mr Paterson's social circle, which no doubt would seem to her to be a group of stuffy businessmen. She had been too miserable to look at the flower paintings. She was bored with embroidery and didn't want to take an interest in the Hall farm because of the smell of sheep. Laura was beginning to rely on Alice as a steadying influence, but she wouldn't be cured until she could take some control herself . . . and accept the idea of marriage to Bradley Paterson, who seemed to be charming and would probably adore her.

Adam Burns cut his hand rather badly one day when Alice was at the Hall, and asked her to dress it. She wiped it with a little lavender oil on a clean cloth, and Mr Burns smiled. 'This is why they call you the lavender girl.'

'It seems to keep wounds from going bad. I often use it, and Dr Dent approves.'

It was, of course, forbidden to talk about employers and their problems, but somehow their conversation came round to Laura. Adam Burns seemed to be interested in Laura. He had heard that Miss Grey was artistic and he knew that her father wanted some landscape design in order to enlarge the grounds. Was she at all interested in landscapes, he wondered. 'I can arrange the practical details, get the men to plant trees, make paths and so on. I thought of a bridge over the end of the lake. But I'm not very artistic, I'm afraid. We need some imagination – and the colonel admits he's no good. He arranges everything in straight lines, like soldiers on parade.' Adam winced as the dressing was placed over the wound.

'It would be good for Miss Grey, if we could get her to take on a project such as landscape design,' Alice agreed as she tied the bandage in place. 'She needs something to raise her spirits.'

'You think so, too.' Adam Burns looked at her. 'Do you think you could persuade Miss Grey to take an interest? For her own good, of course?'

Later that day on their walk, Alice turned the conversation to Laura's art, and then to the composition of landscapes. 'What would you know about it, Alice?' Laura asked, with her usual hauteur. At least she didn't call her 'Greenwood' any more, and 'market girl' was seldom mentioned.

'I learned something about landscaping when I was a lady's maid, Miss,' Alice explained quietly. 'My lady took a great interest in the work and they had alleys, follies, surprise views, all planned to look natural.' She looked round her, at the sweep of the land down to the river. 'The grounds here were planned long ago, of course, but they could be extended. It's rather like composing a picture. Have a think about it, Miss Laura. I expect the colonel might be interested in improvements, if you were to ask him.'

Two weeks went by before Alice was able to visit Laura again, but the next time she went to the Hall she found a very different girl. Laura was ready to go out when Alice arrived; she was waiting with a sketch pad under her arm. 'I talked to him about it, and Papa has asked me to look at the gardens and grounds, to see where they can be extended.' Happily she told Alice how Papa had driven her to see Studley Park and other famous gardens, to gather ideas for their own estate. She had found books about the eighteenth-century landscape gardeners in the library – a collection that Papa had acquired when he bought the Hall. It was all most interesting, and Laura felt that as an artist she could make a contribution to the plans. 'And so, each time we go for a walk, I must make sketches and plan vistas . . . there is a great deal to consider.'

The colonel was a strange man, it seemed to Alice; immovable about his daughter's marriage, but happy to indulge her in small things. Laura was to consult Mr Burns about the practical details of the plan. Laura had managed to bring herself to see her suitor once, and now seemed to have put Mr Paterson out of her mind, which was easier while he was in Bradford on business.

Mercifully, Mrs Grey decided on most days that it was too cold to go out, and wondered at length why they could not have resided at Brighton, or somewhere warmer on the south coast. 'It must seem cold, after India, madam,' said Alice politely. They were enjoying a good summer for Masham, long sunny days for the most part, with a few refreshing showers, and at times a cool breeze blowing from the moors above the town.

With a light heart, Alice took the lead with Hamish; she had not realized how worried she'd been until the young lady's spirits improved. They set out on a walk to look at the park, which ran from the back of the town across undulating land to the river. On the far bank she could see workers in the fields, and she felt rather guilty to be paid for such light work as looking after Laura. But the Greys had decided that Alice was responsible for their daughter's improvement and Laura herself had asked for Alice. Paterson was still there in the background, of course, but perhaps Laura would get used to the idea in time.

Laura spoke about a ha-ha, and this had to be explained to Alice, who admitted that she could not see why a dip in the ground would keep sheep in the park from invading the gardens. 'You don't know our local sheep; they're very good at getting into where they oughtn't,' Alice argued from bitter experience. It was a constant battle to keep Gabriel's sheep out of her herb garden, especially when grass was short in early spring.

They sat on a bank so that Laura could sketch in the positions of existing trees, as a foundation for her vista. 'If I were a man,' the artist said as she worked, 'I would take up a career and become a famous artist, or a landscape designer—' She broke off and looked at Alice, sitting so quietly beside her. 'What would you do, if you were a man, Alice?' She sometimes made an effort, these days, to see the servants as real people.

Alice considered. 'If I were a man, or even a woman with money, I would buy a little farm and grow useful plants, and employ girls to dry the herbs and pack them, and start a little business.' There had been no time to dream of what she would like to do. For the last few years, Alice was proud that she had managed to survive. Early thoughts of the future had included children, but now that she was thirty and a widow, that dream had slipped away. 'I would really like to own a still, so that I could distil lavender oil, but nobody does that round here. The lavender growers are all in the south of England, and in France, I think. It would be good to have a proper still-room, and make up perfumes and hand creams for ladies. And I'd make more salve for the poor farm women's hands, that get so rough with hard work—'

Alice stopped speaking as Adam came up on a chestnut horse almost the same colour as his hair; both horse and rider shone in the sun and Alice was almost dazzled. What would be the effect on young Laura? Adam beamed at them and dismounted, patting little Hamish on the head. Blushing a little, Laura showed her sketches and then looked at the sheep grazing under the trees. 'I suppose we couldn't have deer in the park, could we? So picturesque, Mr Burns! I saw deer at Studley with Papa, and thought how beautiful they were.'

The manager looked across the park. 'I think we would need more land for a deer herd, Miss Laura. They browse, you know, and that means they eat tree foliage. They could damage the trees in a wee park like this one. Relatively wee, of course!' he added hurriedly. There was a twinkle in his eye.

They talked for some time about how the park could be made more interesting, and Laura showed that she had some ideas and an artistic eye. Maybe in the future she would be able to take up some form of design? But then, there was always the marriage – and Laura would have little chance to develop her own interests. Adam evidently was thinking on the same lines. 'You could learn more from a school of landscape design, Miss Laura, if you're interested. Ladies are now accepted and there is a college for young women in Berkshire, where they tell me there are classes in botany and so on.'

It was all very pleasant, but was the young man just a bit keen on Laura? Did Adam Burns now have an interest in Miss Grey, and her fortune? Masham folks said he was the son of a poor crofter who had scrimped and saved to send his son to university. It was surprising how much you could pick up from the gossip round the market stalls. And in that case, a good marriage might bring him an estate of his own in due course. Young Laura was an only child and would inherit the estate. Mr Burns didn't look as though he wanted to go back to a crofter's life.

A few weeks later Adam Burns asked Laura – with Alice of course, as was proper – to meet him in the park. He had made a point of meeting Laura on a Tuesday, when Alice was with her. The sketching and planning had been enjoyable and the project seemed to be making progress. Walking along with the puppy at their heels, Laura and Alice were absorbed in plans and were surprised when Adam emerged suddenly from a little wood. 'What do you think of the new arrivals?'

There, in the distant park, was a group of cattle; shaggy, with long horns, posing dramatically with lifted heads, sniffing the breeze like their wild ancestors. Laura clasped her hands. 'Just like a painting! Oh Adam, how lovely! We have Scottish cattle, here in Masham!' She blushed and looked away. 'Thank you so much, Mr Burns. They are delightful, just what the park needs for interest. I suppose Papa knows about them?'

Adam looked pleased. 'They are Highland cattle, Miss Laura. The colonel had them sent down by rail. I'm glad you like them.'

Alice was helping out in her sister's dairy one day when the doctor called. While she was wrapping his cheese, Dr Dent gave a big sigh. 'I suppose you couldn't spare a few days to work for my wife, Alice? Our maid has gone off to care for her sick mother, and my wife hasn't found anyone to help. Actually, what she said was, "James, bring someone home tonight or I'm leaving." But I don't suppose she meant it.'

Mrs Emily Dent was feared by some as being very forthright, but not by Alice, who smiled at the thought. She could imagine working with Mrs Dent. And a spell in the doctor's house, even though it would be spent mainly in the kitchen, would earn some welcome shillings. 'Yes, Doctor, I could help – so long as I can have some time for the herbs, and the market stall on Wednesdays.' And a day for Laura. Before the doctor could thank her, she added, 'I can manage only the odd day, I'm afraid. But I'm not sure about your man, Fowler. I should think he might have something to say, and I don't want to have to fight all the time. I like a quiet life, Doctor.' The thought of working in the same household with a misery like that was not pleasant; Jacob had made it quite clear that he despised the lavender girl.

'The housekeeping has nothing to do with Jacob,' Dr Dent said briskly. 'Dammit, he doesn't rule the roost! In any case, he's a decent fellow, underneath. It's just that he's had . . . a difficult life.' He shook his silver head sadly.

With Dr Dent, Alice could say what she thought. 'A lot of folks have difficult lives, don't they? You must see a lot of pain and suffering, a lot of loss.' Dr Dent had tried to save her father, and failed. He knew that Alice had felt the pain of loss.

'I agree, and Jacob should get over it. I think it must be three years now since it happened.' He looked at Alice and she was conscious of her grubby apron. 'I suppose I might as well tell you, Alice. He was working on a farm and became very, very attached to the farmer's daughter. They were engaged to be married, and Jacob had been promised a farm to rent. But another man managed to talk his own way into the farm Jacob wanted, and worse, he married the girl very quickly, before she had time to think about it.' He turned for the door. 'I believe they are very happy, but poor Jacob has never been the same since. It's a sad business.'

Clean and tidy in a print dress and apron, Alice started work the next day in the doctor's kitchen. Mrs Dent did not issue strict orders, but told her what was needed and then wisely left her to it and went to do something upstairs. 'It's more of a house-keeper's role, Alice,' she said comfortably. 'I'm grateful for any help you can give me, and I know you're not a kitchen maid. We will share the work, but there's too much for me on my own.'

Peeling potatoes at the sink, the new 'housekeeper' enjoyed the change of scene. But not for long; the kitchen door burst open and Jacob appeared, a dressed chicken in his hand. He laid it on the table and then he saw Alice. 'What the heck are you doing here, woman?' As a greeting, it was predictable. Jacob, looking shocked, went out muttering 'Women!' and banged the door. Just outside he met the doctor, and Alice could hear the conversation through the open window. She had a feeling that Jacob meant her to hear it.

'No good'll come of it, you'll see! That lass will have no sense, she'll be under our feet. I don't hold with it, Doctor. She's a market girl, that one, bound to be as common as muck and as rough as they come. Not fit company for the missis, if you know what I mean. She swears something horrid, I'm sure. Maybe I'll ask about, there's some good girls in the villages that could come in, I'll be bound.'

'Thank you, Jacob, that will be helpful. Alice can only spare us a few days. But I am sure you're wrong, you know. You will find that Mrs Greenwood is a refined sort of woman.' The doctor's quiet voice was soothing.

The only answer to that was a loud snort as Jacob went about his business.

THREE

'Surely you've heard of Felix Mayo? Everybody has heard of Felix Mayo. He's a portrait painter, you know. He has painted royalty. And Papa has asked him to paint my portrait, before . . .' Laura faltered. 'Before I leave home to get married.' Laura had seemed to be less violently opposed to the marriage since she had taken an interest in landscaping, but Alice thought that this might be because Mr Paterson was still away in Bradford.

'Very good, miss.'

'I shall wear my lavender dress, I think. Papa says he likes it the best. Now, Alice, you're the lavender girl – can you bring me some lavender, for a spray? For the portrait?'

This was another interest for Laura, and Alice felt bound to encourage her. 'Where will you be painted? In the drawing room, with a vase of flowers?'

Laura smiled, a more frequent event these days. She was quite likeable now that the spoiled, imperious miss was gradually being replaced by a real person, even if that person was some-what immature. 'No . . . not indoors. Down by the lake, so I can have my little Hamish there. I am not sure whether the artist will want to include a dog, but at least Hamish can play, and chase ducks off the lake.'

And annoy Papa or the keepers if they see him. Alice turned as a man came towards them as they sat in the garden, a slender young man with long dark hair and a floppy tie. He must be the artist; he was certainly dressed for the part.

Laura looked at Alice. 'I suggested he comes on Tuesdays . . . so we don't have to put up with Mama.' Alice could imagine only too well a sitting in the drawing-room, with Mrs Grey in full flow. Mr Mayo had been spared that, at least.

Fortunately the sun was shining on the day the artist arrived, and a small breeze ruffled the surface of the lake. The light was bright but not glaring, the park looked its best and the cattle posed just as they should.

Mr Mayo may have looked artistic, but he was brisk and businesslike. 'Please sit here, Miss Grey, so that you have the lake and the grove of silver birches behind you. Thank you. Now, the hat obscures your face too much . . . but leave it on until I have sketched the outline. We must not allow the sun to spoil your complexion.'

Alice smiled to herself; she never covered her face from the sun these days, and Laura had said once that she looked like a gypsy. But then, she was not a lady.

Mr Mayo made friends with Hamish the terrier at the start, so that the dog accepted him and played happily, while Laura sat as still as she could. Talking while he worked to set Laura at ease, Felix Mayo confessed that he studied the market for art most carefully. 'Rural scenes are popular in London.' He deftly pencilled in the trees. 'And of course, Highland scenes, since our dear Queen has set a fashion for everything Scottish. We should perhaps include your little dog in the portrait, to be quite in fashion. And I see you have Highland cattle down there, under the oaks, just the latest thing. No doubt your father would allow me to paint them?'

Enjoying the occasion, Laura told him of her plans for improvements to the park and gardens. 'Would you – I would very much appreciate your opinion, Mr Mayo, if you would care to look at my sketches. Alice, would you fetch the plans from the house? I think they are in the drawing-room.'

Hamish trotted along beside Alice as she went back to the house; she was as glad as he was of the chance to stretch her legs.

This sitting about and chaperoning was not what she was used to, although it was pleasant to sit down for a while, as a change from scrubbing out the doctor's kitchen.

As Alice went back to the lake, the dog bounded ahead. She was at the top of the bank and about to take the path down to the water, when a figure on horseback came towards them from the park. The horse was big and black. It was Mr Paterson.

At that moment, Felix Mayo stood back and looked at his work. He said something to Laura and then he moved forward, gently put his hand under her chin and tipped her head up and slightly to the right. His other hand adjusted the set of her shoulders.

Paterson spurred his horse forward and shouted hoarsely. Then he jumped off the horse, strode up to Mayo and punched him hard on the chin. The artist went down and Paterson seemed inclined to hit him again, but little Hamish intervened. The terrier fastened his teeth into Paterson's leg in a most determined way, growling and shaking his head as though killing a rat.

The sitting was at an end; Alice ran down the path to the lake. Paterson was shaking with rage, and after a few minutes Laura managed to control her dog. Mayo sat up groggily and Alice helped him to his feet. 'Come and sit down, sir.'

Felix Mayo looked at Paterson with a neutral expression. 'Whatever your reason for that attack, it is your affair. I refuse to indulge in violence.' He turned his back on the bigger man.

Paterson looked round at the chairs, the easel and the artist's gear. 'I apologize,' he said stiffly. 'I came home early from Bradford and I was looking forward to seeing my future fiancée. It was a shock to see her with another man., laying hands on her in a most intimate manner.' He mopped his bleeding leg with a handkerchief. Hamish, held by Laura, growled when Paterson approached her.

'This is Felix Mayo, Mr Paterson,' said Laura helpfully.

'The artist? My dear fellow, I had no idea! I believe we have met . . . I attended your Leeds exhibition last year.' Paterson held out his hand, but Mayo ignored it. Paterson bit his lip and then turned to Laura, who handed the dog to Alice and then allowed her suitor to take her hand. 'You must understand that I have very strong feelings,' Patterson said urgently to Laura in a low voice. 'Especially where you are concerned, my dearest. I was too hasty, of course, but you must forgive me. I have ruined your sitting. And how lovely you look in that dress!'

'I will go now, and continue the portrait another day.' Mayo stood up, still looking very white. Laura went over to him.

'My father will give you a glass of brandy. I am sorry this has happened, Mr Mayo.' She put her hand on his arm and Paterson looked grim.

The artist smiled faintly and packed up his easel. 'I must say, this is not the way that sittings are usually conducted.' He walked off slowly and Alice felt compelled to help him.

'Let me carry the easel, sir. Is your jaw – damaged?'

Mayo felt his face gingerly. 'It's bruised, of course, but I don't think anything is broken. What an uncouth man! I wish Miss Grey joy of her marriage . . . I only hope he treats her well. I shall say as much, to the colonel.'

Alice saw the artist to the gate; he declined to go into the house, saying he wanted to go home. Meanwhile, Paterson had limped back to the house, with Hamish growling at him all the way. Surprisingly, Laura seemed almost impressed by the show of aggression. 'Do come into the drawing-room for tea, Mr Paterson. The grooms will see to the horse, and will you take Hamish too, Alice?'

When Paterson had gone, Laura laughed. 'He was jealous! Bradley was jealous! He must think something of me, after all.'

'I think you will be quite well suited to each other, once you get used to the idea.' Alice hoped she was right. 'He seems to be a devoted gentleman. You will have a pleasant life, a beautiful house, travel – a lot of women would envy you.'

Laura frowned a little, as though Alice had gone too far. 'But he's so old! And Hamish doesn't like him. I wonder why? I thought Hamish liked everybody. Oh, dear . . . I really don't want to marry him, Alice.'

The weather turned wet and the next sitting for Laura's portrait was held indoors. Alice sat quietly at the back of the big drawing-room, sewing for Laura and remembering her days as a lady's maid. The endless mending, cleaning muddy shoes, braid-ing hair . . . no, she did not want to go back to service. She had enjoyed making skin lotions and perfumes, but she was still working with the scents of herbs and selling some of her lotions on the market stall; not so respectable, but much freer, more enjoyable.

Laura and the artist were in the big bay window, making the most of the light. Felix Mayo was animated, chatting to Laura about her plans for a garden colour scheme. He seemed to have recovered from the attack.

'The gardeners jumble up all the colours in the herbaceous borders, just like a cottage garden. Now, I would like a scheme for each season. I think that cool blues, violets and whites would look pretty in summer, at different heights, of course.' Laura considered, looking out into the wet garden and the despised riot of colour, where broad borders flanked the lawns.

'Very pretty. I would add some plants with silver leaves, Miss Laura. I tried to get that sort of colour into the portrait—' Mayo broke off rather nervously as the door opened, as though he expected Paterson to walk in.

Colonel Grey, white-haired, straight-backed and yellow of face, strode forward and shook the artist's hand. He looked briefly at the painting. 'Excellent.' Then he cleared his throat. 'Er – Mayo, I was very sorry to hear of the unfortunate incident the other day. It seems that my future son-in-law is rather too impetuous.'

Mayo was cool and self-possessed. 'The incident is forgotten, Colonel. It arose from a mistake.'

'You are very generous to say so. I would like to double the fee, for Laura's portrait; it is the least I can do.' The bitten-off words sounded very little like an apology.

Mayo looked amused. 'Not at all. Thank you, sir, but I am enjoying the commission and I dare to hope that the result will be good. Miss Laura has plenty of character, as well as youthful beauty.'

Miss Laura blushed as her father said quickly, 'I hope she hasn't got too much character. Young ladies should be meek and dutiful, preparing to be good wives and mothers.' He glared at his daughter.

Alice jabbed impatiently at her sewing, unnoticed at the back of the room. Women are people, not just bargaining pieces . . . why were the Greys so set on this marriage? Probably because they thought that young Laura did not know her own mind and had to be told what was good for her, poor lass.

When the sitting was finished, Alice went quietly up to look at the painting. Laura's delicate blonde beauty was echoed by the graceful silver birches in the background, but there was a hint of mischief in the slight smile. The eyes had a thoughtful look. Mayo had somehow managed to spot the strong personality, and then brought it out in the painting. The artist stood beside her. 'Do you like it?'

Alice nodded. 'How did you do it, sir?'

'It was when I got her to talk about her plans for the park. Miss Laura is an interesting person – I tried to capture that.'

As soon as the artist packed up his brushes, Mrs Grey sailed into the drawing-room, rustling in dark-red silk. A maid brought in a tray of coffee and biscuits, which Alice handed round. Laura sat beside her mother on a sofa. There was polite conversation for a few minutes, but Laura was uneasy. When the empty cups were being collected, she said quietly, 'Mama, I would like to take drawing lessons from Mr Mayo, if you agree.'

Her mother looked across, but the artist was carrying the easel out into the hall. 'Laura, are you bent on upsetting Mr Paterson? You know that Bradley was most angry when he saw you together and we could hardly cancel the commission, but I will be relieved when it is over; why you should want to continue the acquaintance I do not know; he may be a successful artist, but what is his background? And in any case, Mr Mayo lives in London, does he not?'

'Yes, Mama, but Mr Mayo has rented a house in Masham for the summer. He has commissions at the castle.' Laura paused to allow this to sink in. 'The suggestion was made by His Lordship, I believe – two or three young ladies could be taught drawing – by one of the most successful artists of the day. We could meet at the Mechanics' Institute near the Town Hall; it would be most convenient. I would so like to take up art again, and there will never be another chance.'

Mrs Grey interrupted angrily. 'Your father and I will not allow anything to upset Mr Paterson, and your marriage arrangements; I absolutely forbid it, so pray do not ask again, Laura. I half suspect that Mayo has designs on you; he probably thinks of making a good marriage; artists are usually short of money and to suggest drawing lessons was most improper; I shall make sure that I am present for the rest of your sittings and I hope the painting is finished as soon as may be. Now go upstairs and change your dress; that muslin is too thin for such a cold day and we have not yet adjusted to this dreadful climate.'

'Yes, Mama.' Laura went to the door and looked at Alice, who followed like a dutiful maid. They walked upstairs in silence and Alice helped the girl to find warmer clothes. Tears were not far away, but Laura bit them back.

'Let's go into the garden, Miss Laura, the rain has stopped. Fresh air will do you good. Here's a dark skirt, and you could wear the riding boots.' Alice was bent on a diversion; anything was better than one of Laura's bad moods.

Laura brightened when they reached the walled kitchen garden, where the sun was now struggling though. Steam was rising from the hotbeds and each plant glistened with gilded raindrops. Lance Drake, the head gardener, a solid man with a grey beard, was tying up climbing beans at the far side. 'Do you know Mr Drake? You should talk to him about the plans, let him know what you're thinking of doing.' The poor man could well resent a replanning of the garden, done without his knowledge. Why didn't employers remember that servants sometimes have an opinion of their own?

'Mama says not to talk to the servants,' Laura whispered.

Alice laughed in spite of herself. 'If you talk to Mr Drake, you will learn a great deal. He's been here for twenty years and he doesn't mind answering questions. He has helped me several times with advice about growing herbs.'

Laura gave Alice a thoughtful look, but she took the hint. Walking up to the gardener she said, 'Mr Drake, will you show me the greenhouses? I am trying to learn about gardening . . . but I don't know where to start.'

'Certainly, Miss Laura.' Drake smiled with pleasure. He led the way to where several large glasshouses stood against the high garden wall, facing south. Alice was enchanted. Under the glass was another world, warm and green. Young grapes hung in clusters from the roof, the air was soft and full of the scent of growing things. Lemons like yellow lanterns peeped from among glossy, dark green leaves and there were other exotic plants; it would be good to learn their names and uses.

After two hours together, Laura and Mr Drake were on the way to becoming allies and the girl had a new interest; she would not only design gardens, but learn about the plants in them as well. 'You must get your hands dirty if you're to be a gardener, Miss,' Drake said firmly.

'Mama won't like it, though.' Laura looked at Alice, who said nothing. Mama would not be happy until Laura was safely locked up with Mr Paterson, but meanwhile, why should she not enjoy the garden? There were no lurking artists here, only Mr Drake, two or three under-gardeners, and a boy.

'We should take Hamish for a walk; he's been tied up all day.' Alice always remembered the dog, but she wondered how much exercise he got on the other days of the week. So they left the gardens and went down to the stables, where Hamish now had a splendid kennel to himself and a couple of canine friends, sheepdogs who worked with the shepherds. As Alice slipped on the dog's lead, Adam Burns came up to them. Fresh-faced and smiling, the farm manager looked pleased to see Laura.

Miss Grey was full of her new knowledge and enthusiastic about Mr Drake. 'When we have planned the vistas, Mr Drake will grow the shrubs and trees for us, or know where to get them . . . he knows so much!' She dropped her voice. 'Oh, Mr Burns, the people one employs are so different here! Our Indian servants – well, they have the caste system of course, they keep their heads down and say nothing. It was a different culture, different food . . . the warmth and the hothouse brought it all back to me.' She stopped and blushed, as though suddenly remembering that Mr Burns was one of the people one employs.

Alice watched them. It was a pity about Mr Burns's humble Scottish background, and the poor crofter father. If he had been Laura's social equal, things would have been interesting. Burns laughed. 'There's a lot of wisdom to be learned from talking to ordinary folk, I agree. Look, Miss Laura, I have some acorns here. Would you like to try to grow them? Drake will give you some pots.' He led the way into his office in the stable yard and foraged in a cupboard.

There was more trouble for Laura that day; on their return from the walk with Hamish, Adam came out of the office to meet them. 'Mrs Grey has come here to look for you, Miss Laura.' He tactfully disappeared into the stables.

Mrs Grey, looking flushed and panting slightly, was sitting in the office.

'There you are, Laura! I never know where to find you! I should have sent one of the servants, if I had known how far I would have to walk. You spend too much time out of doors and your complexion will coarsen dreadfully; I don't know what Mr Paterson will say to all this hoydenish behaviour—'

'We took the dog for a walk, Mama, that was all,' Laura said wearily, all her joy in life gone. 'And Mr Burns gave me some acorns—'

That was the wrong thing to say. Mrs Grey seemed to swell with anger and Alice tried, but failed, to move out of earshot. Outside the office door, the tirade floated past. 'I must say, my girl, that you are very bold and forward for your age. Spending so much time with the servants cannot be good for you and I really feel that it is most unseemly for you to be seen with Mr Burns. We do not invite him to the house; he is not in our social class, of course, but you seem determined to spend time running about with him on these hare-brained schemes for the grounds, schemes which should be left to servants; I shall tell your father that the sooner you are safely married the better; now come back with me to the house at once and take up some occupation that is more ladylike, more becoming to your station; there is some sewing—' Mrs Grey struggled to her feet and started to walk slowly back to the house, but Laura did not follow. She ran back to the kennel with the dog in her arms, tears running down her face, no doubt to get away from that grating voice. Alice followed and saw her run straight into Adam Burns.

'What is it, lassie? We can't have this!' The manager's blue eyes were anxious. 'What has upset you, Miss Laura?'

'My mother.' There was no need to explain.

Burns shook his head and changed the subject. 'Come with me to see the colonel, Miss Laura. I have a proposal for him and you can help, if you like.'

What would Mama say to this? Perhaps Laura could hide behind her father. Alice passed her a clean handkerchief and Laura dried her eyes. She swallowed. 'What's the plan?'

The manager laughed, a pleasant, carefree sound. 'That's better. Come along, and you'll see.'

When they reached the house Dr Dent was just getting into his gig, driven by the sour-faced Jacob. He hopped out again when he saw Laura and greeted her warmly. 'Out in the fresh air, that's the way! You look much better than the last time I visited,

39

Miss Grey. Good day, Mr Burns,' he nodded at the young man. 'I've just paid a visit to the colonel.'

So whatever Laura did, she couldn't please everybody. Alice withdrew slightly, earning a smile from the doctor.

'Please go in, Mr Burns, I'll join you in a minute.' Laura was suddenly decisive. 'I would like a quick word with you, Doctor, if I may. Stay with us, Alice.' The doctor steered her down the drive but Laura was twisting her hands as though ill at ease. 'I wonder whether – Doctor, would you do something for me? Would you tell my parents that I need more time to recover? That I should not have to marry, just yet?'

There was a silence, while Dr Dent looked at Laura carefully. 'What will you gain by a delay, Miss Laura? I gather that you don't want to marry him at all, now or in the future. And that your parents insist – mmm – as many parents do, when they feel it is for their daughter's good.'

Laura shook her head and brushed some mud off her skirt. 'I just thought . . . if it were put off, he might get tired of waiting and find somebody else. He often goes to Bradford and York on business. He will meet plenty of women, I am sure.'

The dear old doctor smiled; he wasn't going to be pompous, after all. 'I can say with truth that you are not yet ready for marriage – that might help. But don't raise your hopes too high, my dear. I should say that Mr Paterson is a most determined man and that the marriage is bound to happen, sooner or later. So' – he moved a little nearer and spoke into Laura's ear – 'take an old man's advice. Don't go falling in love with anyone else; it will only make for unhappiness, you know.'

Laura looked at him in surprise, but the doctor was examining a scratch on the side of his vehicle. Her chin went up. 'If you mean Mr Burns, I am quite aware of the difference in our stations in life. I would really like to stay here in Masham for at least a few years, and work at garden design.'

It was a busy day at the Hall; the next visitor was Bradley Paterson. He rode briskly up the drive and threw his reins to a groom, who leapt to help him. He acknowledged the doctor and strode up to Laura. 'My dear girl!' He took her hand and then swept her up in a hard embrace, and Alice thought she saw a look of panic on Laura's face. The poor girl was being suffocated.

'I want to talk to you, Laura!' Paterson's voice was low and urgent. Alice backed off again, embarrassed.

Dr Dent came up and cleared his throat, and Paterson released Laura. 'Excuse me, Mr Paterson, but there is something I must tell you. I am afraid,' and he dropped his voice, 'that Miss Grey has health problems . . . this is a delicate matter, you understand.' He waved a hand vaguely. Laura stood demurely with downcast eyes and Alice dared not look at her. The doctor had done as he'd been asked. 'Therefore, I would not recommend marriage at present. The young lady needs time to recover.' The quiet voice was full of authority.

Bradley Paterson tapped his riding crop on the side of his boot. 'I am sorry to hear it, and even more sorry that there will be another delay.' His tone was not too sympathetic. He turned to go into the house. 'It is high time we set a firm date. I will tell your father now, Laura, that we will become engaged in February – the fourteenth will be sufficiently romantic, don't you think, my dear? We will arrange the marriage for the end of Lent, just after Easter.'

'Mmm, well, I hope your wish comes true. Goodbye, Miss Laura.' The doctor smiled encouragingly at his young patient. Jacob must have been asleep; the doctor had to dig him in the ribs before the trap moved off down the drive.

Later, when they reached the colonel's office, Alice was invited in too. 'You're interested, Alice, I know,' Laura said with a faint smile. She seemed to need support. The colonel was complaining to Mr Burns about the doctor. 'I ask him about dyspepsia, but his only advice is to eat less curry. We practically live on curry! Ah, there you are, Laura. Now, what's this new project, Burns? Speak up, man!'

Adam spoke up, with a twinkle in his eye. 'I'd like to talk to you about a new cottage on one of the estate farms. Perhaps Miss Grey could help to design it. You may remember, sir, that the worker's cottage at Mickley Bank has fallen down. It's not been used for years, but the tenant, James Gill, wants to put a man in it.'

The colonel nodded. 'I don't see why not. You'd better prepare an estimate of the cost, and perhaps you could have a look at some good examples? I believe the Brayshaw estate have been building lately.'

FOUR

'Can you come quickly, Mrs Dent? I think the doctor's fainted.' Knees shaking, Alice ran back to where the doctor lay on the surgery floor, breathing harshly. Moments before he had been talking to her as she brought in coals for the fire.

As his wife came in, Dr Dent stirred, tried to sit up and then collapsed again. 'Overwork,' Mrs Dent said grimly. 'I told him so, only this morning.'

Eventually the patient was got to bed with the help of Jacob, who seemed a little less surly and quite anxious. With eyes closed, the doctor gave them his diagnosis. 'I'm just tired. Heart going too fast, but nothing to worry about. I will go to sleep.'

Crossing the square on her way home, Alice shivered and drew the shawl closer as the wind whipped dancing leaves along the cobbles. Autumn had come to Masham, along with an outbreak of measles; Dr Dent had been out on his rounds day and night for weeks, trying to save the children. Alice had done what she could to help in the house, hoping that a new maid would soon be found, because the season brought extra work for a 'lavender girl' with herbs to dry and syrups to make for the winter.

They were all worried about little Bobby, Alice's nephew. But the school had been closed on the doctor's advice, and Bobby had escaped the measles, thank goodness. The little lad had been delighted to be kept from school and had spent some days with Gabriel, who was digging drains on the farm they had bought from Paterson; it was safely away from Masham and the risk of infection.

The morning after the doctor's collapse, Alice went to the surgery early. She took up breakfast to him on a tray, and thought how worn he looked. Dr Dent was slim and sprightly, but he was the wrong side of sixty. His patients respected his long experience, but how long could he continue to visit them in all weathers?

'I think you should stay in bed, James,' his wife told him as he sipped the tea.

Dr Dent smiled faintly at Alice. 'I try to get my patients out of bed as soon as possible . . . you tend to feel worse, lying down. I'll come downstairs and give myself a day off, or perhaps half a day. Mrs Hammond's baby is due at any time.'

Mrs Dent followed Alice down to the kitchen. 'It is impossible to get him to rest, I'm afraid. The patients always come first, and lately, there have been too many. I've been thinking half the night, and I've decided that the only answer is to take a holiday, to go right away.' She adjusted the spectacles on her nose and looked at Alice with her mild brown eyes. 'But that would mean getting in a locum, another doctor to look after the practice. There's no one near enough to do that, so we'll have to bring someone in, and let him stay here.' She paused and Alice dreaded what was coming. 'Could you . . . would you be able to spare some time to look after him, Alice? You and Jacob would be able to help him out, with your local knowledge. I think we really need to go away for a month or two.'

'Do you think the doctor will agree, ma'am?'

His wife shook her head sadly. 'He will, if he knows what's good for him. He really does need a rest.'

The other question was, what would the grumpy groom say? Jacob was appalled when this plan was explained to him at a household conference round the kitchen table. Mrs Dent was taking charge of the holiday plans, and had called in Jacob and Alice, to enlist their help. 'We can't do it without your help, both of you.'

'You're going to let some city doctor loose on the patients, poor beggars? I don't believe it. And run horses into the mire? Mark my words, Boss, you'll live to regret it.' The right-hand man did not approve.

'As long as I do live,' the doctor replied drily, smiling benignly at him. 'You can drive him round the parish, Jacob, if you don't trust him with the horses.'

'Honey will throw him off, most likely. And then, you need a proper housekeeper, not a part-time wench who keeps a market stall.' Jacob shot a look of pure dislike at Alice and she glared back. The temperature in the kitchen appeared to drop several degrees. 'What will an off-comer think he's walked into? It's not respectable, that it isn't. A market girl likely doesn't know how to set a table for dinner properly.'

Alice was stung to reply. 'Jacob Fowler, I'll thank you to keep your insults for those that deserve them. Sorry, Mrs Dent, but I am respectable.'

The doctor's wife nodded sympathetically. 'I am sure of it. You've been very well trained, at the castle.' She paused, to let the significance of this sink in, in case Jacob didn't know Alice's background. 'But Jacob is right, the house will need a house-keeper while I am away. Will you be able to live in for those few weeks, Alice?'

It was going back into service again. It meant leaving her cottage and the herb garden, and the little cat, to live at the Dents', and to see miserable old Jacob every day. 'Er—' If she refused, there would be no holiday for the doctor. She would have to fit in the herbs as best she could, and ask Ruby to look after the market stall. 'Well, Mrs Dent, I'd rather you brought in someone else. But if you can't do that, I will stay.'

The horseman got to his feet and put on his cap. 'More's the pity. I'll be off; I've got work to do. I just hope you get a bloke that can stand up to the hill men, that's all, and find his way round in the dark of the moon.'

'With you to lay out the welcome mat, Jacob, the locum will have to be strong-minded from the start. Now look here, both of you. I would rather not impose another doctor on you, but I have no choice. I expect you to behave in a civilized fashion, try to agree, and to give the new man all the help he needs. The patients will depend upon it, and so will we.' Dr Dent looked stern, but why had he let Jacob get away with rudeness for so long?

For the sake of Dr Dent, it was all arranged. Ruby would hire a young girl who had just left school, who could help with the dairy, and she herself would feed Alice's cat and look after the market stall for a few hours on a Wednesday. 'I've been thinking,' her sister said diffidently to Alice one day, 'that we could share the stall, and maybe I could sell butter and eggs, and a bit of cheese.'

'What a good idea!' It was a great relief to think of sharing the stall, especially just now, when Alice would be too busy at the surgery.

It proved difficult to find a doctor who was free to take over the practice for a few weeks, but Alice told Laura of the problem and she was keen to help Dr Dent, who had been so sympathetic to her. So she told her papa, and the colonel organized a locum from Harrogate, in brisk military fashion. It seemed that there was nothing a soldier couldn't arrange.

Some weeks later, Alice was alone in the doctor's house. From her seat beside the fire the kitchen looked orderly, with a gleaming black-leaded stove and sparkling plates on the dresser. She'd been given permission to dry herbs there, and her bunches of sage and mint hung at the back of the room, scenting the air. But the house was uneasy. The new doctor was expected that night: Dr Cecil Fanshawe, an unknown quantity, apart from what Laura had said. He had visited Masham briefly and met Dr Dent, but Alice had been with Laura that day and had not seen him. Jacob was scathing about the man, but that was to be expected. It would be best to keep an open mind. Laura said her father had recommended the doctor for the job. 'He used to ride out on an elephant, in India. He was an army surgeon, you see.' She pulled a little face.

It would have been far easier if the Dents had been there, to help the new doctor to settle in. But Alice understood quite well that Dr Dent had to get away. He had developed a bad cough, and the milder air of the south of England might do him good.

Jacob had taken the trap down to meet the locum off the train in Ripon. Why couldn't he travel on the branch line up to Masham? They were now very late, and no wonder; the night was foggy and the trains would be running late. Alice had looked out earlier and seen the fog swirling across the square, drifting round the church spire. It was a bad night for travellers in an open trap. No doubt the doctor would wear a thick cape, but Jacob seemed to wear the same jacket all the year round. He would have been waiting on Ripon station, growing colder each hour.

Alice looked at the pan of soup bubbling gently on the stove, and made up her mind. Even though Jacob was doing his best to be to be her enemy, she felt sorry for him in his loneliness. Why not take him a little comfort? Quickly, she poured the soup into a jug and went over the yard with a basket to Jacob's house beside the stables, taking a candle with her.

The groom's house was surprisingly neat and clean. The horse brasses on the wall shone with polish, the red tiled floor was damp from washing . . . but it was cold, so cold. The fire was laid ready to light, so Alice lit it and put the soup down beside it to keep warm, with a fresh new loaf. Then she shivered her way back across the yard.

There were noises coming from the direction of the Bruce Arms, the public house in a little square at the back of the doctor's house; there must be something going on there tonight. It was a meeting place for farmers, shepherds and gamekeepers, but they were not usually so noisy. There were lanterns in the yard, and a general air of bustle.

Half an hour went by slowly, but at last Alice heard the horse turn into the stable yard. Relieved, she hurried out with a lantern. A bulky shape huffed and puffed up the path and looked back at Jacob. 'Bring my bags in, man; look sharp!'

Alice hid a smile as Jacob deliberately laid the suitcases on the cobbles, turned back and led Honey away. Horses should come first, of course. It was left to the temporary housekeeper to lug the heavy cases into the house and to welcome the doctor to his new home. 'There's a fire in the drawing-room, sir; you could have supper there. Jacob will carry your cases upstairs to your room in a moment.'

Seen up close, Dr Cecil Fanshawe was short and fat, with round spectacles, and the long driving coat made him look even shorter. His hair and eyes were pale and the eyes looked at a point about a foot above Alice's head as he spoke to her.

'You must be Greenwood. I will start as I mean to go on, and I will take my meals in the dining-room.' The doctor unwound the muffler from his neck, took off the heavy coat and stalked into the dining-room. A blast of cold air met him; the fire was not lit, the room smelled unused and a portrait of Dr Dent's grandfather stared down repressively from a heavy gilt frame. That was strange; the old boy had never seemed to look so grim before. So there would be another fire to light.

'Just as you wish, sir.' Alice stood and looked at him without moving. It was a battle of wills.

Taking a gold watch from his waistcoat pocket, Fanshawe conceded. 'For this evening, I will dine by the fire. But in future, you will light a fire in the dining-room. I intend to live as a gentleman should. Now, where is that infernal groom?' He strode to the door, flung it open and looked out into the night. 'Fowler!' It was like a bull's bellow, but it did not produce Jacob Fowler. Honey would be rubbed down and given her evening feed before they saw Jacob again.

The minutes ticked by, with Fanshawe pacing up and down, refusing to do anything until his luggage was taken up to his room. At length, he opened the door again and looked out into the fog.

At that moment a shrill, piercing scream echoed across the square, as of someone in agony. It died away on a long, shuddering wail. Fanshawe started back for a moment, but then he seemed to pull himself together. 'I must go to help – there has been an accident!'

'That's the Bruce Arms, sir, where all the noise is coming from. Maybe there was a fight.' It was a dreadful sound and perhaps it would be wiser to keep away.

'I am appalled. An inn? A common public house, a few doors from my residence? I was not told of this.' Fanshawe took up a walking stick from the hall stand, holding it like a weapon, and went out into the night.

It was hard to know whether to laugh or cry. Jacob appeared, fuming. 'Greenwood and Fowler!' he snorted. The Dents had always used their Christian names and treated them with respect. 'Where is he?'

'Did you hear the scream? He's gone to find out what's going on. I hope it's not a murder.'

Jacob laughed grimly. 'He'll find out soon enough – it's nowt to worry about. I'll take his bags up and then I'm off home. You're welcome to him.'

A light and fluffy cheese omelette was waiting for the doctor when he returned. Soup was not on the menu, having gone elsewhere. Alice tried to escape to the kitchen, but Fanshawe seemed to want an audience for his indignation. 'Those peasants, those primitive savages – they were killing a pig in the inn yard!' The doctor tucked his napkin under his chin and waved a knife in the air. 'There were even women in the yard, catching the blood in a tub . . . the pig was cut clean in two! The scene was indescribable – a great deal of smoke as well as the fog. They had a fire somewhere, and the lanterns flickered – it was a scene from hell! I have never seen anything like it, not even in India, which was primitive enough.'

Well, that explained all the activity at the Bruce. 'We'll probably get some pork soon,' Alice consoled the doctor. 'Mrs Dent has been saving scraps to feed that pig, and everybody gets a share . . . it's the time of year, you see.'

Fanshawe finished his mouthful of food and laid down his fork. 'But they were enjoying it! And on a dark night . . . surely a butcher should do such a thing in the daytime, and decently out of sight? I never saw such a scene in Harrogate. My mother resides in Harrogate, and I was brought up there. It is not so very far from Masham, I suppose about twenty miles, but I fear this is a very different world, Greeenwood.'

It was no good. If this man was going to compare Masham with Harrogate he would be disappointed, every time. It was impossible to explain how everybody worked together, how pig killing was a community event. How the children learned about where their food came from, in all the rituals of the farming year. 'Would you like some apple pie, sir? And coffee to follow?'

Tucking into a large slice of bread, Fanshawe nodded. 'I would. . . . I am sure to have nightmares after witnessing such a scene.'

'I will put hot bricks in your bed, sir.' If anything did, the pie might keep him awake.

The next morning the fog had gone and Masham went back to normality; but the new doctor was not impressed. 'We are on the edge of desolate moors here, and I expected to be far from polite society, but I had not realized that the town of Masham was so . . . uncouth. More tea, Greenwood. Now, I must tell you that I am accustomed to the very best of food and service.' The man looked as though he had eaten too much food, over a considerable time. There was a pompous pause.

'Yes, sir. Will there be anything more, sir?' There was a great deal to do in the kitchen and not enough time to listen to Dr Fanshawe.

'Certainly, Greenwood. I have not finished. I was about to say that I expect three good meals a day, in the dining-room, with everything set out and the silver in place. For breakfast, I usually take porridge, followed by kippers or ham and eggs, and toast. I take coffee for breakfast . . .' he looked with disdain at the Dents' teapot '. . . and after dinner. I never touch alcohol of any kind, and with lunch, I drink water. I trust you know where to obtain some good ham?'

'Yes, sir. But we can't always get kippers . . . they come from up the coast.' Better not mention the fact that last night's pig killing was necessary before they could have some ham. Of course, it could be bought at the grocer's, but home-cured ham was better than the bought variety.

'For lunch . . .' the doctor continued, listing his preferences in great detail. 'And dinner is important, my main meal. I will be giving some small dinner parties and I expect you to produce some memorable menus.'

How can a lady's maid and herb grower turn herself into a cook? Think about the Dents, this is all for them. The new man would probably settle down, once he found out how much travelling was involved. The Dents rarely gave dinner parties; they didn't have the time. By the time Dr Dent finished evening surgery, all he wanted was a quiet supper and an early night.

Back in the kitchen, it was hard not to panic. Would Alice's plain cooking be good enough for Dr Fanshawe? Jacob came in, grim as usual, with a bucket of potatoes; he was the gardener as well as the groom and it was well to remember to try to be civil to him; fresh vegetables would be very necessary. 'Good morning, Fowler!' She decided to start with a joke – he had never been called by his surname, until last night.

To Alice's surprise, a faint twitch of a smile lit Jacob's stern face. 'Morning, Greenwood. Still here? I'd ha' thought you'd have gone back to the market stall by now.' He went to the door and then turned back, rather awkwardly. 'That soup was grand last night; my word, it was just the thing. I was fair nithered, when we got back from Ripon.'

Jacob was thanking her, almost graciously. Shock made Alice blush and say sternly, 'Bring the jug back; it's wanted.' Then another wave of panic hit her. 'Jacob, I don't know how I'm going to go on, with his meals . . . he says he expects the best.'

'You must start as you mean to go on!' That was what Fanshawe had said. 'Tell him we can give him good, plain local food, but nowt fancy or French. I've got some grand cabbages and sprouts, we've plenty . . . tell you what, lass, I'll tell him all about prize-winning local cheese and the like, and you make sure you get the best cream and eggs.' He sighed. 'When did doctor say he'd be back?'

If Jacob would at least speak to her, produce vegetables and keep Fanshawe out of the house as much as possible, it might be possible to survive. But after a few days, it was not clear how. Dr Fanshawe was tiring; not just the large meals, but his fussing over the laundry, and giving Alice advice all the time. The fact that he knew nothing at all about housekeeping did not deter him for a moment. 'Greenwood, I will thank you to iron my shirts correctly.' It was very hard to take, after a week of this, when the humour of the situation had worn off a little.

Jacob was not impressed. 'He hasn't learned owt about this place; he's over busy telling me how much better things are in Harrogate,' he grumbled. 'He doesn't like the moors, he thinks old farmers are peasants, and some on 'em will be worth more than he is, for sure. No. Doctor Fanshawe likes the big houses, he only wants to talk to patients with plenty of brass, and he likes the military, the colonels and majors. He's a snob, that's what he is; a snob.'

'Greenwood!' Fanshawe strutted out of the dining room one cold evening and Alice paused on her way to the kitchen with the dessert plates. 'Greenwood, I plan to give a small dinner party next week. There will be a full moon, will there not? I will invite Colonel and Mrs Grey, of course; I knew them in India, and their delightful daughter, should she be well enough to come out at night. Miss Laura plays the piano very well, so you must make sure that the instrument is dusted, Greenwood. I will ask her to bring some music.'

'Yes, sir.' This was what Alice had been dreading . . . how many is small?

'Who else? Er . . . the vicar, Mr Carr is a Cambridge man, I believe. He should be good company. And the Scott-Joneses . . . and it would only be polite to invite Dr and Mrs Poole, from Tanfield, my medical colleague . . . Dr Poole has been most helpful.'

What would Jacob say to that? He knew that Daniel Poole was Dr Dent's rival, very keen and successful, and much younger than the Dents. If he was helpful to Fanshawe, it could only mean trouble for the practice.

Fanshawe was looking at Alice, but his mind was now on food. 'Since, as you point out so often, we live so far from the city, you had better tell me what rural delicacies are in season. Nothing too coarse, I trust, no pigs' trotters or sows' ears.' He was not joking. 'So that I can plan a menu.' He licked his lips. 'Now, where are the keys to the wine cellar, Greenwood? I do not drink wine myself, of course, but no doubt my guests would enjoy a glass or two.'

Now that the blow had fallen, the only thing to do was to enjoy the challenge. The guests could have a hearty game soup, made from the remains of a brace of pheasant that the fat little doctor would soon be demolishing. He would want a fish course . . . sometimes, fish came up from Ripon on the railway.

'My brother-in-law Gabriel has some fat geese . . . maybe you could give them roast goose. They're big enough to feed a party.' Or two, rich folks eat a lot. 'Did you say nine, including yourself, sir?'

The next day the doctor was fussing about the dinner again; it was time to tell him, not ask him, about the dessert. 'Apple pie and fresh cream, followed by Wensleydale cheese,' Alice said firmly. There were plenty of good cooking apples in the loft.

'Rather simple, a cottage dish, but . . . your pastry is quite good,' the doctor conceded. 'Are you quite sure, Greenwood, that the geese will be ready? I thought geese were only ready at Christmas. We don't want a green goose.'

'Yes, sir, geese are in season from Michaelmas to New Year.'

FIVE

'The man sits a horse like . . . like a sack of potatoes.' Jacob watched as Dr Fanshawe went out of the yard on Honey, bouncing uncomfortably and with elbows and knees sticking out at odd angles. 'Oh, heck. Keep your heels down, man, and go easy on the old girl's mouth—'

'Miss Grey says he used to ride an elephant,' Alice told him gravely, as she crossed the stable yard to collect the washing.

'I can believe it. He should have stayed in India; he's overhelpless here. When did you say doctor's coming back? I hope he gets back before that man spoils the horse's mouth. Honey's been here for nigh on seven years; she's a grand lass. But half the time, he won't let me drive him in the trap, heaven knows why.'

If only Jacob could appreciate people as he did horses, life would be easier. Best catch him in a mellow mood to ask for a favour. 'We've got to get this dinner party organized. Can you help me to extend the dinner table, please?' It was a huge mahogany affair, too heavy for one person. An extra leaf was to be added to accommodate the guests and, possibly, card tables put up in the drawing-room. They might want to play cards, after dinner.

'You helpless, an all, Greenwood?' But Jacob remembered to come in on the morning of the party, to help with the furniture. Sourness was just a habit with him; if you could get past that, there was a human being underneath, deep down in Jacob's lonely soul.

'I'm nervous, Fowler. What if something goes wrong?' Dr Fanshawe would not be forgiving. The dining-room looked very pleasant, with the table extended and a big bowl of red autumn leaves on a side table. They stood back and admired their work.

Jacob flashed her a look with the grey eyes. 'Nowt'll go wrong. Why should it? And anyway, as Boss would say, it's not life threatening. You should only get worried when there's a real emergency. I hope you do tip the soup down his neck, serve young Cecil right!'

'Are you managing to be polite to him, Fowler?' It was hardly likely.

'Aye, well, I promised Boss. Said I'd keep my big mouth shut, I did. But young Cecil is trying, very trying.'

On the night of the party, Jacob was on duty to look after the guests' horses. The vicar and the colonel's party could walk across the square, but the rest would drive in and then throw their reins to the groom, and forget about the horses until it was time to go home. That left Alice to cope with everything else; Jacob was a dubious ally at best, but a helper would have made things easier. 'Next time, I'll dress him up as a waiter,' she told herself, and smiled at the thought of so much animosity in the dining-room, glowering at the guests.

For the first part of the evening Alice concentrated grimly on the work, although she could see that the guests were enjoying themselves. The soup was a success, thank goodness, and the bread rolls came out of the oven just as they should. The old silver shone in the candle light, the fire burned brightly and the portrait on the wall looked almost benign. Dr Fanshawe fussed over his guests, but left Alice to get on with her job. Things were going well and soon it was time to clear the soup plates.

Dr Poole's fair head was bent attentively towards his host, and they seemed to have a lot to say to each other. What would Dr Dent have thought of their alliance? Mrs Grey was directing her usual stream of talk at Mrs Poole, although she was not always heard. Some of the others discussed fishing, of which Fanshawe was ignorant, but he threw in an opinion even so; Jacob would have been delighted to hear his inane remarks.

Miss Laura had appeared with her parents, looking enchanting in a pretty green dress, but not very happy. Her eyes were kept down and she wore a closed expression, although she flashed a smile at Alice.

By the time the cheese was on the table, the worst was over. As Alice presented the Wensleydale to the host, Mrs Scott-Jones looked across the table at him. 'And how do you find the practice, Dr Fanshawe?'

The fat doctor shook his head. 'Rather run down, I would say. There is a distinct lack of civilized people; many of the patients are cottagers, small farmers and the like. I really do not know how poor Dent makes a living. I shall try to improve the level, by engaging with a better type of family, while I am here. I am sure he will thank me for it.'

The Pooles both smiled; Dr Poole had a habit of poaching rich patients from Dr Dent. In fact, it seemed that Dr Poole was trying to impress Miss Grey, who of course was a firm Dent supporter. In spite of knowing everything, Fanshawe did not seem to notice that, being too preoccupied with the food. Thank goodness the meal had been up to standard; the geese had been fat and the cheese was a beauty, white and crumbly, impressive in its laced-up calico cover. Sister Ruby certainly made a good cheese, although Alice had seldom tasted it. The family usually ate the more economical skimmed-milk cheeses.

The vicar asked whether Miss Grey would oblige them with a piano piece after dinner, and Laura quietly agreed and began to look through her music. They all removed to the drawing-room, where coffee would be served. Walking behind Laura with the coffee pot, Alice noticed that she'd had a pencil and a sheet of paper hidden under the music. She had made a quick sketch of Dr Fanshawe; there were the fat cheeks, the plastered-down hair, the pebble spectacles – and the pompous expression. For a moment, Laura and Alice exchanged a look of understanding. So other people found him pompous too, and that was a comfort, of sorts.

'Can you come to see me one day next week? I want to start a new project.' Laura spoke to Alice so that no one else could hear, as she took her seat at the piano.

'I'll try, Miss, but it's hard to get away from here.'

Laura smiled. 'I expect so!' She turned to Beethoven and played with a light touch. The vicar hummed in a clear tenor, and so, of course, he was asked to sing.

'Oh, please do, Vicar, we hear so little music, and I do love it so,' Mrs Grey gushed. She had talked all the way though Laura's piece. Mr Carr and Miss Grey conferred; they chose a song, and Mrs Grey continued to talk. Laura became a little more animated and then chose to play 'The Last Rose of Summer', as appropriate for the time of year.

The kitchen door banged as Alice went back to face the washing up, and Jacob appeared. 'Have you come to dry the dishes, Fowler?' she asked brightly.

Jacob was grim, as usual. 'Nay, I've not. There's an old lad here with a bad cut that needs stitches. Do you think Cecil would do it tonight – or maybe not? I doubt he'll be too busy with his dinner.' Outside the open door was a dark shape, waiting. 'Didn't bring him in – he's bleeding like a stuck pig.'

They had no idea how Fanshawe would react. 'I'll go and tell doctor . . . see what he says.' The drawing-room was bright with lamps and full of chatter; this interruption would not be welcome.

The guests looked up as Alice went to stand by Fanshawe's chair and said quietly, 'I am afraid there's an emergency, sir, a farmer, with a badly cut hand. Will you see him tonight, or shall I tell him to come back in the morning?'

The whole room fell quiet, enjoying the drama, waiting for Fanshawe's reply. Surely he wouldn't turn the man away with an audience like this? The doctor's fat jowls shook as he turned to glare at Alice, as though it were her fault. There was a silence before he pushed back his chair. 'A doctor's work is never done.' He held out his hands in front of him. 'Perfectly steady, as you see. I never drink, because at any time I may be required to perform surgery. Greenwood, please make sure that my guests have everything they need.' He strutted out into the hall. 'Wrap the wound in a cloth, Fowler, before you bring the man in. We don't want blood all over the floor.' He took off his jacket and rolled up the snowy sleeves of his dress shirt.

In the drawing-room, Alice served more coffee round the fire and found another bottle of port for the colonel, who was smirking. 'I knew Fanshawe was a competent surgeon when I recommended him. Had plenty of practice, cutting off limbs in the army. You should get him to talk about India.'

Mrs Grey shuddered. 'Please, we want no gory details, my dear.'

'Certainly not!' echoed Mrs Scott-Jones, although her husband looked disappointed.

Alice took a deep breath and went into the surgery, where Sam Brown was sitting at the table, looking very pale. He had nearly severed two fingers with a turnip chopper. Jacob stood by while the doctor concentrated on the job, instructing the groom to hand him what he needed, a task that Jacob had obviously done before. Alice was allowed to make the poor man a cup of tea before they sent him home.

Dr Fanshawe did not, as expected, complain; he seemed to be in his element. 'A very neat job, you will agree, Mr Brown. Keep the hand clean and covered, and come back to see me in two days.'

Back in the kitchen, Jacob lingered long enough to say, 'Well, it takes all sorts. He's a city man, young Cecil, but he can sew folks up well enough.'

'I shall not require dinner tonight, nor breakfast in the morning. I must go to Harrogate,' Dr Fanshawe informed Alice one cold day as she served his porridge.

Snow was falling outside the window, lighting up the winter garden, swirling down from a leaden sky. "Do you think it's wise to go far, sir? The weather could get worse.' Harrogate was a long journey in winter; trains out of Ripon were often cancelled or delayed.

'Nonsense, Greenwood. I never allow the weather to interfere with my plans. I am not a timid man. I shall wear my warm cape and Fowler shall take me to the train in Ripon. The Masham–Melmerby line is slow and tedious.' The doctor attacked his porridge.

Jacob would no doubt have an opinion on Fanshawe's plan, but neither of them could offer advice to such a pig-headed man. On the other hand, a visit to Laura would be possible, if dinner was not required. 'Yes, sir.'

'Colonel and Mrs Grey have kindly said they will bring me back from Ripon on Thursday afternoon. No doubt the weather will be cold, but I can bear it, in spite of my years in India.'

'Well, sir, it is only November, and the worst snowfalls are usually after Christmas.' Perhaps he was right, but did the doctor know what the weather here could do? They were on the edge of the moorland and sheltered from westerly gales; but if the wind came from the east, it swept through the town straight from the cold North Sea.

Jacob came in for the doctor's overnight bag, muttering. 'Is he helpless? We might be in for some bad weather, or we might not. I'm coming home as fast as I can, once I've done the errands and delivered "sir" to the station.' It seemed to irritate him when Alice called Fanshawe 'sir'.

'You miss Dr Dent, don't you, Fowler? You must have a heart, after all.'

'Not so you'd notice,' Jacob growled as he picked up the bag in the hall. 'If we perish in the storm, look after the rest of the horses.' The door banged, but not quite so nastily as before.

The weather did not worsen and when Jacob came home there was only a little powdering of snow on the cobbles of the market square; but the dreaded easterly wind sprang up as darkness fell and the kitchen fire burned up brightly.

The next morning, a blue sky mocked fears of bad weather. The carrier's cart set off for Ripon, two horses pulling an assortment of farmers' wives, bound for the Thursday market. Dr Fanshawe would want a hearty dinner after his journey; a piece of pickled beef cooked with spices, and a suet pudding . . . although he might find it rather common. The fire was drawing well and the stove roared; Alice made a batch of scones and wondered whether to give a few to Jacob, or not.

In a few hours, there was a different world outside the kitchen window The heavy grey sky was full of snow; large flakes were tumbling down and already there was a white cover on the cobbles, a white lining on the bare winter branches. By midday, the snow was thick and a keen wind was moaning through the little town, drifting the snow against the stone houses. Jacob brought in some Brussels sprouts from the garden, blowing on his frozen fingers. 'It looks bad. The market folks'll have a sore job getting back to Masham. And our doctor might get his little feet wet, if he has to walk home.'

'Those poor folks, struggling to get home. What can we do, Jacob?'

'Wait and see.' But the snowfall increased and by mid afternoon there was no traffic coming into Masham from any direction.

Jacob came into the kitchen and to Alice's surprise accepted a cup of tea and a scone. He was worried. 'We can't dig the road out through to Ripon, you daft lass. But . . . there's often a bad drift just t'other side of the bridge. If I go down there with a couple of lads, we might be able to pull 'em out, if they're in that there drift.'

'It might be best to go down there before dark,' Alice suggested. 'Er . . . can I come and help? There's no point in cooking any more, doctor's not back.'

Jacob made an impatient noise. 'Of course you can't go

digging folks out of drifts; that's man's work. I'm off to find a few lads.'

Half an hour later, he was back, looking rather sheepish. 'There's no lads about, happen they're all looking to their own folks. You'll have to do, Greenwood. Put your boots on and carry the lantern.'

Two faithful servants trudging through the snow; it was like one of those stories in *Leisure Hour* in the doctor's waiting room. It would be interesting to see just how rude Jacob could be when he got cold and tired. They went down the slope to the river, and where the road narrowed at the other side of the bridge in the failing light there was the scene of a disaster. But at least the snow had stopped.

Alice could just make out several vehicles stuck in deep snow; one was tipped over on its side and the driver was struggling to free himself. It was Mr Carr, the parson.

Jacob righted the horse and then pulled the cap down a little further on his head. 'Just you bide there a little, Vicar. We'll get to you later, there's folks we need to get out first, mothers that have to go home to their families.' It was very heartless and quite in character.

Alice held the lantern as Jacob dug heroically, helped by a farmer who was one of the victims, and who had thought to stow a shovel in his cart. When they came to the carrier's cart, they managed to free the occupants and help them to the bridge, after which the walking would be easier. They could manage now there was light and the grateful travellers called out, 'Thank you, Jacob!' as they set out on the last half mile to Masham, clutching their coats round them against the wind. The drivers led their horses; the carts could wait until another day.

Just as they were turning away, Alice heard a low moan from the inside of the carrier's cart. By the lantern light she could see a huddled shape at the far end, where one wheel was suspended over a bank. 'Oh, Oh!'

Jacob came, and together they hauled out the pathetic figure of Dr Fanshawe. He was wet, bedraggled, pale with cold and bleeding from a cut on the cheek.

'Doctor! Didn't expect to find you here!' Jacob managed to catch him before he fell over. 'Steady, now!'

'What a dreadful time I have had!' moaned the little man as they helped him up the road.

'We thought you were travelling with the colonel, sir?' Alice ventured.

'The colonel decided not to travel today, because of the weather. So I took the carrier, in order to get back to my duty. But what an experience! I shall never do so again.'

Someone had brought a pony and trap down to the drift by then, so they bundled the doctor into it and also the parson, whom Jacob kindly helped out of his predicament. Alice and Jacob walked home, tired and wet but, strangely enough, not at all grumpy. Their feet crunched on the cold ground and, as the sky cleared, a few stars came out.

Everybody had been rescued and all the horses were safe. The disaster was over, apart from the splintered carts. Jacob looked weary, but he smiled, actually smiled, at Alice, as he turned for his cottage across the yard. 'A lot of women would have stayed at home,' was all he said.

Alice laughed. 'You did a grand job, Fowler, but you were rough on the parson!'

As she made dinner for the shivering doctor, Alice thought about the strange character of Jacob and how contrary he could be, but how dependable. He was the first man out there in the terrible weather, and knew just where help would be needed He was a man you could trust, unless you wanted polite conversation.

The next morning, Dr Fanshawe was sneezing and in a very stern mood. He called both his servants into the dining-room after breakfast and had them stand in front of him as he sat at the big table. 'I will not go into the details of my terrible journey last night,' he began. 'But I must say, I find you very remiss in your duty to me, on several counts. Why was I not warned of the likelihood of bad weather? I had no idea that these roads would be blocked by snow.'

Alice choked back a quick reply. You were told, you stupid man—

'Further, I had not been informed that there are several people here, competing with the practice in a most shameful way, unqualified women who take money from the gullible cottagers and purport to cure their ills. And you, Greenwood, are one of them! I could hardly believe it. This is not to be tolerated.' Fanshawe was getting worked up into a rage.

Not daring to look at Jacob, who was shifting from one foot to the other, Alice looked the doctor in the eye. 'What do you mean, sir?'

'There was talk in the carrier's cart, which I was forced to overhear. They spoke of diseases, and treatments. They did not know who I am!' The doctor seemed amazed. 'There was even a smell of alcohol in the vehicle. Some of the passengers had been drinking.'

The farmers' wives would all have known very well who he was, and talked about ailments on purpose to annoy him, with the grim Dales humour. 'That's a pity, sir.'

Dr Fanshawe was red in the face; he was working up a great deal of righteous anger. 'I have to tell you that I was absolutely appalled to hear what they said. It was agreed among these ignorant people that a certain herb woman named Greenwood can help them with their petty ailments. In direct competition with the practice! Did Dr Dent know of this? You must have been deceiving him! It cannot be allowed to go on. You must cease your illegal activities at once.'

'But Dr Dent—' Jacob began.

Alice could feel laughter bubbling up inside her. The man was absurd.

'I will take no argument from you, Fowler. And I must insist that there is too much collusion between you and Greenwood. It is to be discouraged. To outsiders, it could appear to be immoral.'

'What?' The servants glared at each other. They hated each other, didn't they? Except that Jacob had a twitch in the corner of his mouth as his glare changed to what was almost a wink, and Alice suddenly wanted to laugh again. They disliked Dr Fanshawe much more than they hated each other.

'Excuse me sir, I have something boiling on the stove,' Alice said quietly, and left the room. There was no sense in getting worked up about what Fanshawe said. The man must be mad.

The next evening, it was Jacob's turn to get into trouble. Dr Fanshawe discovered at eight o'clock that Jacob had gone over to the Bruce Arms for a pint. 'How dare he? We could be called out to an emergency at any time! Bring him back immediately!' The squeaky voice rose to a crescendo.

Alice went unwillingly round the corner, found a young lad and asked him to fetch Jacob out of the inn. 'Come back immediately!' She managed to imitate the doctor's voice.

Jacob shook his head. 'Drat him. I was winning at dominoes.'

Time went by slowly; the last autumn leaves fell on the cobbles of Masham square, and winter winds swept them away. One day, with Dr Fanshawe bouncing his way on horseback to see patients over the common, Alice breathed a sigh of relief. There would be a couple of hours of peace, before he came back. The doctor's outbursts had not really worried her; he was only a temporary problem. But worse was to come.

Alice's sister Ruby called in to see her, when she knew the doctor was out; it was asking for trouble to call when he was at home. With a worried look on her brown face, she sat down thankfully on a kitchen chair. 'Is it true that Dr Dent isn't coming back? That Dr Fanshawe's here for good?'

Alice felt herself go pale. 'What do you mean, Ruby?'

'It says here in the paper. Doctor's going to retire.'

SIX

This was a shock. Alice could hardly wait for the Dents' return, and many of the patients felt the same way. The only way that she and Jacob could survive was to think of Fanshawe as a temporary irritation. 'Who said doctor wasn't coming back?'

'Well, it's in the *Clarion*, so it must be true! I mean, you have plenty of other work, you can leave if you want, but it would be a sad loss to Masham.' Ruby brought out a copy of the local paper.

Jacob came in with some potatoes, and almost jumped when he saw Ruby. 'Women!' he growled in the usual way, but with not quite the usual spirit. He was only going through the motions. Since Fanshawe's rage, he had been almost polite to Alice, as though he sympathized with her.

'Stop, Jacob, listen to this!' Alice halted him at the door. It would be worse for Jacob than for any of them, if it were true. The groom took off his cap and sat down opposite Ruby. 'All right, if you're not going to attack me with a rolling pin, like cooks usually do.'

In the local news section, there was the bad news. 'Our reporter was sorry to hear that the highly esteemed Dr Dent of Masham is in failing health. He is currently on vacation, but will probably not return to the practice. His medical colleague, Dr Poole, said that it was a sad case, a man not able to continue with his life's work. He felt sympathy for both Dr and Mrs Dent.'

There was a horrified silence. Alice moved the kettle onto the range; a cup of tea was called for. Then Jacob drew out of his pocket a postcard from Weston-super-Mare. 'Look at this . . . from the missis. Doctor's feeling better. Back by the middle of January, will tell you everything then, remember us to Alice. That's friendly, like.'

'From the horse's mouth, Fowler,' Alice couldn't resist saying.

'Aye, but what does it mean?' Jacob frowned. 'I took it to mean they'll be back to work, but now, I'm not so sure. "Tell you everything then." They could be coming back to tell us he's retiring.'

It was too awful to contemplate.

Currant scones, with Ruby's butter on them, made everybody feel a little more settled, but Ruby thought there must be a plot. 'I reckon that Dr Poole is trying to get all your patients. If folks think that Dr Dent isn't coming back, they'll change to Dr Poole; it stands to reason. Nobody likes Fanshawe. Mrs Sanderson told me last week they only stay for Dr Dent. Loyal to the Dents, most folks are.'

Jacob drained his tea. 'Cecil's off to the big nobs again today. Sir does like to mix with the gentry,' he said sourly. 'Don't know how he worms his way in. But if this tale gets about, we're done for.'

'You thought he was good, when he stitched up Sam Brown,' Alice reminded him.

'And so he was, those fingers healed up quick, I took particular notice. But these rich folk, they only need liver pills and something for sleepless nights, because they don't work hard enough to get tired. Boss always told them to stick to a low diet. It didn't suit, as a rule.' He smiled sadly. 'How long is it to the middle of January?'

Alice was thinking as she poured Ruby a second cup of tea. 'We might be able to do something, with a bit of help from the patients.'

'Doubt it.' Jacob stood up and replaced his cap. 'Thanks for the tea.'

'Just a minute, Jacob. We need a way to let folks know that Dr Dent is coming back. Even if the worst happens and he decides to go, he'll need to sell the practice. So it's up to us to keep it together for him, stop Poole nibbling away at the boundary.'

'Daft lass, what can we do?' Jacob growled. 'We're the servants.'

'We could have a special welcome home, with the vicar to make a speech, in the Mechanics' Institute.' She indicated the chair next to her and rather to her surprise, Jacob sat down again, quite close to Alice. It was like taming a wild horse; a little bit closer, but no sudden movements. He had been so very edgy, up to now.

Ruby seemed to like the idea. 'We could put on a supper. And somebody could put up posters in the town in good time, that would advertise it. And have the choir sing . . . folks like a bit of a concert in winter, to liven things up.'

'But not the Kirkby handbells!' Jacob shuddered. They knew what he meant; the handbells were deafening, that would be going too far. 'But who'd take any notice of us? We're only the servants, I keep telling you.'

Alice smiled. 'But we know folks with influence. It needs to come from the vicar. And Miss Grey is just the lass – sorry, young lady – to persuade the vicar that it's all his idea.'

Ruby and Jacob were doubtful of Laura, but Alice explained that she was more human of late. 'She is not too fond of Fanshawe, and she likes Dr Dent. She goes to church, and she's pretty enough to persuade anybody—'

With a loud crash the door flew open to reveal the purple, enraged face of Dr Fanshawe. He was panting heavily. 'Fowler, what are you doing in the kitchen? Sitting so close to Greenwood – what are you two up to? The infernal horse has cast a shoe. I had to walk for miles. WHO IS THIS WOMAN?'

Dr Fanshawe may have had right on his side, but it was hard to keep calm, with all his purple fury. Servants should have been working at three in the afternoon, of course. But they worked such long hours, well into the evening, that the Dents had let them have an hour or so free in the afternoons, on days when there was nothing urgent to be done. This was not a formal arrangement, but it gave them a breathing space before the evening chores.

Jacob looked his temporary employer in the eye. 'Mrs Greenwood is on duty, Doctor, and Mrs Turner is her sister. We were having a cup of tea, that was all. Now, I'd better get that mare shod afore the blacksmith shuts down for the night.' He nodded to the women and walked to the door, cool in the face of Fanshawe, who was almost dancing with rage.

'Your conduct is disgusting. I come back unexpectedly to find you lounging with women, when you should be working. I will deal with you later.' He turned to Alice. 'Greenwood, go into the dining-room and wait for me. You are compromising the morals of this household, consorting with the groom and feeding your family—'

Jacob put his head round the door. 'Brought the shoe back, of course, Doctor?'

'No, I did not! Now be off with you, and see me when you come back.'

Naturally enough, Seth Watson, the smith, held out his huge hand for the missing shoe as soon as Jacob and Honey walked in. 'Where is it, lad? It was nearly new.'

'Nay, he left it behind. Typical. I'll have a look on the Thorpe road, next time I go by.' Jacob ran his hand over Honey's legs, always anxious when she had been ridden by Fanshawe.

The smith shrugged. 'Blow us up fire then; we'll see what we can do.'

The forge was warm, lit by the red glow of the fire. Seth walked to a row of shoes hanging on the wall, horseshoes of different sizes, individually made for regular customers. 'Here are Honey's.'

Jacob seized the bellows and Honey stood patiently waiting.

'You've seen it all before, girl, haven't you?'

'What manner of man is this new doctor, then?' The smith picked up Honey's foot and she leaned against him like an old friend. 'Seems like a bouncy little city bloke, to me. Came to see the missis, but she wasn't keen. All he wanted to do was to give her some medicine and get out of the house. Dr Dent, now, he'd have stopped to ask after the bairns and take a cup of tea. New one won't last long, that's for sure.' The hoof was trimmed, and the smith eased his back. 'I hear tell as Dr Dent's not coming back . . . that's a shame, if it's true.' He grunted, and pushed Honey back. 'This little mare has sound feet, Jacob.'

Jacob grinned, an unfamiliar feeling to him. 'Young Cecil won't be here much longer, Seth. The boss is coming back, sure enough.' Seth would spread the word; the blacksmith's shop was a focal point for news, a place where folks often came to get warm by the fire in winter. 'Now listen here, Seth Watson, you can put it about that Dr Dent is well, very well. They'll be back after Christmas. So there's no call for folks to go flocking to Dr Poole.' He watched as the red-hot shoe was drawn from the fire.

After a bath and a change of clothing, the doctor seemed to simmer down. Jacob came back from the forge and together the staff were summoned to the dining-room. Alice had already listened to one tirade, and her head ached.

'I have decided that there is no point in talking to you. You are probably immoral; you are not to be trusted and you are both dismissed, without a character. You will leave as soon as I can find replacements.' The doctor's tone was icy.

Alice felt compelled to speak up. 'You may have treated folks like that in India, Doctor, but you can't do it here. We don't believe we are immoral, and neither will anyone else.' She felt shaky. It would be so good to walk out, go back to her little cottage and the other work . . . and to get away from this furious little man, who seemed to see immorality at every turn. 'I intend to leave immediately.'

69

She was breaking the sacred rule that servants should never answer back, and in her days as lady's maid, Alice would never have dreamed of speaking up, no matter what the provocation. You should never show an employer what you really feel, she knew. But the work with the herbs, and the little cottage of her own, had given her a new freedom that had hardly been realized until now. Perhaps this was another sign of change; the twentieth century was going to be different. If servants could choose where they worked, employers would need to be a little more reasonable.

Jacob gave her a look. 'Steady, lass, not so hasty. Dr Fanshawe can't manage on his own.' Speaking slowly and clearly, he faced the doctor with some dignity. 'The truth is, Dr Dent is our boss, and here we stay until he tells us to go. Now, Doctor, it's only a few weeks till Dr Dent comes back, and we must get over them as best we can. No call to get agitated. Just remember, you need us more than we need you.' He put on his cap and turned away.

Unlike Alice, Jacob would be homeless if he were turned off by Fanshawe, but this had not stopped him from telling the truth. What he said made sense, and you had to admire his coolness.

Amazingly, Fanshawe seemed to accept this. He appeared to be thinking. 'It is hardly worth my while to find new servants for a few weeks ... you may stay for the present, but you may be sure that I shall report your behaviour to Dr Dent. I have no doubt that he will dismiss you, if and when he comes home. But I will tolerate no more slacking, and no more consorting with each other in the kitchen. The good name of the practice must be preserved.'

Alice went back into the kitchen to prepare the doctor's dinner. She had never 'consorted' with Jacob. Was the man obsessed with morals? Why had she left her own life, to come here and be treated like this?

Jacob followed her into the kitchen and they looked at each other across the big table. 'I'm off, Jacob. Back home, to my other jobs. I won't be called immoral by anyone.'

Ruby had warned her once that widows could be suspected of all kinds of things, just because they lived alone. 'Once, they would have called you a witch, what with the herbs and such,' Ruby had said. She had to look after her reputation, to keep her pride.

'Don't go.' Jacob's face was expressionless. Did he mean it?

'How did you keep so cool, Jacob? I – I could have hit him!' Alice was still trembling a little, chopping up onions for a stew as fiercely as if they were parts of Cecil Fanshawe.

'Easy. Young Cecil means nothing to me, so it doesn't matter what he thinks. We just have to put up with him, he's all bark and no bite. That youth has a lot to learn. Now . . . did you want a few carrots for that stew?'

He was trying to calm her down. If Jacob would work with her, things might be bearable. Impulsively, Alice put a hand on his arm. 'Thanks, Jacob, I suppose you're right.'

The groom leaped back as though she had stung him. 'Hands off me, woman! No woman lays a hand on me!' The door banged and he was gone. Jacob was not so calm as he pretended.

Alice peeled potatoes, thinking deeply. Why should she not go home? All this unpleasantness was making her nervous; the quiet life she had striven for, and nearly achieved, was slipping away. But Jacob, prickly though he was, had asked her to stay – and the thought of Jacob facing Fanshawe alone was not at all pleasant. The Dents would certainly expect her to stay, although they would be horrified if they knew what was going on. Fanshawe had said he was going away for Christmas, so that would be a respite, of a sort. Maybe a strong-minded woman would stick it out?

As the stew went onto the stove Jacob appeared with some carrots, not only trimmed of their tops, but washed as well. Perhaps he was trying to tell her something. Alice pushed her hair back under the white cap and stood up straight, prepared to be firm. 'Thank you, Jacob, for the carrots. Now, can you tell me why I should stay in this house a moment longer, with a mad boss and a groom who seems to make a point of being unfriendly?'

There was a silence. Then the groom picked up his empty bucket and turned for the door. 'Suit yourself; it's nowt to me.'

Alice felt let down. She had thought the two of them were making a little progress, until this afternoon. She turned away sadly, wondering what to do, and Jacob must have caught her expression. 'Don't mind me, lass,' he said in a softer tone. 'I'm just a misery, I know.'

'Well, why can't you be more normal? Jacob Fowler, there is no need to go through life being a misery, and you must know it. If you could only treat me half as well as you treat Honey, we should get on. But I don't want to be stuck here all on my own, with him raging about like a bull and you as sour as – as a wet hen.'

This time, she was rewarded with a chuckle. 'Mares are a mite easier than women.' The grey eyes were almost kind. 'Well, lass, you're a stayer, and no mistake. The boss and the missis would be proud of the job you're doing with Young Cecil. We'll have to stick together, I suppose . . . only I'm not used to women, and that's a fact.'

'Well, you'd better get used to them, otherwise you're cutting yourself off from half the folks in the world. Can't you think of women as people?' Alice remembered the doctor's sad tale of Jacob's lost love; a pity he had let it spoil his life. And yet, she could understand it in a way. Tom had been a rather irresponsible husband, but when she lost him, it had been a blow.

'Laying the law down already?' Jacob pretended to be alarmed. 'I'd better be off, or we'll be accused of consorting again. Don't let Cecil get you down, Alice.'

Jacob had actually called her by her name.

'Miss Grey has asked me to allow you to work at the Hall this afternoon.' Fanshawe spoke stiffly, but a little smiled played round his thick lips when he spoke of Laura. 'Provided that you have prepared my dinner, you may go to the Hall for a few hours after lunch.'

'Very good, sir.' Alice and Jacob had both reverted to the conventional reply to the doctor; in fact, Alice spoke to him as little as possible. How clever of Laura to ask for her! To get away from the doctor's house, even for a few hours, would be heaven.

Laura looked quite animated when Alice arrived; she was wearing outdoor clothes. 'Don't take your shawl off, Alice. We'll take the dog for a walk, and I have to see Mr Burns. We have a new plan. I am so pleased you could come; Mama is much happier about me when you are here.' As they walked down to the stables, the girl asked curiously, 'How are you getting on with Dr Fanshawe?' She giggled a little.

'Well—' What could she say? Telling Cecil what she thought was one thing, but talking behind his back was quite another. 'Dr Fanshawe is a very good surgeon.' It was the only good thing they could say about him. He was a good GP, but only if the patient was worth over two thousand a year. Alice said no more.

'I believe so, but he's a funny little man, isn't he?' Laura looked down demurely. 'I think he may be going to propose to me, but of course Papa won't allow that; he had other plans.' She sighed at the thought of the other plans. 'Dr Fanshawe keeps telling me of his expectations . . . his mother is to leave him a fortune, and he is looking for a wife. He may go back to India, he says – perhaps he thought I would like the idea. But – not now. I prefer the climate here.'

'But surely, you wouldn't—?' It was impossible to imagine Cecil and Laura together, although the pompous little man was nearer her age than was Paterson. Here it was again, a changing of relationships between servant and employer. Laura sometimes spoke to Alice as one young woman to another.

Laura shook her head, smiling, and then they were at the stables and Hamish claimed all her attention. 'Now for the farm office.'

Mr Adam Burns was sitting back in his office chair, hands behind his head, looking at the plan of the Hall estate, but when Laura knocked and walked in, he jumped to his feet. 'It's coming on, you must agree. We've planted a lot of trees as well as land improvements, and next summer, we'll see the difference.' He brushed the gleaming copper hair out of his eyes and beamed happily at Laura and Alice. Mr Burns was a cheerful soul and seemed to enjoy life.

Laura waved Alice to a seat and took the chair opposite Adam. 'A lot has happened since you were here, Alice. We've actually started to build a lovely cottage for Mickley Bank. I never realized that planning could be so interesting . . . I am learning so many new things, all the time.'

Alice looked at the sketches and plans on the table. 'Why a new cottage?'

'Well, you know Mr Gill? He's one of our tenants, of course. His farm foreman is to be married, and the worker's cottage there is falling down.'

'And I suggested that Miss Grey could help with the planning. She is good at drawing and maths, and meticulous about detail.' Adam looked approvingly at Laura.

'Mama, of course, thinks it is not a proper occupation for a young lady, but Papa has given me books about architecture, and Adam – Mr Burns – has experience of building, in Scotland. He helped to design a whole new village, to improve the health of estate workers. And I really believe that it is our duty to provide good housing, where we can.' She handed Alice the plan of the new house.

The people who lived in them knew all about damp, over-crowded cottages; Alice's little home had once housed a shepherd, his wife and five children, and it had been very damp before Gabriel Turner relaid the floors.

'Brick would look dreadful, of course, in this district, so we have talked to a stone mason and we will build it in sandstone – we can use some of the stones from the old cottage, I think. So

74

today, I hoped we could ride out in the trap to look at—' Laura broke off abruptly, as a commotion in the yard made her look through the window. Mr Paterson was dismounting from his horse.

'Please stay, both of you – don't leave me alone with him!' Laura's whisper was urgent.

Paterson knocked briefly and walked in; Hamish the terrier growled deep in his throat, full of hate. Adam picked up the dog quickly.

'My dear Laura! You father tells me that you are working hard for the good of the estate. Good day, Burns. This is a pleasant little office.' Paterson went to stand with his back to the fire with his hands in the pockets of his riding breeches. He ignored the dog, and of course Alice, who as a servant was like part of the furniture.

There was a pause, and Paterson seemed to expect Adam to leave. The manager tied Hamish to a chair with a cattle halter but the little dog continued to growl, eying Paterson as though he was longing to attack. Laura smiled at the dog, but said nothing.

'Would you care to take a walk, Laura?' Her suitor glanced out of the window. 'But perhaps not – it's starting to rain.'

'There's another office through here, if you would like to speak to Miss Laura. The foreman is just leaving.' Adam led the way to the farm foreman's office, where the chairs were of wood instead of leather.

Alice realized that he was quite determined; Paterson would have his interview alone. He steered the girl though the door with a hand under her elbow, but she managed to leave the door open. Adam quietly went into the yard, and Alice was left, an unwilling eavesdropper with nowhere to go.

'We are nearly at the end of the year, my dear, and I need not remind you that our engagement will be celebrated in February. I take it you would prefer a diamond ring? I have to go away on business again soon, but of course I will be back before then.

Your parents have offered to host a dinner party in our honour. All you need to do is to choose a new dress!'

Alice could hear Laura pacing up and down the room, her little boots drumming on the bare boards. 'To tell you the truth, Mr Paterson, I had hoped—' she tailed off.

'Bradley, my darling, Bradley. You will soon be my wife, we live in modern times and I do not wish you to address me formally.'

'Well . . . I thought that you might find someone more, more suitable than me, when you were in London. Or Leeds, or somewhere.' To Alice, Laura sounded very young and desperate. Why should she have to marry the man, if she didn't want to?

'Laura, you must know by now that I will never, ever, give up until you are mine. I am completely – obsessed, if you like. I am determined to own you, body and soul—' the deep voice faltered, and then Paterson forced a laugh. 'You should be flattered, you know! Come here.'

He spoke very quietly and there was the sound of a movement, then a cry from the girl, as though he had restrained her. The footsteps ceased. Paterson laughed again as he said, 'Don't worry, dearest. This is natural pre-wedding nerves, very becoming in a modest young girl. You will have plenty of time to settle down, Laura. I've planned a wedding tour of Europe, of about three months on our own. We'll visit all the art galleries, and you can do some sketching. You will learn a great deal about history and art, as well as enjoying the climate. Look forward to it, Laura! We'll have a wonderful time.'

Paterson spoke in a pleasant voice, and he spoke gently. To Alice, it held a deep kindliness, a desire to please his young bride. What a pity she could not see it! She couldn't appreciate Paterson, because of his age.

Paterson and Laura came back into the estate office as Adam returned; Laura had tears in her eyes, but said nothing. The suitor looked pleased with himself. 'Burns, I wanted to see you, too. The colonel has given permission for me to borrow you again, this time for a tour of my home farm, and I'd appreciate your advice. We need to improve production on a new intake. When can you come over?'

Adam consulted his diary and a date was agreed.

'The days are very short now, so we'll have to make it a quick tour,' Paterson reminded him.

After the visitor had gone, Alice tried to take Laura's mind away from him and from the future. 'We've a plan for a welcome home to Dr and Mrs Dent, in January. Will you help with it, Miss Laura? And Mr Burns? We need someone in authority to set things going, and wondered whether you would talk to the vicar.'

Laura smiled, much happier at the thought of more planning. 'Of course, Alice. A party is just what we need! And Mr Burns can help.'

SEVEN

Adam Burns rode over the moor the next week on his way to visit Mr Paterson, picking his way between the peat bogs on the chestnut from the Hall stables. Advising Bradley Paterson was quite a responsibility, come to think of it. He made you feel like standing up straight and watching your words in his presence. Poor Laura might well be overawed, but then, she would no doubt enjoy the money and position. Some said that he was in line for a title and that his wife might one day be Lady Paterson. She might like that. She would have several delightful blue-eyed children, just like herself.

What would happen if Adam's suggestions went wrong, the improvements didn't work and the landowner lost money? It might be prudent to consult someone local, some farmer who knew the land and the conditions; perhaps Gabriel Turner would be able to help. Alice's brother-in-law had seemed to be a practical man, and one not afraid of change; he could look at the draft plan before Paterson saw it.

'Burns, you're just on time! Well done.' Paterson met Adam at the boundary, mounted on his frisky black mare. Under low cloud, they rode over the neglected fields of a vacant farm. 'It's certainly ready for improvement.' Adam commented. Whatever he suggested was bound to have a good effect; the grass was sour and the fields where oats had been grown were full of weeds.

'I thought of making it part of the home farm, and running it myself. I want your opinion because I knew you've studied farming at Edinburgh. I haven't really time to go into the new ideas in depth,' Paterson confessed. 'My textile interests pay so much better, of course.'

'You were not bred to farming, perhaps?' Adam enquired politely.

'Unfortunately, no . . . the family owns woollen mills. My father sent me to school in York – Bootham, actually – and then I went to university, to study economics. When I was twenty-one he gave me this estate, and eventually I decided to live here for part of the time.'

Adam offered various suggestions as they rode over the land, but promised to write up a more detailed analysis. Once or twice he jumped down from his horse and kicked over a mole hill, looking carefully at the soil, running it through his fingers. Paterson looked and listened attentively. The landowner sat his horse so well and talked such good sense . . . surely, Laura could be happy with him? He'd mentioned a Quaker school, too – that should have given him a good moral base.

'It's past lunchtime, Burns. Come and have some lunch at the house, before you go.' As they arrived at the gates to the big house, a trap was driving by. Jacob Fowler, the groom, cap pulled down so far as to make his face invisible, was driving Dr Fanshawe on his rounds. Paterson waved and Jacob slowly pulled up.

'How very pleasant to see you! How are you, Mr Paterson? Good day to you, Mr Burns.' The little doctor was beaming from ear to ear, delighted to be noticed by Paterson.

'I'm busy, Fanshawe, as always. I must tell you, the groom you stitched up last week is improving every day. It was a very neat job. Congratulations. And now, would you care to step in for a bite to eat? Burns and I are just about to go in.'

A meal was welcome, but it would have been more pleasant without the little doctor, who would probably not want to talk about land improvement. Adam took off his riding cape in the big panelled hall. So this was Laura's future home – had she seen it yet?

While the doctor dominated the conversation, on the lines of 'when I was in India', Adam ate his cold beef and pickles and looked round the dining-room, which was immaculate. The silver sparkled and the big mahogany table gleamed with a soft glow, the result of much polishing. There was a well-arranged bowl of chrysanthemums on the table. Mr Paterson, although his house was on the edge of the moor, evidently lived in considerable, if rather sombre, comfort. Through the long windows Adam could see a well-kept garden with gravelled paths and lawns, and beyond them, the walls of a kitchen garden, with a row of glasshouses on the south wall.

Laura would need those blue-eyed children to enliven the house; once she'd got used to the idea, she would probably enjoy living here. Would Paterson allow her to 'improve' his gardens or his estate? Like most of his generation, he would probably expect his wife to be a good wife and mother and a decorative hostess, but certainly do nothing that might take her into a man's world.

'Of course, we rode out on elephants after tiger—' Fanshawe's voice was droning on. 'Miss Grey was superb, I must say, she looked wonderful, riding an elephant – no fear whatsoever. I do so admire Miss Grey . . . and she is a most accomplished artist. Have you seen her water colours? She prefers flower studies, of course, but her scenes of India were wonderful. It was, of course, Colonel Grey who recommended me for my present position in Masham, and I did venture to wonder whether he intended to encourage my . . . ah . . . attentions to Miss Grey.'

As Fanshawe rattled on, Paterson's face seemed to grow darker. Eventually he said in a low voice, 'I suppose you realize, Fanshawe, that Miss Grey is already engaged to be married?'

The doctor laughed. 'Not quite yet, I understand, Mr Paterson. I have not heard of any such arrangement. I flatter myself that I may still have a chance, although naturally, I have not yet spoken to the colonel. My expectations are excellent and I will be able to keep a wife in some comfort. I plan eventually to reside in Harrogate, with a fashionable practice, perhaps, or even in a better part of York.'

'And how is Miss Grey's health, these days?' Paterson appeared to be gritting his teeth. With great restraint, he had evidently decided not to tell Fanshawe that he considered the lady to be his property. But he shifted in his seat and seemed very restless.

Fanshawe sniffed. 'To be honest, I find that Dr Dent has somewhat encouraged the young lady to cultivate ill-health.' He looked meaningly at Paterson, who nodded. 'Miss Grey keeps referring to the fact that Dr Dent told her not to do this or do that, and yet, in India, she was perfectly well, in spite of the heat. I knew her well there, of course. In fact, Mr Paterson, I am forced to conclude that Dr Dent is far too soft with his patients. Of course, Miss Grey was bound to take her doctor's advice; there is no blame attached to her, at all. Her poor mother has been most concerned . . . she is a delightful lady, is she not? And now, I really must go; I have more calls to make; a doctor's work is never done! But first, may I have another cup of your admirable coffee?'

As the doctor sipped his coffee, Adam excused himself and went out to the stables to see Jacob. He had met Jacob with Dr Dent and admired his horsemanship. As he passed the sideboard, he picked up a piece of cheese and a few biscuits. Chances were that the groom had not been fed.

Jacob was sitting gloomily on the feed bin in the stable, talking to Honey, who was in a stall next to Adam's horse. His eyes lit up when he saw the food. 'It's not that I'm starving,' he admitted, 'but it's just that young, er, Dr Fanshawe would never think of it. Thanks very much, Mr Burns.'

'That's what I thought. Never mind, the Dents will be back in January. Miss Grey tells me there's to be a public welcome home for them. Did you know about it?'

'Yes, sir. We were hoping that you'd play the bagpipes, sir, on the evening. Mrs Greenwood spoke to Miss Grey, and it was her idea.' Jacob grinned. 'In a kilt, of course, sir.'

Miss Grey suggested it, did she? 'I'm sorry, Jacob.' Adam laughed. 'I'm a Lowlander, you know, not a stage Scotsman.'

'Fowler! Where are you? The horse should be yoked up and ready for me! Get moving!' Fanshawe bustled in and Jacob, after an eloquent look at Adam, got moving.

'Dear me, I shall never get round before dark at this rate,' Fanshawe fussed.

'Have you enjoyed your spell in the Dales, Doctor?' Adam was helping with the trap.

'In part, yes, Mr Burns, and I flatter myself that I have improved the practice. But I had no idea when I took it on how uncouth the people were, or what large tracts of desolate land I should have to travel. And the other problem,' he dropped his voice, 'has been the servants. I really cannot think why Dent would not be able to find some properly trained people. It has been most trying, coping with insubordination and complete inefficiency . . . so unlike India. I shall say as much to Dent, when he returns.'

'So Dr Dent is coming back?' This would try him out.

Fanshawe permitted himself a podgy smile. 'I believe so, although Dr Poole thinks not. It may only be to say goodbye. If the Dents do not return, Dr Poole and I may work together. The practice is not worth much, so I shall buy it and then Poole and I will cover the area between us. My speciality is surgery, as you may know, while he is a physician. I rather think Poole is look-ing forward to it, you know. But on the whole, I have decided to seek a city practice eventually, as I said earlier, and so if I am to stay in Masham, it will not be for a very long period of time.'

'Very wise!' Adam left it at that.

As Jacob drove Honey sedately down the road, Paterson suggested a walk round the cattle sheds. Adam nodded, always interested in livestock. 'Yes, I can spare a few minutes, and I'd like to see the cattle.'

The sleek shorthorn cows were in their winter quarters,

bedded on clean yellow straw. 'This is my best bull – he's won prizes at several shows.' Paterson was obviously proud of his animals.

There was a row of bull pens down one side of the yard, where the animals could see other cattle and watch the farm men coming and going. The prize bull was handsome, with elegant horns and above his head was a board covered in rosettes and ribbons. 'Is he quiet? Shorthorn bulls can be a wee bit short-tempered!'

Paterson smiled. 'Well, you can never trust a bull, of course. But he seems quite good to handle – he's only three years old, quite young for a bull. We let them out to pasture in the summer, of course.' A young worker came along to give the bull his evening feed, and Paterson opened the door of the pen for him.

'Well, Joseph, you can be proud of him. He looks extremely fit. Mr Burns, this is Joseph Wood, he's a good stockman.'

Joseph was in his twenties; he looked alert and interested in his work. 'Have you heard of the black Scottish cattle, Joseph? They're my favourites,' Adam admitted.

'Yes, sir, I've seen them at shows. They might do well, up here, I reckon, but of course Mr Paterson favours shorthorns. I am learning all I can here, because I want to farm myself, one day.'

Paterson turned away to speak to a shepherd who had come up to him, and Joseph looked at Adam.' Do you think I've got a hope, sir? I'm going to ask Mr P to rent me a little farm, in a few years. I'm saving up and I've got that many plans!'

'Best of luck, Joseph. I hope you succeed.' Paterson seemed to be a benign employer; perhaps Joseph would get his wish.

Another man came past with a barrow, an older man with a sour expression. 'Young Joe's all right, Mr Paterson, but he needs a good man with him. It's me you've got to thank, for winning all your prizes.'

Paterson laughed rather shortly. 'Of course we all play our part, Henry. Even me – I pay the huge food bills!'

Henry shook his head and went on with his work, a typical case of jealousy. You often saw it on big estates, where farm workers lived for their animals and took immense pride in them. Showing cattle was competitive and Paterson obviously enjoyed it.

It was nearly dusk as Adam rode into the farmyard at Masham, to stable his horse for the night. Alice and Laura were feeding the little dog and they both looked up as he came into the stables. 'I've been up to Paterson's place, Linley Grange. Have you seen the house, Miss Grey? It's quite impressive, I think, with a lot of history.'

Laura turned away. 'No . . . I was to visit with Papa and Mama, but I wasn't well enough. So – did you like it?'

'I did – it's elegant, and I think you'll enjoy living there.'

Laura seemed to shudder.

'We talked about farm improvements, of course. He's a man of good sense, very . . . intelligent. He's bound to be a very good businessman.'

Laura looked at Alice. 'That's what you've told me.'

Good, so the little maid was trying to make Miss Laura see sense.

'Yes, my brother-in-law thinks highly of him; he's bought a farm from Mr Paterson recently,' Alice said quietly.

Laura gave the dog a last pat and turned for the door. 'Mama will be looking for me again; it's getting dark. Running round the estate is not how a young lady should behave . . . oh dear! I don't want to get married. I'd much rather stay here!'

Poor lass. 'Miss Laura, you are just like my sister!' Better try to cheer her up.

They were walking up the yard to the house and Laura stopped outside the door. 'What happened to your sister, Mr Burns?'

'Well, she cried a lot about getting married, but she's happy now, with two bonny bairns.' The Scottish tone of voice lightened the mood a little.

'What sort of man did she marry?' Laura was interested.

'He's older than she is . . . a farmer. It's a big step, of course; you're bound to feel nervous. But I think Paterson will be good to you . . . I do hope so,' he added under his breath. He smiled at the girls, willing Laura to smile back, to look on the bright side. 'I'd better be off; dinner will be waiting. I'd like to see Gabriel Turner for advice, some time soon, Alice . . . when it's convenient, of course.'

'I'll tell him, Mr Burns. I don't see him very often since I've been working at the doctor's.'

December wore on; goose feathers began to float over the village as Christmas drew near, and carol singers practised. Ruby Turner was very busy selling the fat cheeses that had been maturing since the summer. One day, she was brave enough to visit her sister Alice in the doctor's kitchen, having seen Fanshawe set out on his rounds.

'I don't want to get you into trouble,' she began, as soon as she was over the threshold.

'Young Cecil's fairly quiet these days,' Alice told her. 'I think he's realized that Dr Dent will soon be back, and he'll be off home to his mama.' She checked herself; this irreverent tone of Jacob's was catching.

Ruby looked shocked. 'Goodness, you never spoke so about gentlefolk when you were at the castle! Well, those posters have certainly told folks what's really happening,' she went on happily. Mrs Watson said she was that pleased to see that there's going to be a concert, when they get back! She can't abide Dr Fanshawe, of course—'

Jacob appeared at the door, but backed off when he saw Ruby. 'I'm not coming in! Got me into trouble last time, Ruby Turner. Lounging with women, he said.'

'Nay, lad. If I remember right, you got me into far more trouble at school, putting frogs in the girls' desks. Surely you're not scared of doctor?'

That was challenge enough; Jacob came in and took off his

cap. 'I find I have just the time to partake of a cup of tea,' he announced, in a fair imitation of Fanshawe's pompous manner. 'I require very hot tea, with a little milk and two teaspoons of sugah.' There was a general laugh, and the three settled down round the table. Jacob had certainly changed, since Alice came to the doctor's house. He was gradually revealing a sardonic sense of humour.

'It'll soon be Christmas,' Ruby said as she passed a cup to Jacob. 'And did you say doctor's going away?' They all smiled.

Alice pointed to a corner of the kitchen, where sewing stood on a table. 'I'm trying to make a few extra things for the stall . . . lavender bags and such. They make nice little presents.'

The talk of Christmas went on, but Jacob was quiet, drinking his tea and looking out of the window. Eventually, Alice tried to bring him back into the conversation. 'What will you do for Christmas, Jacob? Didn't you have a sister?' There was a dim memory of a female Fowler, rather older than Alice.

'Aye, but our Betty's in Canada. So she doesn't ask me to go for Christmas dinner. And I can't leave the horses, in any case.'

Ruby looked over at him, considering. 'Well, why not come to our place for your dinner? There's no call to be sitting on your own. There'll be just Gabriel and me, and little Bobby, and Alice. That's all, and the goose in the yard is big enough for twenty folks!' She smiled happily.

Jacob shuffled and looked uncomfortable. 'There's no call to spoil your family Christmas with the likes of me.'

'The sort of gracious reply I'd expect from you, Fowler.' Alice looked at him severely. 'If Ruby says you're coming, then you are.'

Jacob got up to go. 'Aye, well. Thank you kindly, Ruby. I'll be there.'

The next day, Alice went into the stables and found Jacob working at something, whistling under his breath. He wouldn't say what it was.

For three peaceful days, there was no Fanshawe at Masham.

Dr Poole was to be called in case of an emergency and everyone hoped that no emergency would occur.

Expectant mothers had been warned to contact Dr Poole; there were no cases of pneumonia, in spite of the cold weather, and the children were all healthy. They probably wouldn't need Dr Poole at all. And then there was an accident.

On Christmas Eve, Alice was cleaning the front windows when she heard a commotion at the far side of the square. A runaway horse was careering wildly across the cobbles, evading the farmer who was bravely trying to catch it.

Jacob was sweeping the gateway of the doctor's house, and when he saw the horse he dropped the broom and leaped forward. He caught the loose bridle but he was dragged along the ground, until gradually the horse slowed down and stopped just short of a small child, playing in the gutter. Gasping, Jacob patted the horse and calmed it. The animal's sides were heaving and steam was rising from the sweating flanks.

The owner of the horse collected it and thanked Jacob profusely. He was a stranger, visiting Masham for Christmas, and the horse was young and only just broken in. It had panicked at the sight of a flapping flag and had run through the town. It was very lucky that no one had been hurt.

Jacob went back into his stable like a rabbit into a hole, refusing the reward that the horse's owner offered. Alice found him sitting on his usual feed bin, nursing his arm. 'Let's have a look at the arm, Jacob. You must have grazed it badly.'

'It's nowt.' Jacob backed off, as she had suspected he might. With a lot of persuasion, she managed to get a look at the wound and was horrified. There was a deep hole in Jacob's left arm. Thank goodness, the elbow seemed to be intact.

'We need Dr Poole to see to this. I'll drive you there,' Alice offered. 'Can you bend the arm? I don't think the bone is broken, but the wound is very deep.'

'Bugger Dr Poole.' Jacob turned away, biting his lip. 'I'll be right, I tell you.'

It wasn't going to be possible to drag Jacob down to Tanfield against his will; something else would have to be done. 'We must stop the bleeding, first,' Alice told him, trying to sound as firm as possible. 'Come into the kitchen, where the light is better.'

Jacob staggered a little as he walked into the kitchen; reaction was setting in. 'And what makes you think you can do anything?' He sounded like the grumpy old Jacob.

Alice made Jacob sit down then gave him a cup of hot, sweet tea. 'And now, let me at it, lad. I know what I'm doing.' She saw his dubious expression, and sighed. 'As a matter of fact, I am not just a stallholder who sells herbs. I have actually learned how to use them, from the housekeeper up at the castle.' As she spoke, she was quietly getting together what she needed. 'The old lass up there could heal most cuts and bruises. If the arm isn't broken, I reckon we can heal it with—'

'Some of your blasted lavender, I suppose.' Jacob's face, rath-white, had the ghost of a sneer. 'Well, if it's choice between thee and Dr Poole—'

'Yes?' Alice's voice held the steel she had once observed in a hospital matron. 'If you won't go to Poole, I can't force you. So, Fowler, for heaven's sake, let me see to it! Have some common sense!' In spite of the firm tone, she laid gentle hands on Jacob as he sat at the table, and he did not flinch. His arm was held over a bowl, and the wound was swabbed clean of gravel with a generous flooding of cold lavender tea. Even the scent of laven-der was soothing; Alice felt a little less agitated, and she hoped that Jacob was influenced, too. He sat still for the operation. All he said was, 'They call you the lavender girl.'

Alice then applied a soothing green cream to a pad of clean cotton cloth, and held it close until it covered the wound. Then she wrapped a bandage round the arm to hold the pad in place; the bleeding had stopped. Satisfied, she looked into the groom's face. 'Is that better? Last summer, I made a cream with chick-weed and daisy leaves, both good for fresh wounds. Little Bobby's always falling down and grazing his knees.'

Jacob looked at Alice and a slow smile spread over the pale face. 'Well done, lavender girl. It's grand, Alice. Better than Young Cecil himself.' For a fleeting moment, he put a hand over hers. 'Thank you, lass. Now, I require another cup of tea with lots of sugah.'

'Of course, Fowler. That's the next stage of the treatment for shock.'

On Christmas Day, Greenwood and Fowler walked decorously, but in full view, across the market square at Masham and down the lane to where Gabriel and Ruby Turner lived. They were 'consorting', but Dr Fanshawe was safely away in Harrogate. 'Let's not think about Young Cecil today,' Alice said. Jacob carried a parcel rather awkwardly with his good arm and Alice had a big basket of Christmas cheer: mince pies on top and mysterious objects underneath.

Little Bobby met them at the gate, coming forward eagerly at first and then hanging back when he saw Jacob. But not for long; when he saw the contents of Jacob's parcel, Bobby could not believe his eyes. 'For me? Just for me? A little train, and little wagons full of coal, just like Masham station!'

Alice looked at the groom. 'So that's what you were busy with, in the stable! What a good idea. Well done, Fowler.' The man was not nearly so horrible as he believed himself to be.

Bobby's happiness was infectious and it was a cheerful party that gathered round the dinner table. Gabriel and Ruby both knew Jacob fairly well, since they were all Masham folk; but his recent reputation for sourness had kept everybody at arm's length. Today, he seemed to be trying hard. 'This is grand,' he exclaimed when he saw the table, decorated with holly. He thanked Ruby graciously when she cut up his meat, seeing that he had only one arm; the other was still in a sling.

'I remember your dad farmed at Low Moor, over the common,' Gabriel said thoughtfully. 'You never got the chance to take it yourself?' He passed the gravy.

Jacob poured some more gravy over his dinner before answering. 'Nay, the chance was never mine. Landlord took the farm over, when my old man retired. I did have a mind to farm, but,' he sighed, 'it'll likely not happen now.'

Dusk was settling down over Masham when Gabriel went out for the evening chores and Jacob stood up reluctantly. 'Horses will be looking for their evening feed.' Ruby persuaded him to come back for the evening and he seemed quite pleased.

When Jacob had gone, Ruby made up the fire with fresh logs and looked over at Alice. 'What do you really think of him, lass?'

'He's rude, of course, but underneath, Jacob is . . . well, he's a good lad. Very cool, very capable. Much better than me, with Fanshawe.'

'Gabriel is still looking for a tenant for Ellershaw,' Ruby reminded her. 'Jacob Fowler might make a good tenant, if he could find himself a wife.'

'Never!' Alice scoffed.' He's frightened of women and I dare say they feel the same about him. Anyway, he's very loyal to the Dents.'

EIGHT

'Fowler, you really should tell Dr Fanshawe about that arm.' Alice was helping Jacob to saddle Honey for the doctor's rounds, because the groom was obviously in difficulty, although he never mentioned it. The little doctor was back from his Christmas leave, but he had hardly noticed Jacob's plight. 'Cut yourself, did you? That was careless,' was all he said when he saw the bandage.

'Nay, Boss will be back next week; I'll hang on until then.' The groom gritted his teeth as he fastened the girth. 'I reckon the muscles have torn, or the shoulder's out, or summat. The sore's healing, but I can't manage very well, as you see. There's no strength in this arm.'

'Well, let me know when you need a hand.' Turning to go back to the kitchen, Alice suddenly realized that Jacob had not been rude to her – not very rude, anyway – for some time. 'Dr Fanshawe seems to be out a lot this week.'

Honey's hoofs clattered as Jacob brought her out of the stall, ready for the day's work. 'I reckon Young Cecil's trying to get round all the patients before Boss comes back, so they tell Boss how good he is.' Honey gave a sardonic neigh at that, and they both laughed. 'He's off Bedale way, over Watlass moor, said he'd call in on Mr Paterson's groom on the way back. Likes the posh houses, Cecil does.'

Dr Fanshawe bounced off on his rounds, Jacob cleaned out the stable as best he could with one arm, and Alice went back to preparing the lunch; the doctor would expect to be served punctually at one o'clock. The morning went quickly; the house needed an extra clean before the Dents came back and there were cakes to make for the welcome home party. Most of the patients knew about the party by now, and many of them had said that they would be there.

One o'clock came and went, but Fanshawe did not return. Alice looked in at the stables. 'Are you sure doctor said he'd be back for lunch?' It sometimes happened that he would stay out all day, and perhaps they were the days when he met Dr Poole down at Tanfield and told him the secrets of the practice. The sooner Dr Dent came back, the better.

Jacob was certain. 'He promised to be back; Honey had a long day in the trap yesterday. That mare needs a rest.' He stroked the silky nose of the second horse, Silver, a shining dappled grey. 'He should have taken Silver here, but the lad's a bit too frisky a ride for Young Cecil.'

By three o'clock, it was beginning to look as though Fanshawe had met with an accident. Evidently worried more about Honey that about her rider, Jacob came into the kitchen, his good arm in the sleeve of his coat. 'Give us a hand, lass? That's better. Now, I think I'd better take Silver out in the trap, and look for Young Cecil. I allus get him to tell me which way he's going, in case he falls off. You just never know, with him.'

Between them, Alice and Jacob yoked Silver. 'I think I'd better come with you, Fowler,' Alice said firmly. 'You can't drive too well, now can you?'

The groom looked at her critically. 'I can likely drive better with one arm than you can with two, woman.'

Alice had brought out a heavy shawl and she now wrapped it round her. 'But what if you find him and have to bring Honey home . . . or go for help, or something. . . ? I'm coming with you.' They didn't know what they might be facing, on the long road to Bedale.

Of course, Jacob insisted on driving, the reins bunched in his good hand, which mercifully was his right. They bowled along at a brisk pace, over the bridge and up from the valley onto the higher land at the other side of the river. Once out of the town they saw no one; the winter dusk would soon be closing in, but a ragged sunset lit the western sky and gave them a golden, late afternoon light.

Looking for Cecil made them uneasy, but it was pleasant all the same to ride out on a fine afternoon. Would they be accused, once more, of 'consorting'? But if the doctor needed help, he might be pleased to see them. Trying not to feel guilty about deserting the kitchen, Alice sat decorously in the trap as far as possible from Jacob.

The groom was looking about him, watching for any sign of the missing horse. He pointed out a stoat in the hedge, and they saw a couple of hovering hawks. 'It beats me where he's got to,' Jacob muttered. The air was getting colder as the sun went down behind the ridge.

On the brow of a little hill was a thick grove of trees, at a crossroads where farm lanes led off from the main road. Jacob slowed to a walk, and then stopped. 'Look at yon tracks.' He pointed to where the grass had been churned to mud by a horse's hoofs; the trail led into the wood. They both held their breath and listened.

Rooks were homing to the wood, cawing in the trees; there was the trickle of a beck somewhere near at hand. Then they heard a muffled cry, very faint. Throwing the reins to Alice, Jacob hopped down to the road and walked into the bushes. In a few minutes he reappeared. 'Tie Silver up to this tree here, lass. Doctor's in there, and we'll have all on to get him out.'

It was so dark in the wood that at first Alice could see nothing, but then Fanshawe's pale face showed in the gloom. He was half sitting, half lying near a bed of nettles and he seemed to be confused. 'Help . . . help,' he murmured. 'Is that you, Fowler? Thank God for that! I thought I was done for.'

'Can you walk, sir? Please try – we have the trap here, to take you home.' Heaven help them if he couldn't heave himself up into the trap; he was far too heavy to lift. Alice offered him a hand.

'Go away, Greenwood. I can't have a woman seeing me like this.' Fanshawe spoke hoarsely, tugging at his coat. 'Oh my head, my head—' Blood trickled down his face.

Alice looked down and saw that his legs were bare, fat little white legs with an ugly nettle rash where the plants had stung him. 'What happened to your trousers, Dr Fanshawe?' She managed to remain quite grave and decorous, but behind her Jacob gave a snort.

The little man pointed to a tree far above his head, where the trousers were draped across a branch. 'My . . . nether garments are up there.' He could hardly speak.

With a look at Jacob, Alice found a long stick and managed to unhook the trousers and bring them down. Fanshawe turned his back and put them on in silence.

'Where's the horse?' Jacob demanded, but Fanshawe shook his head. It took him a few minutes to be able to walk, and the light was failing by the time they half dragged him to the trap.

Fanshawe was still rather dazed, but he was seething with fury. 'This is the second time! First the snow, and then this! I will never set foot in this parish again.' Jacob grinned at Alice, over the doctor's head. That would suit Fowler down to the ground.

Alice lit the carriage lamps and they jogged slowly back to Masham in the winter dusk, the doctor moaning softly the whole way. He was battered and bruised, stung with nettles, and covered in mud. But he was not talking; his servants were left to wonder what had happened. The trousers in the tree hinted at malice, something more than falling off a horse. Some enemy to Dr Fanshawe had stripped him and thrown them up there. But who?

Jacob graciously allowed Alice to drive the trap; he had probably wrenched his arm, helping Fanshawe into the vehicle. Although it was a long time ago, Alice had often driven her father's cart, taking vegetables to market, and she felt quite confident with the reins. The lights were being lit in the little town, the windows had a golden glow and chimneys were smoking, as folk stoked up their fires. It was a relief to get out of the wild wood, back into civilization again.

'You must have taken a rare tumble, Doctor,' Jacob offered, not quite sympathetically. 'Just how did you fall off?'

'I did not fall off!' the little man was indignant. 'I was brutally attacked and dragged into the bushes!'

Jacob was alarmed. 'Was you robbed? The villains have taken Honey?'

'N-no, not robbed.' The doctor was quiet for a moment, and then sighed deeply. 'I was . . . warned by a . . . ruffian with a club . . . to . . . to leave the area immediately, and that it what I intend to do. I will go to Harrogate tomorrow.' He nursed his jaw.

But Dr Dent was not due back until next week. 'Very good, sir, we'll manage,' Alice decided.

Jacob persisted. 'And who was so keen to get rid of you?'

Silence. Then the doctor said stiffly, 'I do not know who the ruffian was; I have never seen him before and I am quite determined never to see him again, or to stay in this uncouth country any longer than necessary. I have had enough.' His jaw shut with a snap, and then he winced.

Alice looked grimly at the road ahead. Most people would be glad to see the doctor go, but who would feel so strongly as to take a club to him? 'What did he look like, Doctor?'

'Huge, ferocious. I would have fought anyone of my own size. With red hair. He hit me on the head, and uttered awful threats,' Fanshawe shuddered. 'I shall never get over it, never.'

'And the horse?' the groom persisted.

'The horse galloped off – he hit the horse too. It went over the moor.'

'Most people know that Honey is Dr Dent's mare,' Alice said to Jacob, to comfort him a little. 'Someone will stable her for the night, and let us know where she is. Do you know anyone of that description, Jacob?' Huge, ferocious. It was not very precise.

Dr Fanshawe was helped to bed, after supper and a hot bath. The next day he packed his bags, left a note for the Dents and departed on the noon train. Whoever it was who had a grudge against him had truly run him out of town. The little doctor had nothing to say to his servants, and they kept as quiet as possible. It was all over so quickly that it left Alice with a feeling of shock.

'Best day since the Boss went away,' Jacob said with satisfaction as the train steamed out of Masham. 'Now, we'd best try to find that mare. I dare not face the boss. We've got to find her before he comes back.'

'And we'd best start getting ready for the party, too.' Alice had her own worries. She was in charge of the food for the party, which was to follow a concert and might be the biggest event in Masham for some time.

That afternoon, Adam Burns called in at the doctor's yard, while Alice was there. 'I was up at Paterson's this morning; they've a chestnut mare in the stable. Nobody mentioned it to me, but I think it might be yours, Jacob, and Dr Fanshawe wasn't there. I wouldn't swear to it, but I think it could be the mare you had in the trap, the day Dr Fanshawe had lunch there.'

'Thank you kindly, sir, it's sure to be Honey. She ran off yesterday on Dr Fanshawe. Was she injured, sir?'

Adam smiled. 'She looked tired, head down and very muddy, but I think she's sound. But what about the doctor?'

'Nay, he'll survive.' Jacob paused. 'Matter of fact, Mr Burns, he's gone. Said he'd been attacked and threatened up on Watlass Moor, and he's gone, that's a fact.' Alice thought he was trying to hide his jubilation.

Adam looked serious. 'That's bad . . . if ordinary, decent citizens are in danger on our moor roads. I wonder what the motive was?'

Alice shook her head. She noticed Jacob looking at the sky; it was too late to go to Paterson's that night.

Of course, the next day Jacob insisted that he had to bring Honey home, and that involved Alice because once again, she would not let him go alone. 'Yes, you can tie Honey to the back of the trap to come home, but no, you can't manage it all with one arm.' Then she changed her approach. 'Please let me come with you, Fowler, I've never seen Paterson's place.' She had been in favour of waiting until one of Paterson's men came down to Masham; surely they'd bring the horse back. But Jacob would not wait.

Leaving a note on the door directing emergencies to Dr Poole, Alice joined Jacob, who could not conceal his impatience to be off and to get the horse back again. 'I'll give her extra oats,' he muttered as they went up the road. 'Linseed oil, an' all. She's got to look fit when Boss comes back.' He sighed. 'It's been a right strain, I can tell you, letting Cecil loose with the horses. I allus knew something like this would happen.'

'Do you think it will rain?' Alice wanted to change the subject, to get away from thinking about Fanshawe. The clouds were low and the tops of the moors hidden by mist; it was a gloomy January day and the countryside was sleeping, waiting for the spring.

It would be good to see Laura's future home, even though Alice would probably not get a glimpse of the inside of the house. As a lady's maid, she had enjoyed visiting beautiful houses with her employer; it was probably the only aspect of her old life that she missed.

The day got darker and there seemed to be an almost ominous gloom hanging over Linley Grange, even before they had passed the huge Tudor gateposts of the drive. 'We'll have to go careful,' Jacob warned her. 'We've no message from the boss; we're here on our own. But they must know who she is,' he added, as if to convince himself.

Jacob drove slowly into the farm yard, and it was soon obvious that there was something wrong at the Grange farm. Cattle were bellowing, farm men huddled in groups. They hardly glanced at the visitors; all their attention was elsewhere. They were looking at a shape on the ground. A figure was lying face down in the dirt, very still. Another man knelt beside him. Alice got down from the trap hurriedly. 'Can we do anything?'

'Nay, he's dead. I dragged the young fool out of the bull pen and then I went to tell Mr Paterson; he's sent for Dr Fanshawe. We thought it was him coming now, in the trap. Where's doctor?' The man's face was grey; his eyes were hopeless, defeated.

Jacob had tied up their horse and he came over. 'Good day, Henry.' He looked down at the body. 'Poor young Joseph . . . the bull did for him, then.'

Alice felt sick. Young Joseph Wood, whom she'd seen often enough in Masham, lying there covered in muck and straw; what a waste of a life. Impulsively, she knelt beside the lad and felt his wrist gently; was it possible that they were wrong? She wanted to bathe his wounds, to try to revive him. But there was no flicker of life; and then she saw the hole in his chest that the bull had gored, and bowed her head.

Paterson strode across the yard, flushed and agitated. 'Where's Fanshawe? Unfortunately it's too late to save Joseph's life, but we will need a death certificate. This is . . . this is a terrible shock to us all.' He looked hard at Jacob Fowler. 'Where's the doctor, man? I thought you'd brought him.'

Another group of men came into the yard with a load of turnips and they rushed over to the bull pen and then stood back, obviously horrified by what they saw. Jacob said quietly,' I'm sorry, sir. Dr Fanshawe has left for Harrogate; you will have to send for Dr Poole from Tanfield, who is standing in for him. We are here to collect the mare. Dr Dent's mare.' There was a silence; nobody seemed to know what to do.

'He were a good lad, wanted to be a farmer,' one older man said, tears on his cheeks. Paterson seemed stunned. His handsome face a dark red, he stood looking at the body.

Two men put the body on a hurdle and went into the big barn. Jacob spoke to the grooms about his horse; Honey was there, they at least knew why he had turned up. Paterson paced up and down, breathing fast.

'Did you see the accident?' Alice asked Henry, who was shaking.

Henry looked across the yard to the rain clouds sweeping across the moor, and down at the cobbles of the yard. 'I told him!' he muttered. 'But I never saw him go in, that last time. I . . . I just heard old bull roaring, like, and went to see what was up.'

The doctor would want to know who saw poor Joseph go into the pen, all the details. But nobody had seen what happened. 'I heard bull bellowing and came over to see what was up,' Henry repeated uneasily. 'That lad was always taking risks. I only hope as they don't blame me. I might ha' been a bit hard on the lad, but I'd never—' The man's eyes were darting about, not looking at Alice.

Why should they blame Henry? The bull was to blame.

Jacob had collected Honey; there was nothing they could do, so they'd better get home before dark. A woman came into the yard, carrying a basket. A shawl hid most of her face, but she walked quickly, with a straight back.

Henry groaned. 'His mother. She's bringing eggs for the kitchen. She don't know, of course. Could you talk to her for a bit, lass?' he asked Alice. 'Another woman would be better—'

Quickly, Alice said to Jacob, 'Can you wait a little while? I've been asked to talk to this poor woman.' It would have been easier to refuse, to hop into the trap and drive back to Masham, but it was the least she could do.

Jacob was busy tying Honey to the back of the trap. 'Aye, do what you can, lass. I'll keep away, there's nowt I can do.'

Mrs Wood came across the yard with a confident stride and looked round at the men, as they stood silent, with bare heads. 'What's up, then?'

Nobody spoke. The boy's mother looked round in sudden doubt. 'Where's our Joey?'

'I'm afraid that Joseph has had . . . an accident.' Paterson led the woman into the barn and Alice followed. Mrs Wood sagged visibly when she saw the lifeless body and the truth dawned on her. She sat down on a feed bin, white and shaking, but not weeping. Alice went up quietly and stood by her side.

Paterson touched her shoulder compassionately. 'My dear Mrs Wood, I am so sorry that this has happened.'

The woman turned on him suddenly. 'You should have taken better care of him! He were only a lad! But you didn't care about poor Joey.' She put her head in her hands and Alice stood by uncomfortably, not knowing what to do or say. Anger was natural, of course; anger had consumed Alice when Tom died.

The landowner spoke hoarsely. 'Mrs Wood . . . it was an accident.'

Joseph's mother turned savagely. 'You never called me Mrs Wood when you fathered him! When I was a young maid at the hall, only sixteen, and you came to my bed in the night! My name was Maisie then, and you called me a bonny lass.' She broke out in wild, uncontrollable sobbing.

Paterson shook his head. 'Now, now, Mrs Wood. This is a fantasy. You can be punished, you know, for making such a vile accusation. I have warned you before about your delusions.' He turned aside to Alice. 'The poor soul is harmless enough as a rule, but deranged, of course. But I cannot allow this kind of thing. I must speak to the doctor, I am sure he will find evidence of insanity . . . and of course, this death may be the last straw for the poor woman's wits.'

Alice looked round, but no one else had heard the woman's accusation. She felt rather sorry for Paterson, at the mercy of a crazy woman, but surely, he would be believed before she was. His statement would carry the greater weight.

Mrs Wood had not finished. 'You know, Bradley Paterson, with your airs and graces! You know! And now we've lost him, poor little Joseph, your lad and mine. I should never have let him work for you. But I always hoped you'd give him a farm. That was what he wanted, poor lad.' Bending over the body, she sobbed.

Paterson kept his tone low and soothing. 'You have another boy, I believe. I will make sure that you and he are well provided for. The accident happened here, and while I can't be held responsible for Joseph's death, I will try to compensate a little for this terrible loss.'

Alice was at the door, but Paterson came over to her. 'We must allow for the shock, the grief. We have all been shocked by this terrible event, of course. I am sorry that you had to be here. I will be obliged if you would say nothing of this to Miss Grey as it would only distress her.' He looked keenly at Alice. 'I will get an opinion about Mrs Wood in a week or two. I don't need to tell you that she is entirely deluded. So far as I know she has never worked at my house. Joseph's father came from Ripon, and I assume she came with him.'

'Yes, sir.'

Paterson walked across the yard with Alice. 'She was always rather strange, but harmless, we thought. She was allowed to keep the cottage when her husband died, and I employed Joseph, to help her. One tries to look after one's people, of course.'

There was nothing for Alice to say; she was an outsider, and nothing would comfort Mrs Wood. Jacob was waiting with the two horses, the wind was rising and it was time to go home, to get out onto the fresh, cold moor.

Mrs Wood took the eggs to the kitchen door, a true, stoical woman – and not obviously insane. If she persisted in her allegations, what would the Greys think? Paterson was rich and influential, but if he lost his good name and the respect of the community, what then?

Paterson came up to Jacob as Alice climbed into the trap. 'Thank you for looking after the mare, sir,' the groom said politely. 'Dr Dent will be home in a few days. Sorry to hear about the accident, sir – a bad business.'

Paterson sighed. 'Farms are dangerous places, of course. We must design safer bull pens, and I suppose I'd better shoot the animal, before I go away again.'

A black depression seemed to settle on Alice as they jogged back to Masham, with the mare Honey trotting behind them, her reins tied to the back of the trap. Wild rain came sweeping over the heather, backed by the icy wind. Jacob turned up his coat collar and Alice pulled the shawl tightly round her, trying to remember what it was about Joseph's body that had made her uneasy. There was something not quite right, but she couldn't put her finger on it. The image of the poor lad floated before her eyes. He was filthy, there was a huge wound in his chest . . . and yes, there were red weals on his neck.

Alice tried to imagine what might have happened. Henry had seemed to be afraid he would be blamed. Suppose that he had lost his temper and attacked the young man, killed him by accident? He could have dragged the body into the pen, and then stirred up the bull.

'Nasty piece of work, that bull,' Jacob said at length. 'Did you see how he still pawed the ground and roared? There was a pitchfork in the pen, the poor lad probably tried to defend himself.'

'Do you know the workers here, Jacob? What are they like?'

'I know Henry Beal; he was a Masham lad and he worked for my dad over at Low Moor. A good worker, Dad said, but very jealous, old Henry was.' Jacob shook the rain out of his eyes.

'Jacob, I think there was something strange about that accident.' Alice spoke carefully 'Did you see the marks on his neck?'

'Nay, I went to fetch the mare. I was never one to gawp at misfortune.' Jacob looked across at her from under the cap. 'Like . . . he was strangled? That's serious, that is. But I expect doctor will see them, when he comes up for the death certificate.'

NINE

The accident at Linley Grange stayed in Alice's mind, even though they were all busy with the Dents' return and waiting to hear of their plans for the future. It was surprising that there was no mention of the death in the newspaper. Jacob had seen one of the Grange workers at the Bruce Arms, a few days afterwards. He reported to Alice the next day as she hung out washing on the line. 'Yon Joseph's gone to his grave,' he announced gloomily. 'All very quiet – even his ma wasn't there, she's been certified and taken off to the asylum. Mad with grief, they said. They might let her out, later on.'

'Poor woman! I wonder—' Alice finished pegging out a table-cloth and looked across at the groom. 'What did Dr Poole make of it, I wonder? Mr Paterson sent for him, when he found out that Fanshawe had gone.'

'Ha! He didn't turn up; it was too far from Tanfield. Sent back to say he'd issue the certificate without seeing him, as it was obviously an accident. Undertaker said same . . . only, the lad I was talking to wondered if Henry had owt to do with it. Henry's been off work since with the gripes, he said.'

'Goodness.' Alice stood still in the winter garden, thinking about Mrs Wood and her story. Was it the truth, or the ravings of a madwoman? It was hard to believe that such a pleasant man as Paterson, a model employer and a popular landlord, would have seduced a young girl and refused to acknowledge her child as his son. The gentry sometimes had their little fling, but they usually put it right with money, and Paterson had plenty of that. But, why had Joseph died? 'Do you think we should say anything, Jacob?' The truth was important, for Laura's sake.

'I've been wondering that myself, but we can't bring the lad back, or help his ma. The only thing we can do is keep our ears open. The truth might come out, in the end.'

'Wherever can they be? They should all be here by now!' Laura drummed imperiously on the table and then looked guiltily at Alice, probably remembering that she wasn't supposed to be imperious. Alice had recently let her know, quite tactfully, how much she had improved since 'Greenwood' first came to work at the Hall. One must remember the difference between Yorkshire and India, she had learned.

The Masham Mechanics' Institute was a good place for community events, but it was probably going to be a squeeze to pack in all the patients tonight. 'The only place where Church and Chapel can meet,' Ruby had commented. Tonight they could forget about the things that divided them; everybody in Masham, it seemed, wanted to welcome back their doctor. Tonight the large room was bright with oil lamps and the glow of a good fire.

There was a hum of activity in the kitchen, where a huge kettle sat on the range and the central table was laden with good things. Cakes, sandwiches and pies stood ready for the feast, many of them made by Alice, who was wondering whether there was enough food. This was the first time that young Laura had mixed with the lower classes, but there she was, talking happily to Ruby, although heaven knew what they found to talk about.

The scene was set, but some of the players were missing. Dr and Mrs Dent, the guests of honour, safely back from the south, were sitting by the fire with the vicar. Jacob, pale and unfamiliar in collar and tie, was arranging chairs for the concert, with one hand because his damaged arm was in a sling; Dr Dent had treated it immediately. Alice thought privately that the fact that

Fanshawe had not treated Jacob must have told Dr Dent a lot. But where were the patients? The loyal supporters hadn't yet turned up.

Jacob sidled up as Alice laid out cups and saucers on a side table at the back of the room. 'Wonder where they are?' Alice shook her head and he continued, 'Boss had a talk to me, but he hasn't said owt yet, about whether he's staying or going. Has he told you?'

'No, Jacob. I think he'll tell us all, when he makes his speech.' And let's hope for Jacob's sake that they're staying. Alice glanced over to the group by the fire. Dr Dent looked relaxed and cheerful, but his wife was rather strained, to judge from her expression. Was she dreading his resignation?

'I feel responsible,' Laura said, coming over to Alice. 'If nobody comes tonight . . . we've invited everybody, the villagers as well as townsfolk. Papa and Mama agreed to be here. What will Papa say if there is no audience for his speech?' The colonel was pacing up and down, looking at his watch every few minutes. This event was not running on army lines, Alice could hear him thinking. 'And does it mean that they've already gone over to Dr Poole?' She frowned anxiously.

Mrs Grey, on the other hand, was sitting in an armchair by the fire and looked as though she were enjoying the occasion. 'I suppose dear Dr Fanshawe will be coming tonight? He is such an excellent doctor, I am sure all your patients will agree. My husband knew that he was exactly the right person to look after the practice for you, Dr Dent; I would not be surprised if he has gained more patients for you.'

Dr Dent shook his head. 'I'm afraid he won't be here, Mrs Grey. He was unwell, and went home to Harrogate. But we have had a very good holiday and we are grateful to him.' Alice busied herself with the plates to hide a smile. The Dents had read Cecil's letter, and they had been told quite forcibly by their groom that Dr Fanshawe had been far from an excellent employer.

'I don't think Dr Fanshawe enjoyed his stay in Masham very much,' Mrs Dent said demurely.

'Can't think why.' The colonel was brisk. 'Colder than India, of course, but no cholera to speak of.'

The door opened and a group of people came in, people from the farms round Fearby and Healey. Adam Burns was among them and Alice thought how fresh and healthy he looked; he was just the opposite of Fanshawe. Adam seemed to get on well with people in all walks of life, but that might be because of his humble background – and then, he'd had a good education. He came over to Jacob and Alice. 'You got the horse back safely, then, before Dr Dent came back?' The farm manager spoke quietly to them both.

'Aye, we did, thanks to you, Mr Burns.' The surly Jacob could be gracious when he felt like it. 'She was mucky, but no worse, thank goodness. It beats me what happened to Young – to Dr Fanshawe, though.' Jacob looked round, but nobody was listening. 'Who would want to attack him? It's a mystery to me.' Smiling, Jacob looked as though he enjoyed the mystery.

Adam laughed quietly. 'Perhaps a jealous lover?' he murmured.

Alice looked over at Laura thoughtfully. Laura had told her that Fanshawe could possibly be about to propose marriage. What if Mr Paterson had heard of it? He had been quite violent with the artist, Felix Mayo . . . but no, that had been a misunderstanding. Mr Paterson was far too civilized to send a man out to remove Dr Fanshawe's trousers, through jealousy over Laura.

Laura joined the party round the fire, in time to hear the Dents being happy about their homecoming. 'It is so good to be home,' Emily Dent said with feeling. 'And everything is in such good order, too. The house is gleaming, the pantry is full of good food and, of course, the horses are in good health.'

'Thanks to our wonderful staff,' Dr Dent smiled. 'Alice has baked a magnificent cake!' Alice was placing the iced cake in the centre of the table at that moment, and blushed to be the centre of attention. But the warm glow persisted; the Dents had been so pleased with her efforts, and Alice and Jacob were both to receive a bonus in addition to their wages. She would buy some stuff for a new dress, and perhaps some little pots for her hand cream.

The waiting went on; Laura was talking to the Dents about how much her health had improved in the last few weeks. 'Alice has encouraged me to walk, and of course we have the dog . . . I feel so much more alive! And then, too, we have been planning changes to the grounds and I've been asked to design a cottage.'

Dr Dent looked suitably impressed. 'For once, somebody has taken my advice. Well done, Miss Laura. Exercise, I believe, is always important; many ladies in your situation sit down far too much.' He dropped his voice a little. 'It's not always easy, I suppose, when mamas want their girls to be thoroughly ladylike.'

'I'm painting again now, as well.' Laura smiled. 'Dr Fanshawe thought you had encouraged me to be ill, he said.'

The doctor raised his eyebrows; he must be hearing many stories about his locum tonight. 'But Alice is bracing, is she not? That was the intention!'

After consideration, Alice decided that to be bracing was not a bad thing. It had been what Laura needed, at the time. And here came the patients, at last, a throng of people, laughing and talking, with the big blacksmith towering above the crowd.

Seth Watson, the smith, was pushed forward with a bulky parcel, which he set down on the floor in front of the Dents. The vicar spoke gracious words and the guests of honour unwrapped the parcel. It was a set of wrought-iron fireside tools, poker, brush, shovel and stand, made by Seth in his forge. The work was almost delicate and the design included an owl, which may have been a tribute to the doctor's wisdom, or there because folks knew he loved birds.

Dr Dent looked at his wife speechlessly and she spoke first. 'We've always admired the craftsmen of Masham. We will treasure this gift as a memento of Masham, made here and given to us by our friends; we will never forget you.'

Oh, dear. Laura and Alice looked at each other. It sounded as though this was a farewell speech. Jacob was swallowing nervously.

'Well,' Seth said, with his huge hands still black from the forge and twisting with nerves. 'That's very kind of you, Missis. I'm sorry we're a mite late, but I've just finished it, you see.'

Dr Dent stood up and there was a hush. He looked round the crowded room and raised his voice to carry to the far end. 'What can I say? My wife speaks for us both. We are both thankful to be home again, with better health. I would like to think that I've completely recovered. But,' his voice deepened a little, 'I must tell you that we have decided to make changes, to try to prevent such a thing occurring again.'

Alice heard Jacob breathing heavily beside her.

'Dr Poole has agreed to take over the eastern part of the practice, from Tanfield down to Ripon. That leaves me with Masham and the moorland, so most of you here tonight are still my patients.' There was a general sigh of relief. The lowlanders on the other side of the river were a separate community, even though they often appeared at Masham markets; they wouldn't be missed too much.

Then the applause broke out, spontaneous applause for the speech; people were smiling at each other. The vicar stood up again. 'Thank you, doctor, for putting our minds at rest. The *Clarion* reported, you see, that you were not coming back to us at all and some of us have been anxious to hear your good news. And now, I call upon Colonel Grey to say a few words of official welcome.'

The colonel rose, the choir fiddled with their music sheets and the evening was under way.

Later that night, Alice went back to the surgery when the first guests left the party. She wanted to pull the kitchen fire together and to boil a kettle for the doctor's hot drink. The supper had been a success, the concert was bearable and no quarrels had broken out; a thoroughly satisfactory evening, in fact. She was thinking about the speeches when there was a light rap on the kitchen door. 'Who is it?' The Dents would come home through the front door, and the rule was that doors must be locked at night.

'It's me, you daft besom, who d'ye think?' The familiar insult made her smile as Jacob stepped into the kitchen. He was carrying some of the baskets in which food had been taken to the party. 'I fetched a bit of cake and pie home. Is that kettle boiling? I wouldn't mind another cup of tea.' He put down the baskets and loosened his tie. His lean, freshly shaved face, with the wide brow and determined chin, looked almost handsome. He could be quite attractive sometimes, when he lightened up a little. It was a pity that he was so miserable, as a rule.

'Thanks, Jacob Didn't they give you any supper?'

'Well, aye, but I was over-busy talking to eat much.' The groom sat down at the kitchen table and leaned back in the chair contentedly. 'Boss and Missis look right well. Boss came into the stable tonight, told me a few things.'

Alice poured the tea. 'What did he say about Dr Fanshawe?'

'Oh, Young Cecil told him he might as well give up. Practice is finished. Nobody can be expected to gallop about moors like Boss does, he said. No wonder it broke his health.' Jacob reached for a slice of fruit cake.

'What did he say about the patients?' Alice sat down with her own cup.

'Home visits to farms should be stopped!' Jacob managed to imitate Fanshawe's high, querulous voice. 'He reckons that if folks are daft enough, or so poor, that they have to bide out there in the country, they should either put up with their ailments, or bring 'em down to Masham to be cured. Of course, he said Dr Poole would be pleased to take over, if the patients are clean and in their right minds, and specially if they're guaranteed to pay. It was all in a great fat letter, along with the stuff about getting rid of the servants, who are most unsatisfactory. Boss reckons nowt to it, thank goodness.' He laughed shortly. 'So I told him that Cecil didn't understand the country, couldn't ride a horse, and should go back to the army.'

There was a sound in the passage and Dr Dent came into the kitchen. 'Poor Dr Fanshawe still catching it? Well, Jacob, you must understand that a doctor never hires a locum who is better than he is. It stands to reason; it would show him up! Thank you, Alice, we'll have a cup of hot milk and one of your oat biscuits.' He smiled at them both and disappeared.

'And never a word about us consorting.' Jacob's grey eyes were clear and guileless as he looked across the table. 'I suppose doctor knows well enough that I never get friendly with women. Cecil hadn't worked that out.'

'Well, and why not?' Alice put a pan of milk on the stove. Maybe it was time for a few home truths. 'There's no call to keep on being so miserable, Fowler, especially now that doctor's home. Just look at you tonight, clean and tidy, talking away to folks and enjoying the company. You are quite presentable, you know. I'm sure you'll find a good lass somewhere to keep you company, but you have to be in the right frame of mind.' She took out a tray and spread it with a cloth.

'Who says I want a lass? I'm right enough as I am.' It was a growl, but only a token one.

'Don't you think that your cottage would be brighter with a nice lass in it, and a little bairn or two? And then, your wife could clean for Mrs Dent,' Alice continued feelingly, 'and I could go home. See? I've worked it all out.'

Jacob snorted. 'So I see. Have you picked out the lass yet, or do I have any say in the matter?' He held out his cup for a refill.

'This is just a suggestion, Jacob. It's up to you.'

Jacob sighed as he put down his cup. His table manners were quite good, when you thought about it. 'Nay, I'm getting too old for a young lass, I'm over thirty. And to tell you the truth, Alice, when it comes to it, I . . . I'm too shy.'

'If shy people never got married, the human race would die out pretty soon. I think we're all shy, in different ways. I'd better take their milk in.' Alice went though to the sitting-room, where the doctor and his wife sat before a bright fire as if they had never been away. They both smiled and thanked her and Alice realized how much Fanshawe had made her appreciate ordinary courtesy.

'You seem to have tamed Jacob, Alice,' the doctor smiled.

'Well sir, it was more a case of, well, supporting each other when Dr Fanshawe was here.'

When she got back to the kitchen, the groom was still sitting at the table. 'Would you like to take some cake home, Jacob?' Alice was trying to suppress a yawn; it was time for bed.

'Aye, well, I suppose it's time to go – I'll take the hint.' But the groom seemed reluctant to leave. 'What about you, anyway? Maybe it's time you were wed, give you somebody to boss about.'

Alice laughed. 'I am not that bad, am I? But to tell you the truth, I was widowed and so it's over for me.'

'What happened to him? Who was he, anyway? I know you're a local lass, but I don't remember a Greenwood.' Jacob stood up and went to the door.

Alice wrapped up the rest of the fruit cake quickly. 'Tom was a fisherman. We went for holidays to Whitby when I was young, and Tom and his brother Andrew took us out in their boat – that's how we met.' She shook her head. 'It seems a long time ago. I went to live at Whitby when we got married, left Masham for a while. But I was only married for a couple of years, and then . . . Tom was drowned at sea. They never found his body. It's more than five years ago now. I was terribly shocked, of course, but . . . time heals.' If only Jacob would learn that for himself, and stop hankering after the girl he lost in the past. She handed him the cake.

'I'm sorry, lass,' Jacob said gently. He looked at the floor. 'Well, it applies to you, same advice as you've given me. Maybe it's time you took a fresh grip. You're better than a maid of all work. Why clean other peoples' houses for the rest of your life?' He slipped out of the door quickly, before Alice had time to answer.

Alice did not object to cleaning, but she had been hoping that the Dents would get their regular maid back, and let her go. It would soon be spring, with plenty to do in the herb garden, and she was still committed to Laura for one day a week. But Emily Dent brought bad news into the kitchen, the day after the party.

'Could you possibly stay a little longer, Alice? We won't get our maid back until March, at the earliest.'

'Er . . . I was hoping . . . but yes, if you need me, I will stay.' Alice sat down suddenly. It was loyalty that kept her here, but there was so much to do at home.

'Just a few weeks; it can't be too hard for you, now that Jacob is – shall we say – on your side?'

'Yes, Mrs Dent. Jacob was very – well, we worked together quite well. But I have my herb business to run—'

'I understand, Alice. We will try to let you do what is necessary, for the herbs.'

TEN

'Where's Jacob?' Dr Dent strode into the kitchen one Saturday afternoon, about two weeks after his return. Alice was washing dishes at the sink and watching whirling snowflakes through the window. 'He's not in the stables and we have an emergency at Healey.'

Alice took off her apron. 'He sometimes watches the football match on a Saturday, Doctor . . . but no, I remember now he said he was going to my brother-in-law's farm, to mouth a young horse for Gabriel.' She knew that Jacob was needed by the doctor sometimes not just as a driver, but as a second, steady pair of hands. Putting on her big shawl and boots, Alice went across the town to fetch the groom.

As expected, she found Gabriel leaning on the stable door and Jacob in the box with a young horse that was being introduced to the bit. The horse was chewing and frothing and Jacob had a quieting hand on its neck, and was talking to it softly.

'What's up, woman?' Jacob said surlily when he saw Alice, sprinkled in snowflakes, come into the stable yard. 'You should have the sense to stay in the kitchen, this weather.'

Gabriel looked stern, but Alice knew that Jacob was just reacting automatically, while he was running through what he needed to do to get the medical team on the road as quickly as possible. He would have known there was an emergency, as soon as she appeared. 'You're wanted, Fowler.' She smiled at Gabriel. 'Doctor asked me to fetch him; I'm sorry if you've not finished.'

Gabriel waved an arm. 'Nay, doctor's work comes first. It might be a case of saving life; we can't hold that up. Young hoss has likely had enough for one day. Er . . . Ruby wants to see you, lass. She's in the dairy.' He looked worried.

'Later, Gabriel. I'll be free about four o'clock.'

Alice and Jacob walked back together through the snow, which was melting as it touched the cobbles. 'Shouldn't hold us up too much, as this rate. Where are we off?' Jacob looked up at the clouds.

'Healey, I think he said.' Trotting beside him and trying to keep up with Jacob's long stride, Alice felt thankful that they remained on fairly good terms. They hadn't talked very much since the night of the party, but since the Dents came back he had been quite considerate and only occasionally rude. It seemed that Jacob was often asked to break in horses. 'Do you like it?' Alice asked him. She had seen horses broken with whips and curses to impose obedience through fear; it could be a thoroughly unpleasant exercise. Horsebreakers, in her experience, were rough and callous.

'I like to make sure it's done right.' Jacob's face was set. 'There's no call for cruelty, only patience – which some folks haven't got. You can gentle them into it, if they haven't been spoiled.' As they reached the surgery he added, 'Horses are better treated with kindness, than curses.'

Alice couldn't resist a parting shot. 'And so are men and women, Fowler.' Come to think of it, any lass who wanted Jacob would have to approach him with great gentleness, as though he were a scared young horse. And she wouldn't have to worry about his rudeness, under which, Alice had decided, lay a deep kindness.

Mrs Dent was going out to visit a friend, so Alice was not able to go to see her sister; the surgery must not be left unattended. Quite contentedly, she finished preparing the evening meal and made a batch of biscuits. Kettlewell biscuits, made from oatmeal, were the doctor's favourites. Alice had no inkling that her life was about to change; she was happy in the moment, since the snow had stopped and the medical team should be able to get home safely.

The first hint of change came when Ruby appeared at the kitchen door, seeming very agitated. 'I've got something to tell you, Alice. It will be a shock. Can you talk now?'

Alice drew her sister into the kitchen and shut the door. 'Come and sit down. It's bad news, is it? Yes, I can talk to you; there's nobody in the house. What's wrong, love?'

Ruby was breathing fast. 'I don't know whether it's good or bad. Well, lass, your Tom's come back to look for you. Seems he wasn't drowned, after all. I didn't know how you'd take it, so I never told him where you are. You might need a bit of time to get used to the idea.' She sat down then, looking relieved to have got the news out.

Tom back! The husband she thought she had lost, five years ago. Alice felt the blood drain from her face; she felt sick and giddy. Automatically, she pulled the kettle on to the stove. 'I . . . don't know how I feel,' she said slowly. 'Where has he been, all this time? If he didn't drown . . . he could have let me know, five years ago.' She felt let down; he obviously didn't care about her, after all. Her loving young husband had been all in her imagination.

Tom had been fun, but irresponsible. 'He might have changed in five years, but then, so have I.' Alice was not the young girl who had married her handsome fisherman. Did she still love him? She was not sure.

Ruby was looking anxious again. 'I don't quite know how to put this, but . . . I think you'll find he's changed, Alice. He seems . . . sort of coarser than I remember him, but then, he'll have had a hard life.'

Life with the North Sea fishing fleet was very hard, but Tom had known no other. He'd laughed when she suggested that he take a land job, after they were married. 'So – where is he?' Alice took a deep breath.

115

'Well, he was stopping somewhere in Ripon. He knew our Ma and Pa came from Masham and he thought you might be some-where here.' Ruby paused. 'But then he came up here to stay at the White Bear, and he was in to see us this morning. Did you . . . was you fond of him, Alice?' It was strange that Ruby had to ask the question; but she had seen very little of Alice and Tom during their married life at Whitby. 'I sometimes wondered whether he drank more than he should.'

'At times he did.' Tom had been young and thoughtless; Alice had loved his jokes and lightness of spirit, coming as she did from a serious, responsible family. Her father had been a small farmer and had also been postman who was promoted; he took his work seriously. But after a while she had wondered whether Tom would ever settle down – in fact, whether he would ever grow up. And then he had died, and her memories of their life together had been of the good times. The drinking, the rough-ness had been forgotten.

'He's saying he wants his wife back. "Neat little piece" is how he describes you, and I didn't like that at all.' Ruby shook her head disapprovingly. 'He'll have to learn a bit of respect.'

'Andrew and Tom both used to talk like that, at times,' Alice remembered. 'But Tom was a nicer lad.'

'So I said he could come to our house tonight, and I would try to get you there. You want to make sure you take him back on your terms! You don't have to rush back to live in Whitby, if you don't want to.' Ruby stood up to go.

'Well, I suppose I'll do my duty. I can't see how I can get out of it, even if he does want to go back to the coast.' Alice sighed. Why had he not come back to her until now?

'Why did it take you so long to come back? We were told you were lost when the boat went down, five years ago.' Alice faced Tom Greenwood in her sister's parlour, where Ruby had lit a fire so that they could talk privately; she was dismayed by what she saw. Tom was fair and ruddy as he had always been, but his face was weatherbeaten now, with broken veins on the cheeks. He had thickened up with age and his voice was harsher than she remembered. He looked nervous; he was avoiding her eye and stirring his tea busily.

Tom sighed at the question. 'Well, we got picked up by a Norwegian boat and they took us off to Norway. Of course, it took a long time to get back. It's a long story. But now, lass, I aim on settling down. Maybe take a shore job, mending boats and such. We'll go back to Whitby, of course.' He wasn't trying to act the loving husband, which was a relief, in a way.

Alice had thought about this for hours, and she was now prepared with an answer. Thank goodness Ruby had given her some warning. 'I can't go back to Whitby, Tom. I have a little herb business here, and besides, I've promised my employers that I will stay until the end of March.'

'You mean, you're not coming with me now?' He was surprised.

'I will stay where I am, for the present, Tom. And I think it will be best if I join you when you have found a house for us to live in, and a job of work to earn some money. As I recall, you were quite expensive to keep, what with the drink and the betting on horses.'

Tom looked at Alice then, with slightly bloodshot blue eyes. 'Nay, lass, you never used to snarl at me like that. You was always soft and cuddly.' He grinned, but the old charm had faded, like his looks. He looked rather like a pirate, with wary, calculating eyes.

'I am older now, Tom, and have had to earn my own living, all these years. It hasn't been easy. And you know, I don't trust you any more. Five years it took you to come back to me. You could have written a letter, at the very least! What is a wife to think about that? That's why I say you should find a house and a job before I give up what I have.'

Alice could have told him about her little cottage, but she didn't want him to know about it; the house was far too small for a man like Tom. Her cottage, so near to Ruby, and the herbs, the kind-hearted Dents and even Jacob Fowler, seemed very precious to her now that she was in danger of losing it all. She had a pleasant enough life at Masham; she was looking forward to the summer, and didn't want to leave. But she was shocked at her own cool reaction. If Tom had come home as soon as he was rescued, the younger Alice would have been overjoyed to have him back. It was sad, but there was not much feeling left, possibly not on either side. There was no warmth about the man.

'And as for cuddles, all you'll get from me is a sharp elbow, or a rolling pin, if you come near me. I don't want to see you again, until you can prove you have settled down.' The rolling pin was one of Jacob's jokes, and the thought of him seemed to make her feel stronger. Perhaps she'd learned a few sharp answers from the Dents' groom.

Tom leaned back, looking out of the window. 'Well, Alice, this is a shock, I must say. You've turned sour! Where's the bonny little lass I've been thinking about all these years?' Yes, he was blaming her for the change in their relationship. 'You've kept your looks, neat little waist and big brown eyes, but you sound like an old witch. It's very hard on a man, coming back to this.' He sighed again. 'I suppose you'll be coming at me for brass; women allus do.'

'I am not asking you for anything, Tom, except time to get used to this.' It would be hard to lose her independence, after the freedom she had enjoyed.

'You haven't found another husband, have you? That'd be just like a woman, to take up with somebody else and forget all about her poor old bloke, once his back was turned. How many other lads have you taken to your bed?' He was sneering, even as he reached over to her.

Alice got up, avoiding contact with Tom, and poured another cup of tea with steady hands. She was still surprised at how little emotion she felt. Her surly colleague Jacob was far more considerate and capable than Tom had ever been, she realized. 'Well,

Tom, I believe there are plenty of jobs here in Masham, if you look for them. I will agree to settle with you here if you can find a house, but I am not going back to Whitby.' To the isolation, the loneliness she had felt there; the cry of seagulls always reminded her of walking by the sea on her own, with Tom on a boat far away. 'So . . . will you settle in Masham? Or will you run away to sea?'

Tom Greenwood looked up at the beamed ceiling and groaned. 'Ties a man down, doesn't it? Cramps his style. You might have to work an' all, lass. Take in washing, or something of that.'

'I'll only work with herbs, Tom, no washing, thank you! And no drinking for you, if you live with me. I will keep you on the straight and narrow.' Her voice was quiet, but Alice put as much determination into it as she could. She was not going to let Tom drag her down.

'I'm a happy drunk, you know that. Never beat you once, did I? There you are, then. You never had nought to complain about, Alice.' Tom sat back with an air of satisfaction.

The next day, Alice was thinking over her predicament as she worked. There was now the possibility of children; she hadn't thought of that before. She could imagine that one or two babies might make up for a disappointing marriage, and she wasn't too old for that yet, was she? But was Tom mature enough to be a father? That might be the question. Children would make her more dependent on him to provide a living.

Jacob came into the kitchen with the eggs. 'What's up, woman?' he growled. 'Look as if you've lost a sovereign.'

Should she tell him? Dr and Mrs Dent had not been told; Alice had talked to nobody except her sister. 'Well, Jacob—' it would be interesting to see what his reaction would be. 'I'll tell you, but not a word to anybody, just yet. My husband Tom, that was drowned five years ago, he's turned up, alive and well. And he wants me to go back and live with him, of course.'

119

Jacob whistled. 'After five years, and you thinking he was dead? He's treated you rough, Greenwood, very rough. He could have sent a message, surely.' Quite unlike Jacob, he looked into her face. 'Do you want him back, lass?'

'Well, it's my duty, but to be honest, Jacob, I dread it. We've both changed . . . he's like a stranger, now, and not a very nice one, I'm afraid.' She picked up the basket of eggs and took it to the pantry.

'And where is the man?' Jacob looked as though he wanted to fight him.

'He's at the White Bear, on the Leyburn road, for a day or two, I think. I told him to find us a house in Masham, but I'm not leaving this job until Mrs Dent's maid comes back. I promised to stay until then.'

'Well, that's a good thing. Gives you a bit of time.' Alice saw that Jacob's eyes were bright with sympathy as he looked at her. 'Mebbe he'll get tired of waiting and go back to sea? He wasn't in a great rush to see you, was he now?' As he reached the door the groom added very quietly, 'I'd have been back right away, if it was me. The man doesn't know how lucky he is.'

Shocked, Alice looked at the door as it closed behind Jacob. It sounded as though he actually liked her, appreciated her worth – what a strange idea!

Jacob thought deeply as he went about his work that day. He had been horrified by Alice's news, on two counts. Firstly, he hated the thought of duty taking her back to a man who had treated her so casually; but that was not all. She was a grand lass, somebody you could get very fond of. Had got fond of, in fact. Whether he would ever have had the courage to tell her so was doubtful; but now, it was all over. Alice was a married woman. Well, he didn't go to church much, but there were principles. Other men's wives were treated with a distant respect.

In spite of the lump of lead in his chest at Alice's news, Jacob decided on action. If he could befriend Tom, he might be able to persuade him to go back to sea, out of Alice's way. He went to the White Bear that evening as soon as his work was done. 'I'm off out for an hour or two, Boss. Be back before nine.' Dr Dent nodded, and that was that. Jacob ate his supper before he set out; no good drinking beer on an empty stomach and he needed a clear head. Many a lad staggered home from the inn, but not Jacob.

The White Bear was full of customers. How could they afford to drink so much? There was a noisy group in one corner and among them was a fair-haired man of about Jacob's own age, with an earring and a sailor's guernsey, as worn by the men of the east coast. Tom Greenwood, it had to be. Best to go cautiously. A couple of the men in the group spoke to Jacob and he worked his way in, drinking as little as possible. It would never do to go home the worse for drink; he and the doctor were never really off duty.

By the time that Dr Dent's groom left for home, having told a few jokes and downed a few glasses, he was a friend of Tom's and had promised to come back the next evening. Fortunately for Jacob, the practice was fairly quiet at the moment and most evenings were free.

It was easy for a man who knew his horses to infiltrate a group of betting men, and most of them knew him for a good judge of horses. They talked about horses all the time, but they were an idle lot, single men for the most part, whiling away their evenings in the bar. Tom seemed to have settled in at the Bear. The next week, Jacob went in armed with newspapers as part of the plan. He also took with him an aged man called Harry Lawson, a retired seaman who wanted to yarn with Tom about the good old days at sea. He was a talkative old boy and Jacob knew he would enjoy the evening.

They bought a drink, the old seaman was introduced and a smaller group than usual settled in the corner. Jacob was quiet as the talk went on, mostly of fishing and the sea; it was outside his experience. But eventually, he brought the conversation round to

121

the subject of houses. 'See here, lad, there's a nice stone house to rent on Ilton road.' Jacob showed Tom the *Clarion*, with its list of houses to rent. 'There's not so many here in Masham . . . more in Ripon, but that's too far away. I would have a look at this one, if I was you, Tom.'

The big sailor looked doubtful. He took a swig of beer and squinted at the paper. 'Who said I'm going to live here? I'm minded to go back to Whitby, to where my folks are. Even if I don't go back to sea.'

Harry Lawson looked at Tom with a grin on his wrinkled face. 'You'll go back to sea, lad, if you have any sense. Do it while you're young enough! You'll regret it later, if you skulk at home when you could be out on a boat. I'm right glad that I took every berth that was offered, when I was your age. Saw a lot of the world and a few bonny lasses, and even managed to save a bit of brass, like, for later on, ha, ha.' He lit his pipe noisily.

Tom appeared to think about this. 'Well, mebbe you're right. I would like to go back to sea. I've had a good offer from my old skipper, but I didn't tell the wife about that.' He frowned. 'But what's the point of renting a house here, then?'

'Wouldn't your wife be better off here, with her own folks, if you're going to be away a lot?' Jacob suggested meekly.

Harry laughed and blew a smoke ring. 'That's the secret, to my mind. If I had a wife, which I managed to avoid, thank goodness, I'd ha' left her with her own folks when I went to sea. Stands to reason, and I've heard many a married man say the same.'

'Well.' Tom looked into the bottom of his empty glass. 'That's what she says.' He sighed. 'I suppose I could look at this here house . . . read it to me, Jacob. Print is over-small for my eyes.'

ELEVEN

'Ha! Caught you this time! I've been looking for you all over town. I thought you'd have a hiding hole of your own, somewhere.' Tom Greenwood loomed in the low doorway of Alice's cottage, grinning. 'Now come here, woman, and be nice to me. It's about time you stopped running away; you're surely over the shock by now.'

Alice had been on the point of moving back to sleep in her own home, but Tom's arrival had changed her mind; she was safer at the Dents' house. That Friday evening, the Dents were eating dinner and Alice had slipped out for half an hour to feed her cat and light a fire in the cottage, to keep away the damp. She loved to get back to the peace of the cottage, but tonight that had been a mistake.

Seen in the leaping firelight, Tom was a menacing figure and Alice fought a rising panic. How could she get away from him? And yet, she had been married to him once; strange how you could change, as you grew older. Why be so scared of someone you used to know well?

'Yes, Tom,' she said soothingly. "This is Gabriel's cottage, I've been using it for a while. But it's too small for you, isn't it? You can hardly stand upright in here. But it's a nice little place, just right for me on my own.'

He was not interested in her cottage. 'Why don't you light a lamp?' Tom moved nearer and she could smell the beer on his breath. He put his hands on her waist, quite clumsily. 'So I can see what I'm getting, my lass.'

'Wha-what do you mean, Tom? I have to go back to work now. To do the washing up.' Alice tried to dodge round him to the door, but Tom grabbed her again.

'You know what I mean. It's time I had my rights, Alice. Every married man has rights, whether you women like it or not, and I'll bet most do like it, but you pretend to be shy.' He licked his lips. 'And I mean to have them now.'

Most men would surely try to be a little more persuasive, but why did she feel so repelled? He was crude, but perhaps it was to be expected from a sailor. Had he always been like this? Alice tried to remember as she looked up at Tom, trying to restrain his hands.

There might be a way to get out, to avoid the worst. 'I haven't got long, but, well . . . the bedroom's up here, under the eaves.' Alice led her husband up the twisting staircase. 'Now, make yourself comfortable, you can light the candle if you like. I'll go down and lock the door, in case Ruby comes over. It wouldn't do if she walked in.'

Alice went down, put out the cat, looked up at the night sky and locked the door on the outside, very quietly. That should keep him in there long enough. She ran all the way back to the doctor's house, her heart pounding, her skirt lifted above the puddles. She might suffer for it later, but for tonight, she was safe. The washing-up was nearly done before Mrs Dent came into the kitchen again.

That night, Alice turned over the problem in her mind. She had evaded Tom tonight, but she couldn't go on like that for ever. Hers was a lonely position; no one, not the Dents and not even her sister, could help her if her lawful husband wanted to claim his wife. Tom had the law on his side, and the opinion of all decent people. A woman's place was with her husband. But she didn't want to be with Tom. She hated the idea of living with him for the rest of her life.

Would it be really sinful to run away from the burden? The

new Tom, coarse and callous, was nothing like the lad Alice had married. It always came back to the fact that he had waited for five years before coming to look for her. Perhaps he had changed as a result of his injuries when the boat went down; you sometimes heard of folks who were completely different after an accident.

Lying in her narrow bed, Alice looked round the attic bedroom. The candlelight flickered over the pine chest of drawers, the washstand and a few bunches of lavender. It was good to be a widow, safe from rough men. Married life with Tom would be a downward spiral, a constant worry about money. If there were children, their mother would have all the responsibility. It was easy to imagine herself on that lonely walk by the shore in Whitby, but in the future, with two little children held by the hand. Poor little mites, with rough Tom for a father.

The next morning Alice was no nearer finding a way out of her trouble, but there was work to be done. The small Saturday market was often busy, and if Alice got up early she could sometimes help Ruby on the stall for an hour or two. Once the morning chores were done and the Dents' breakfast over, she put on a warm shawl and went out to the square with her baskets.

'I've done well with your salve, lass,' Ruby greeted her as she wrapped butter for a customer. 'Salves and creams seem to sell well in winter, and there's a good demand for cough remedies. Have we any coltsfoot syrup?'

Alice spread out her goods on the stall and handed over a small bottle of the syrup. 'The flowers are just up now, so it's fresh.'

'It tastes so bad, it must be good for you,' a farmer grinned.

Trade was quite brisk for a while, then slackened, and Ruby took a turn round the other stalls, leaving Alice feeling nervous. What if Tom turned up now, while she was alone? Surely he wouldn't make a scene in a public place, but you couldn't be sure. She tried to hide behind the two large women who gossiped in front of her stall, ignoring her as if she were a statue, not bothering to lower their voices.

'Pity about poor Billy Ford,' one said. 'You saw death notice in the paper last month? Only forty-five, he was. Died in his sleep . . . heart, doctor said. And his missis left all on her own, no bairns for company and nobody to support her.'

Her friend nodded sadly. 'Aye, it's a sad business, all right. But Maggie Ford's right, she found herself a grand place. She's to be housekeeper to an old lass with plenty of brass, over in Harrogate, she told me. I saw her in Ripon last week.' The woman looked round at Alice, as if including her in the conversation. 'It's all right for some, isn't it? I'll have a packet of dried sage, thanks, lass.'

Alice handed over the sage, wishing she was in the same position as Maggie Ford. With her experience as a lady's maid, she could fit into an old lady's household quite well; and the cooking experience at the Dents' had given her the confidence to – what? Well, she could apply for a job as a housekeeper. Get right away, before it was too late.

That evening while the doctor and his wife ate their dinner, Alice turned over the pages of the *Clarion*, wondering whether she would be brave enough to get away, to find a job where Tom could not find her. There were several pages of appeals for domestic workers; some looked like sheer drudgery. More promising was the lady looking for a refined housekeeper. She lived in Palace Road in Ripon, where the houses were large and prosperous. Ripon was just big enough to hide in at least until Tom went back to Whitby, but near enough for her to come home sometimes.

After the dishes were done, there would be time to write a letter. Applying for the job would not bind her; she could still go back to Tom if her conscience insisted that she should.

Alice went to church on Sunday evening, still wondering what to do. What would the vicar say? Dr Carr usually preached in a very human way, talking about love and forgiveness more than about sin and hell fire. Looking up at the tall figure in the pulpit, it was easy to imagine what he would say. 'Do your duty, Alice, and love will follow. Your place is with your husband.' That was what he would say.

As it happened, the Dents went to Ripon the next day and offered a ride to Alice. Now was a chance to call at the big house on Palace Road and hand in her letter personally. It would be more polite to post the letter and wait for a reply, but how long would it take Tom to find her again?

In her good winter coat, Alice felt quite warm as they jogged down to Ripon in the doctor's trap. The hazy sunshine almost promised an early spring. It had been hard to tell the Dents that she was applying for another place, but they had understood. 'Look after yourself, Alice,' Emily Dent had said. 'Our maid will be coming back soon. We'll give you a good character, of course.' Thank goodness, she had not yet told them about Tom.

Put down in Palace Road, Alice found the right wrought-iron gates and knocked on the big oak door, feeling nervous. 'Mrs Roberts has advertised . . . I have a letter here; my name is Alice Greenwood,' she said to the little maid in the white cap, who thought for a moment, looked her up and down and reluctantly let her in.

For ten minutes Alice stood in the panelled hall, listening to the measured tick of a grandfather clock. At length a door opened and a woman with severe grey hair and pebble spectacles came up to her. 'This is Greenwood? You look too young to be properly responsible. I am looking for a mature woman of forty. And you are rather thin.' She was examined again from head to foot. 'What can you do?' The voice was hard and the face had no expression.

'Well, ma'am, I am thirty, and quite responsible. I am temporary housekeeper to a doctor, and looking for a permanent position.' Stand up straight, speak like they do at the castle. 'And I was trained at the castle, ma'am. Swinton Castle, near Masham.' That sounded quite respectable, but it seemed to have no effect.

'Have you children? We want no children here.' The prim

mouth pursed at the thought. 'My nerves are delicate and I require absolute quiet.'

Alice said nothing; the woman looked as though she would have cast-iron nerves. 'You said you work for a doctor.' The woman managed to make it sound as though she thought it was unlikely. 'Do you have any medical experience, as such? My health is precarious and I may need nursing.'

Heaven forbid; it was time to get away. Alice realized that the atmosphere of the house was pressing down on her, that the woman was cold and hard, and that she would hate to work here. She would not take the job.

'Yes, I know about herbal medicines, I have a herb stall on Masham market,' Alice said cheerfully. 'I'm the lavender girl in Masham.' She stood back to watch the effect.

'A market stall?' It was almost a shriek. 'You would obviously be far too rough here. A low market girl! I shall not waste any more time with you. Good day.' Mrs Roberts marched back through the door, banging it behind her; so much for the nerves. The maid appeared immediately and opened the front door with a smirk.

Alice shook her head as she rejoined the Dents, and the doctor tried to console her. 'Never mind, Alice, there is plenty of time for you to look for another place. I really hope you'll be able to stay in Masham, where your friends are.' Well, that had been the plan, until Tom appeared.

'Here, Tom lad. I've got the key for the front door, do ye want to come for a look at this house that's to rent?' Jacob went into the White Bear the next Saturday, ready to act the hearty mate once more. It would have been good to watch the football match and see Masham beat Leyburn, but he might get there before the end of the game. He was bent on persuading Greenwood to rent a house in Masham and then go back to sea, leaving Alice to her herbs and her own devices.

Unusually for him, Tom Greenwood was drinking tea from a

big mug, his empty dinner plate before him on the table. 'Where's the landlord, then?' The sailor looked round.

'He lives in Darlington, so he leaves the key with Mrs Taylor at the Post Office.' Jacob almost pushed Tom to the door. 'It seems that this here house belonged to his auntie, and she died and left it to him. It's full of furniture, all ready to move in. I think he's even left the bed linen there, it will cost you nowt to set up. It's all very handy.'

Tom took the key from Jacob, thus taking charge. 'Well, I don't fancy staying here for ever, even though the beer in Masham is second to none. They brew a right good ale in Masham. But I suppose you're right. I'm in deep trouble with the missis for staying away so long. I'd better let her choose where we live. You wouldn't believe the trouble I had to get her to bed, last week ... maybe a decent house will settle her down a bit.' He laughed rather self-consciously.

Jacob did not want to hear the details of poor Alice's married life. 'Well, it was a bit of a shock when you suddenly turned up. You've got to give her time to get used to it.' He led the way to the terrace of stone houses on the Ilton road, and stopped at the door of one in the middle of the row. It was solidly built and roofed with slate, respectable enough for anybody, although Tom was not likely to worry about respectability. Best to let him take charge, though, and to think it was all his idea.

'The first thing we do,' Tom said firmly as he turned the big key in the lock, 'Is to look through all the cupboards and such. Under mattresses, an' all. The old girl must have had a sight of brass to own a house like this and she might ha' left some hidden, somewhere, like, for me to find. I'm lucky like that. Found a gold coin in a fish, once.'

'If we find owt, it belongs to landlord,' Jacob said sharply, but Tom only laughed.

After a quick look round, Greenwood nodded. 'Aye, I'll take it, for a year at any rate. After that, we'll see.' There was no mention of whether Alice would like the house, or that her opinion mattered at all.

So far, so good. Jacob shut the front door. 'If you're taking it from now, we'd better get some tidying up done before the lass sees it.' He sniffed. 'I must say, it smells clean enough. I can smell muck a mile off. Let's light a fire, it's cold in here.' He found a few sticks of wood and lit a fire in the back-room grate. 'We'll dump these old newspapers in the yard. Pantry needs a coat of whitewash, but that's about all.'

'That's woman's work; you won't get me doing that,' Tom growled. He was evidently not going to be drawn into anything too demanding.

The house was quiet although it fronted the road, and Jacob could hear a bird singing in the big back garden. Perhaps Alice could be happy here, living quite close to her sister Ruby, if she could put up with Tom's rough ways. It was hard to imagine, but then, she had been married to him before. She had never talked about her old life, but that didn't mean she had been unhappy with Tom.

While Tom rummaged in the cupboards, Jacob inspected the kitchen; Alice would like it, he thought. There was a good coal range with an open fire and side oven, and a hot water boiler. There was a stone sink with a tap and the floor was tiled. A door in the kitchen opened on to steep wooden steps, leading down to a dry cellar that would be useful for storing coal and wood.

'Hey, look here, Jake!' Tom had found a bottle. 'It's gin; that's lucky.' He took a deep swig.

Jacob thought there should be a list of what was in the house when the Greenwoods moved in, and agreed by both parties, to avoid any trouble when they moved out. It would take some time; there was solid old oak furniture in every room and all the pots, pans and utensils you could need. Tom went on prowling through the rooms with bottle in hand, looking for money; Jacob took out a pencil and started a list of the main items of furniture.

Half an hour went by. Tom had drunk a fair amount of gin and was feeling tired, he said, after all this hard work. He went to sit by the fire, which was drawing well; no problems with this chimney at least. There was often trouble when jackdaws built in chimneys that had not been used for a while.

'Find a glass and I'll give you a drink, Jake. We can leave the rest to the missis.'

Greenwood pointed to the chair opposite.

Jacob sat down, but he did not drink. Gin was not his choice, although many of the farmers drank it, neat or with water. Jacob preferred a glass of beer, and in any case, it was too early in the day. What did the future hold for Alice? She was not likely to get much support from this man. Greenwood seemed to be entirely self-absorbed. Now, he was becoming sentimental, talking about his life at sea and the great adventures he had experienced. Life had been wonderful at sea. 'I've been lucky, as a rule, as I said,' he mumbled. 'Except with that lass . . . Alice—' He said something else that Jacob didn't catch.

'Alice should like this house, Tom. I'm sure of it.'

The drink was having an effect on Tom. He looked over at Jacob suspiciously. 'Do you know her?' he demanded truculently.

'Er . . . slightly.' Jacob had never mentioned Alice before.

The sailor took another drink. 'Hands off, then. She's mine! I always fancied her, but Tom got there first.' He slid sideways in the chair. Tom was drunk, and it was best to let him sleep it off. Jacob moved him gently so that he would not fall, and the man opened bleary eyes. 'Always fancied Alice, I did . . . but she married Tom.'

What did he mean? 'She married Tom' – but he was Tom!

TWELVE

Jacob froze in his chair, holding his breath as a possibility struck him with the force of a blow. Greenwood started to snore. Supposing that this man was not Tom Greenwood, returned from the dead, after all? Supposing he was really the brother – what had Alice called him – Andrew? That was it. Sitting alone in his cottage at night, Jacob often went over the conversations of the day and that gave him a good memory of what people told him; especially Alice. The lass talked good sense and she was worth listening to, and sometimes, she made you smile.

Jacob gazed into the fire, thinking. Just suppose that Andrew, because he 'fancied' Alice, had decided to pass himself off as Tom. They were alike, they must have been, but Andrew was older – and rougher, Alice had said. After five years of absence, Alice might easily have been persuaded that Andrew was her husband, allowing for his ageing in the years between.

Honest herself, Alice would never have imagined such a cruel trick. But how long would it have lasted? Alice had only seen Tom briefly since he came back to claim her. They might not have had time to talk about the past, their shared past. That would have been dangerous ground for Andrew. The man had been uneasy and had no explanation of his long absence. It all added up, but Jacob could not see how the deception could last, or how the man could expect any woman to accept him once the truth was out.

If this was the truth, Alice was free. Jacob felt a strange lightening of his spirits. The lass should be told as soon as possible, but it might be best to let the man sleep for a while and then try to check again. He would need to be quite certain, before he raised her hopes. A horse clopped by on the road outside; time passed slowly. The football match would be over by now.

Eventually, the winter dusk came stealing into the room. It was time to move: Jacob made up his mind. He leaned over Greenwood and spoke urgently. 'Andrew! Is it you?'

The man stirred. It's me,' he mumbled. Then he opened one eye. 'Jake! You trying to trick me, or what?'

'You're Andrew Greenwood. You are pretending to be your brother, Tom. The one who drowned. He really did drown, didn't he?'

The sailor jumped up suddenly and deftly twisted Jacob's arm up and back. He was heavier and stronger than the groom. 'Interfering bastard! That's what you get from a man who calls himself a mate! So – what if I am Andrew Greenwood?'

Jacob twisted and turned, but he could not break free.

'You're a big problem for me now, Fowler. You're the only soul in this place that has worked it out, damn you. I should throw you down the cellar steps. Plenty of folks go that way, an arranged accident.' Greenwood started to drag Jacob towards the kitchen, towards the cellar door. His harsh voice was full of menace and he sounded as though he meant every word. From his brief knowledge of the man, Jacob thought that Greenwood was hasty. He might kill a man in the heat of the moment, if it suited him; he seemed to have no principles. During their sessions at the White Bear, it had been clear that when Greenwood drank, he tended to be aggressive.

Relaxing his muscles as though giving in, Jacob asked conversationally, 'How do you plan to go on, with Alice? It won't be easy; she's bound to find out some time. She'll spot the difference between you and Tom, and she'll catch you out on memories, if nowt else. And then you'll have a hard time!' The sailor was surprisingly strong; Jacob was no weakling, but he was held fast in a steel grip that must have been developed by hauling on ropes in the icy North Sea. 'Lay off, mate, you're hurting me.' He was twisting the arm that had been damaged.

Greenwood laughed. 'I'll do worse to you in a minute. She's very moral and all that, our Alice. That's why I could never get near her when she was married to Tom. But now, I got her to bed . . . well, almost, you might say. And when I get her staying with me here, I'll be right. I can tell her we're living in sin, because I'm not her lawful husband. She'll marry me then, just to keep things respectable. And she must fancy me too, I'm sure of it, underneath that old-fashioned look.'

Why would such a brute be so sure of his attraction? Human nature was a strange thing.

A beautiful idea flooded into Jacob's mind, like a burst of sunshine. He forgot the pain in his arm; he knew just what to say. 'As I told you, I know her slightly and I wouldn't want to know her any better, not on your life. She's a sour one, your Alice. That woman,' he spoke slowly and deliberately, 'will make your life a misery, Tom – I mean Andrew. Specially if you've tricked her into marriage. I wouldn't be in your shoes, lad, not for owt! But it's nothing to do with me, of course.'

Andrew Greenwood did not relax his grip on Jacob, but he sounded slightly uncertain. 'I did think she seemed very sour and bossy, what I've seen of her. The bitch was all for giving me the slip last week, and I had to fight for my rights! That's no way for a loving wife to be.'

Poor Alice. Jacob hoped fervently that she was not knocked about. 'Aye, that'd be right,' he agreed quickly. 'Alice is a right tartar and no mistake.'

At last the sailor let go of Jacob; he turned away and drained the gin bottle. 'Is that so?'

Jacob rolled his eyes. 'I could tell you some tales! That Alice is like a madwoman at times; nobody dares to go near her. She kicks, you see. She can reach out and kick you in the you-know-whats as easy as anything. They reckon she would beat the bairns something cruel, only they're safe now, with their auntie.' He rubbed his arms to get the circulation back.

'Bairns? She never had no bairns! What do ye mean?' Greenwood was really alarmed by now.

'Oh, didn't you know she's got three children? All by different fathers, they say, but none of 'em is game to own a bastard.' Jacob sniffed. 'All under five, of course.'

The sailor's mouth dropped open. 'So she's not a prude, after all? She's been with— Oh, my! Three bairns to support! That puts a different face on it, entirely. And she's second-hand, you might say, by now.'

Jacob kept his face in the solemn expression that was natural to him, but it was an effort. Once you started to make things up it was easy, but you had to stay serious. 'Summat wrong with her head, doctor thinks. Of course, I work for Dr Dent, I get to know a lot about his patients,' he added importantly. 'Mind you, they should lock her up, certify her, if it gets too bad. They say she's worse' – he dropped his voice – 'at the full moon.'

'You don't mean it? But I can see you do.' Greenwood sat down, a man in shock. 'Three bairns! You're ruining all my plans, Jake.'

'I thought you was bound to know she was . . . mad, like . . . or I'd have mentioned it before. But you don't go round criticizing other folk's wives, not unless you want a black eye.' Jacob looked innocent. 'It came on worse, I reckon, after Tom died. Went to her head, somehow. They say she was a nice enough lass before, but still – a bit different. Happen Tom didn't like to say owt, but even in those days, he might have had a rough time.'

'No, I never knew about it; Tom never said.' Andrew looked grim. 'But I can believe you, right enough, it all fits. Even last week . . . she looks thin and pale, with great big eyes. Sort of queer, they are. Well, it's a good job I found out in time.' He sighed. 'It's bad enough having to find enough brass to keep her and the brats – three, you're sure? – and lose my freedom, into the bargain. And then, she won't live in Whitby. My old ma won't like that. I'd thought to take her back to my ma, after we were wed. But if she's not going to be sweet and biddable, and look after me – why, I might as well not bother. There's nothing in it for me. She'd be a burden.'

Jacob looked wise. 'You've had a lucky escape, lad. I did wonder why you bothered to come looking for Alice; she was never your problem. You watch out for yourself, that's what I would do. I've managed to keep out of women's clutches and I reckon it's safest, for independent men like me and you. That lass will need a sight of looking after. You'd hardly be able to go down the street on moonlight nights! Going to sea would be out of the question.' He paused to enjoy the effect.

Greenwood shuddered 'Let's go to the pub, I need a drink. It's a bad business, Jacob.'

There was just one more thing to say, to seal it completely. 'You know, all her folks were looking forward to you taking Alice off their hands. Mad Alice, they call her in the township. They won't tell you how bad she is, oh, no. Even if you was to go to her sister Ruby right now this very minute, and ask her, she would deny it. For fear you back off. Stands to reason . . . but I'm your mate and I tell you what's good for you to hear.' And Lord forgive me, Jacob added to himself, rubbing his aching arms again where the sailor had bruised them.

It was getting dark when they left the house, the place that Alice would now never have to live in. Jacob put up a guard before the dying fire and locked the door thankfully; at one point, he had wondered whether he would ever get out alive. 'I'll take key back to Post Office and leave a note for the landlord,' he offered. 'I'll tell him you've changed your mind and you're off back to sea. Folks often change their minds about a letting.'

'What about that drink? I owe you a drink, Jake, for stopping me from ruining me life. And to think that I nearly threw you down the cellar, too. Nay, I owe you a drink for this afternoon.' The effects of the gin were wearing off, but Greenwood still looked a little bleary-eyed.

'I can't come for a drink; there's horses to feed.' Jacob had seen quite enough of Greenwood for one day, and the stables were waiting. He hoped Dr Dent had not noticed his groom's absences in the last few weeks; but even if his wages were docked, it had all been worthwhile.

'Well, mate, let me shake your hand and thank you kindly for all you've done. I'm going to pack my bags and go back to Whitby tomorrow, if there's any trains on a Sunday. I'll go and see Ma, and get a berth on a deep-sea boat as soon as I can. To hell with sour women. I've made my mind up. You can tell her what you like; I won't be going near Alice again.' Greenwood's big, rough face was shining with sweat and gratitude. No doubt his mother would be pleased to see him, but it was hard to imagine him being attractive to a lass.

Suppressing a long sigh of relief, Jacob shook the offered hand. 'She's likely forgotten about you by now; that's the way it takes her. But I'll tell her some tale, if she asks. Good luck, lad.'

'Can I talk to you, lass?' Jacob was at the kitchen door, breathing quickly, as soon as the horses were fed that evening.

'Not now, Jacob, I'm too busy.' Alice pulled a pan of onion soup off the stove just as it boiled over and spilled onto the floor. The dining-room bell was ringing and there was ominous smoke rising from a pan of potatoes.

There was no evening surgery on Saturdays, and so, emergencies permitting, the Dents enjoyed a leisurely meal. But Saturday evening's dinner, the most important of the week, was not going well, and no wonder. The temporary domestic pushed her hair back under the white cap. All the time, at the back of Alice's mind the image of Tom's face grinned at her, whatever she was doing. Perhaps that was why everything had seemed to go wrong that day, in spite of all her efforts. It was so hard to concentrate on the job, to do her best for Dr and Mrs Dent, and Jacob had come in at precisely the wrong moment.

'Suit yourself,' the man muttered and banged the door in the old way as he stumped out. Well, he could wait.

Alice poured what remained of the soup into a tureen, balanced it on a tray and carried it precariously into the dining-room. Even serving the meal seemed difficult, tonight. 'Sorry to keep you waiting, ma'am.'

'Don't look so worried, Alice,' Mrs Dent said comfortably as she passed a plate of soup to her husband. 'The soup smells delicious.' Thank goodness, the Fanshawe days were over. The Dents rarely criticized; they sometimes made suggestions for improvement, but not often, and their advice was always followed.

Alice went back to the kitchen and gradually set things to rights. The top layer of potatoes were not burned and the dinner proceeded. When she took in cheese and biscuits for dessert and cleared the dinner plates, Emily Dent asked, 'Is there any soup left, Alice? Perhaps you could give it to Jacob. I thought he was looking rather pale, when I saw him this evening.'

It would have to be tonight that more soup was wanted. 'I'm sorry, the soup boiled over.' Alice looked guiltily at the doctor. 'But there is some chicken soup left from last night. I'll take that over for him.'

Jacob could wait, since he was so moody. Alice washed the dishes, scoured the pans and made up the fire, before heating up the soup and taking the jug over to the groom's cottage. She was not in the mood for talking to Jacob tonight. It was impossible to tell him how she felt about Tom, but she couldn't think of anything else; he filled her mind.

Alice knocked and there was silence. An owl hooted in the night, and a chilly breeze blew round her ankles. 'Here's some soup, and good night to you, Fowler,' she shouted. 'I know you're in there.'

There was a rattle and the door opened to reveal Jacob's face, glaring out through a froth of lather. 'Can't a man have a shave in peace?'

'Certainly, I won't be bothering you,' Alice said tartly and turned to go, feeling suddenly tired.

Jacob opened the door a little wider. 'You're lucky I wasn't having a bath; that's next on the list. But come in, woman, don't flounce off like that. I've summat to tell you.'

'I'm too tired and too worried—' Alice began, but Jacob put out a damp hand and drew her in, shutting the door firmly behind her.

'Shut up, and listen to me.' Jacob went to the sink, wiped the lather off his face, dried it with a towel and drew up a chair to the fire. 'Sit you down. I'm going to give you a shock – another shock, lass – and I reckon you've had quite a few, lately.'

'I don't want to hear it. What with Tom, and the dinner going wrong, and no chance to do the herb garden and spring coming on—' Alice was near to tears, most unusually. She wasn't a teary female, what was wrong with her?

'Alice!' Jacob sat down opposite and gently took her hands; his touch was reassuring. 'That's no way to go on. Just relax.'

Alice sighed, and felt some of the tension drain away. She noticed then that Jacob was looking happy; he was smiling and appeared to be enjoying something . . . surely he wouldn't enjoy giving her a shock? What had happened to the man, to make him take her hands like this?

'I'll take it slowly. Now . . . do you remember, when you lived in Whitby, Tom's mother was there too, and a brother, Andrew. Can you remember Andrew?'

Alice nodded. What was the man driving at?

'Well, was he very like the man who came here to claim you?' Jacob sat back in his chair and looked into the fire.

There was quiet in the cottage, except for the deliberate ticking of the old wall clock 'Andrew?' Alice felt the room begin to spin and she clutched the arms of the chair. 'Could he be – Andrew? Oh, my goodness!'

Jacob leaned forward earnestly. 'I've found him out, lass. He's Andrew, all right. Tom really was drowned, after all. But Andrew thought he could pass himself off as Tom.'

'I'd kept away from him, as much as I could.' Alice tried to remember what the man had said, why she should not have spotted the difference immediately. 'I . . . I really didn't like him, Jacob, and I felt guilty about it. But this means . . . I am free.'

She looked at him in wonder. 'I needn't worry any more.' It was a shock, but a good one. It was a great relief to think that Tom had not let her down. Poor Tom, he would have come back as soon as he could.

The fire leaped up suddenly and, in the glare, Alice saw that Jacob was watching her anxiously. 'How could he expect to keep it up? Once we got talking about the past, and when I spent some time with him, the truth was bound to come out, in the end.'

Jacob looked embarrassed. 'He was going to pretend he'd lost his memory in the accident, if he had to. But once he – once you – were living together as man and wife, he thought you would agree to marry him, rather than live in sin. You're a decent lass; you might have married him. He said . . . that you'd been together, last week.'

Alice laughed. 'That was his idea, but I ran away. I locked him in the cottage! No, Jacob, I didn't get close to him, at all. I haven't seen him since, thank goodness. But how did you find out? You're a marvel, Jacob Fowler.'

Jacob got up to fill the kettle at the tap. 'We'll have some tea, and I'll tell thee.' It was the old, friendly form of address, the one her father had used.

Dear Jacob was so pleased for her, and proud of his detective work. Thank goodness, it was over . . . the difference should have been obvious, straight away. Andrew had been heavier than Tom, and coarser, although they were similar. Five years on, he could have been Tom, at first sight, but not after a while. Tom, her Tom, would not have stayed away for five years and suddenly appeared. Tom would have written to her, to say he was safe. Poor lad, what would he have thought of all this? Alice felt guilty, that she'd blamed Tom.

Setting out cups and saucers, Jacob looked across at Alice. 'I know there's work waiting, but you'd better have a cup of tea afore you go back to the kitchen. I found out this afternoon, when we looked at a house to rent. Greenwood got drunk, that was all. He mumbled something about Tom. So I let him sleep, and then I shook him and called him Andrew. That's how it all came out.' He smiled modestly. 'So I told him a heap of lies, and he's off back to Whitby on the morning train.'

Alice shook her head. 'I can never thank you enough, Jacob. You're as good as Sherlock Holmes! But was it dangerous? He wouldn't be very pleased at being found out.'

'Nay, I led him to believe he's had a lucky escape. Told him about your three little children, I did.' Jacob kept his face straight.

'My – what?' Alice giggled; she felt light-headed. 'Oh well, if that's what it took to get rid of him . . . but nobody in Masham would believe it, I hope.'

They drank the tea and as she was leaving, Jacob looked at the ceiling and said, 'If you tell me what wants doing in yon herb garden, I can give you an hour or so, tomorrow afternoon.'

With a sigh, Alice opened the door. 'I am so far in your debt . . . and the only thing I can do for you is darn your socks, Jacob.'

'And sew a few buttons on, if you've a mind.' The grumpy old groom actually laughed.

THIRTEEN

'Good morning, ladies! Would you care for a drive?' Adam Burns waved cheerfully and pulled the trap to a halt beside Laura as she stood talking to Alice, in the stable yard.

Alice, having realized her own freedom, had felt a rush of compassion for Laura. The poor girl was about to be pushed into a similar situation to the one she had escaped from: marriage to a man she did not like. And the time was drawing near; they were enjoying pale February sunshine, and the engagement party was only a week away.

'I'm off to look at some pedigree lambs at Mickley, and I thought of calling on the Gills, whose cottage you designed,' Adam said persuasively. 'You might like to see the foundations, I thought.'

Laura looked at Alice, who nodded. 'I can't stay all day, but if we can be back by twelve—' Mrs Dent had given her the morning off.

Laura was keen to go. 'But we will need to find room for Hamish. Poor little dog, he needs a change as much as we do.'

They climbed into the trap and Adam handed them rugs. 'Wrap up; the wind is cold.' Hamish was settled on Laura's lap and they were off.

As they trotted sedately through the ornamental gates, Laura put a hand to her mouth. 'Goodness, I forgot to tell anyone we're going. What if they are looking for me?'

'We'll be back before they notice!' Adam was not for turning back. 'The colonel only buys the very best horses, Miss Laura. We'll do twelve miles an hour, I am sure.'

It felt like twelve fast miles an hour as the trap picked up speed, once they had crossed the river. It was good to be out in the fresh air; Alice felt tired after the strain of the past few days. They turned into a narrow road and she looked out over the River Ure. Far below the road, they could see the gleam of water through a tangle of bare branches. How lucky she was not to have to go back to Whitby, and to have a morning like this, with nothing to do except to accompany a young lady. Perhaps she should go back to being a lady's maid, after all.

'Do you know the names of the trees, Miss Laura?' As usual, Adam was giving Laura a challenge.

'It's not so easy at this time of year, but I think I can name a few.' Laura looked around. 'There are oaks over there in the village street, and those tall trees with smooth trunks are beeches, I believe. I have learned quite a lot about trees and shrubs since I started garden design.'

Adam stopped the trap in a farmyard and tied the horse up to a post. He led Laura and Alice into an old orchard at the back of the house. 'The ewes are put in here for lambing; it's very sheltered,' he explained.

Laura exclaimed when she saw the lambs and Adam picked one up and handed it to her. It snuggled quite happily into her arms. 'Adam, how small and fluffy – how very sweet it is! I would love to have a pet lamb.' She stroked the woolly head gently.

'This is the start of an improved pedigree flock,' Adam told her. 'Part of the plan for improving the estate farms, as you know. But you wouldn't want one. Pet lambs are a nuisance, and they grow up to be very ill-mannered sheep.'

Alice smiled as she said, 'It's true, I'm afraid. You can't really make a pet of a farm animal – and besides, what would Hamish think?' Laura looked so pretty, holding the lamb. The dog was squeaking in the trap, so Alice let him out on a lead, keeping him well away from the sheep.

Adam and Laura spent a few minutes more looking at the ewes, with Laura learning all about their finer points. Reluctantly, she put the lamb back with its rather anxious mother, and they came over to Alice. Laura had tears in her eyes. When Adam went to speak to the farmer, she sighed. 'Soon, I will have to go away, and I'll never be able to spend time with you and Adam again.'

'Let's go to see Mr Gill and ask to see where the house is to be built,' Alice suggested, trying to distract Laura. She knew the farmer slightly, as he was one of Gabriel's friends. But Mrs Gill waylaid them. 'Would the young lady like to step in for a cup of tea? It's cold work, riding in a trap in winter.' So Alice and Laura had tea, and then Adam had tea, and they all went to look at the cottage foundations.

'It looks much smaller than I imagined. Will it be big enough?' asked Laura doubtfully.

'Houses always look small at this stage,' Adam assured her.

They were rather later getting back to the Hall than any of them intended, but it had been a pleasant morning. Even Hamish was contented, having caught a rat in Mr Gill's barn. Alice went to put Hamish away as soon as they reached the stables, but when she rejoined Laura, there was trouble.

The colonel was waiting for them, red in the face. 'Where have you been? Your mother is hysterical!" he was saying to Laura as Alice came up. Adam quietly unyoked and led the horse away to the box. Laura looked at her feet. 'Have you no sense of decency, girl? About to be married, and you go off like a hoyden with a young man, in public and with no chaperone! Your mother has been concerned about you for some time, and I have taken your part. But you go too far!'

'But Papa, it was quite proper, Alice was with us!'

When her father saw her with Adam, Alice was out of sight and he had assumed that Laura was alone with him, but he was not backing down. Colonel Grey ignored Alice. 'You should realize that a young woman in your position is inevitably a target for young men with no fortune. Burns, it is quite obvious, appreciates your attractions as a match. But you have a brilliant marriage before you.' He turned on his heel.

Alice began to creep away uncomfortably, but Laura motioned her to stay and then put a hand on her father's arm. 'Papa, I would like to talk to you. It was a respectable visit to see some sheep. Alice was there the whole time. I am learning a great deal about country life. You said I could study garden design, and the estate—'

The colonel's face turned even redder. 'Tearing round farms is not becoming to a young lady in your station of life, Laura. You seem to have no sense of decorum. Do not let it happen again.'

Laura took a deep breath. 'Women are beginning to be trained as doctors, Papa; they study science and art. I am interested in cottage design,' she was nearly crying. 'If I had been your son instead of your daughter, you would have encouraged me. Why should girls be treated differently?'

'If you do not understand, Laura, you will have to learn quickly; your husband will not tolerate such rebellion. You must realize that the only child of Birchwood Hall would be a very good catch for an estate manager with no prospects of his own. Burns would not be human if he did not think of it himself.'

Laura shook her head and said quietly, 'I am sure Mr Burns has no devious plans . . . he has never tried to influence me at all.'

The colonel only had one theme. 'This marriage to Paterson is the best thing for you, and it must not be jeopardized by flighty behaviour. Paterson would be furious, if he found out where you have been.'

Well, that was true. Alice bent down to fasten her boot, to look as though she was not listening. Paterson had struck the artist; what was he likely to do to Mr Burns?

Laura had a pleading look. 'Papa, may I ask you, one last time? From the bottom of my heart – do I really have to marry Mr Paterson? I would much rather stay here with you!'

Colonel Grey led Laura further away from the stables and Alice followed unwillingly. His tone softened a little. 'Most young girls are hesitant, I am told. Marriage is a big step. But Laura, remember, you will travel in Europe. You can study the best art in the world and the most beautiful gardens. Be thankful you will not have to earn your living.' He glanced at Alice. 'As Paterson's wife, you will have the world at your feet.' He patted his daughter's shoulder. 'It is absolutely imperative that you marry Paterson. He is determined, and he is a man who always gets his way. Now, I wish to hear no more about it. One day, you will thank me for this!' He marched off to the house as though he were on a parade ground.

Poor Laura ran back to the stables and gathered up her little dog, sobbing into his fur. 'And they won't even let me take Hamish with me!' Coming out of the stables, still with her head down, she collided with Adam.

'Steady on, lassie!' Adam's arms went round Laura to stop her from falling and just for a moment she laid her head on his broad shoulder. Tears splashed onto his hand. 'Are you in trouble, Laura? And is it my fault? We should have told them where we were going!'

Laura shook her head miserably and Alice felt like crying herself. 'It's just . . . everything. Papa is angry, and I want to stay here, and I can't. I have to go away and get . . . married!'

'Come in here, both of you.' Adam led the way to the farm office and threw a log on the fire. They sat down, Adam at his desk. 'Let me see whether I can help. It was my fault, I asked you to come. Does the colonel think you have been spending too much time with me? I was rather afraid of it, you know. He's very correct, and would think it not quite the thing.'

'Yes.' Laura looked embarrassed. 'That's it, I'm afraid.'

'Hmm.' Adam stared into the fire. 'Doubtless, he's worried about your fiancé. Perhaps I should put his mind at rest and tell him that I have a lady in mind, myself.'

Laura dried her eyes and stood up. 'Thank you, Adam, but I

don't think you can change anything. It really doesn't matter what they think. I have so enjoyed working with you, and I've learned so much! But – it's over.' She smothered a sob.

Adam opened the door for them and as Laura passed him, he planted a swift kiss on her cheek. 'Don't tell the colonel, Alice! You've been grand company, both you lassies. I will miss you.' He looked at Laura intently. 'I wish you well in the new life and I'm sure you will enjoy it. Paterson is a lucky man!'

The women walked in silence for a while, and then Alice murmured, 'Try to look on the bright side, Miss Laura. Your father's right, it will be a brilliant marriage.'

Laura sighed. 'You know, it would be easy to get fond of Adam. I wonder what his lady is like?'

Worse was to come: when they reached the house, Laura had to be warned again, by both parents this time. Alice was cleaning the young lady's boots, but she could hear snatches of the talk coming down the passage; the Greys never bothered to lower their voices. 'Social inferiors . . . paid servants . . . I think we should dismiss Burns, you never know what Mr Paterson will hear, it is so difficult, why can you not be more. . . .' it was Mama this time. Laura's voice was not heard.

It would be rude to leave without saying goodbye to Laura, so Alice waited for the tirade to end. It was brought to a merciful close by the arrival of Dr Dent, and Laura immediately asked if she might see him.

'Let's take a turn round the garden,' the doctor suggested briskly.

'Alice, come with us.' Laura had just a trace of the imperious manner left, enough to make the doctor smile.

'I am quite well, thank you, but low in spirits,' Laura told her medical adviser precisely. 'I believe you knew Mr Burns in Scotland, Doctor, before he came here?' Her tone was neutral.

'Yes, he's very sound, you know. Likeable fellow.'

'Perhaps you could speak to Papa? He talks of dismissing Mr Burns, and it will be my fault if he does. We went out in the trap with him, and Papa didn't realize at first that Alice was with me.'

The doctor chuckled. 'Unfortunate. Well, I will be pleased to say a few words in his favour. He is a very moral man, Mr Burns.'

'I suppose his position here will be important to him, if the family is poor?' Laura continued. 'Do you know anything about his background?' It was the tone of voice used when speaking of a servant.

Dr Dent was still smiling: the girl must really like Adam Burns. 'Very respectable folk; I know the father. I went salmon fishing up there once.' But, of course, the doctor was used to talking to all classes of people, not just ordering them about, as the colonel did. Alice sighed for Laura as they walked round the garden.

'There's nothing can be done, but I'm really sorry for the lass.' Alice looked across the table at Jacob, smugly ensconced with his cup of tea; Mrs Dent had offered him a hot drink when he came in with the cabbages. 'I only wish I could get Laura to see something good about Mr Paterson.' She shouldn't talk about people she worked for, but Jacob was different; he was very discreet, not a gossip, and even a good detective. He had worked out Andrew Greenwood, before it was too late.

'Well, what do we know that's good about him? You could find out as much as you can, and whisper in her ear.'

Alice remembered Gabriel's comments, when they bought the farm. 'He was good to deal with, quite generous, when Gabriel did business with him.' Perhaps she should tell Laura about it.

Jacob pointed to the *Clarion*, lying on the table. 'I seem to think I saw a mention of him in yon paper. I've had little to do with him, but Bradley Paterson is well spoken of in the township.'

Alice put down her paring knife and picked up the paper. It was easy to find the big headline: LOCAL BENEFACTOR TO HELP MASHAM. 'This is it . . . "Mr Bradley Paterson of Linley Grange wishes to mark his forthcoming marriage to Miss Grey, the only daughter of Colonel and Mrs Grey, formerly of India and now residing. . . ." He should have waited until after the engagement, surely?'

Jacob drained his cup. 'What's he doing for us, then? I didn't read the fine print It might impress the young lady, if he's being generous with his brass.'

Alice smiled. 'Yes, this might help a bit . . . "On this auspicious occasion, the gentleman is to make generous donations to several good causes. He does not seek publicity and had hoped to make his donations anonymously. But the *Clarion* saw it as our public duty to thank Mr Paterson for his generosity." '

Standing up, Jacob clicked his teeth impatiently. 'I've got to get on . . . get to the point, woman.'

'Right!' Alice ran her eye down the column. 'The church gets a new organ, there's a big silver cup for the best ram at the sheep fair, and some money to paint the Mechanics' . . . oh, and a scheme to lend out pedigree rams from the Linley Grange flock, to help local farmers to improve their breeding stock. Now, that's a grand idea. I hope Gabriel gets one. I'll cut out the article for Laura. It might help her to see another side to Mr Paterson.'

'Just going, Doctor,' Jacob muttered as Dr Dent came in at the back door.

'Is poor Alice having to put up with you again? I was looking for you, Jacob, to run up to Linley Grange with one of Mr Paterson's grooms. They've sold a horse and the groom has ridden it down and put it on the train. I should have told you before, but it slipped my mind.' Dr Dent looked round at Alice. 'I'll have a cup of tea too, if you don't mind.'

'Is he here now, Doctor? I'd better take Silver; Honey's been out a lot this week.'

'Yes, it's Jim Thornby; he's in the stable. If you're quick you can be back in a couple of hours.'

A trip out was never too much trouble for Jacob; driving was always a pleasure. Yoking up was done quickly with another groom to help. Jim Thornby slipped the collar over Silver's head and swung it round expertly, and the young horse was soon in the shafts. They trotted briskly up the road, hunched against the bitter wind.

Thornby was a red-haired man and his freckled face was blue with cold; Jacob passed him a rug. This seemed to be a man who liked to talk, judging by his chatter in the stable. It might be a chance to dig for a bit more information about Paterson, to help Alice, but he'd have to go quietly about it. Looking straight between the horse's ears, Jacob ventured a question, to see where it might lead. 'Been at the Grange long?' Thornby was not a local man.

'About a year. It's a good place, boss pays decent wages and there's plenty of us to do the work.' Thornby grinned. 'Not like you, stuck on your own with all to do and no help. You won't get many days off, I bet.' His accent hinted at origins further north, up beyond Northallerton. Geordies always seemed to talk a lot.

This was useful; Alice could tell Miss Grey that Paterson treated his staff well. They talked about some of the Linley Grange workers. 'Henry's right enough,' Jacob offered. 'He worked with my old man, when he was young.' Henry had been well trained by his father, though he wouldn't mention that.

'Aye, well, Henry might not be there much longer. He's thinking of making a move, before he gets a lot older.' This was surprising; Henry had been the foreman on the Grange home farm for twenty years. As they came level with the little wood where Young Cecil had been rescued, Thornby laughed. 'Yon's the spot where poor little doctor got himself attacked, isn't it?'

Jacob turned to look at the man. 'Did the whole parish get to hear about that?' All signs of the tracks into the wood had disappeared; nothing disturbed the smooth green cover of vegetation. 'And where might you have got the tale from?' Neither he nor Alice had told anyone about it, although Fanshawe's version would probably have been in his letter to Dr Dent, as an explanation of why he was leaving in such a hurry.

'Doctor hisself. He were right indignant. Well, it did make you laugh, he was such a pompous little – but you worked for him, you'll know better than I do. Folks at the Grange thought it was droll . . . especially his trousers, hanging up in a tree! That was a right laugh.'

This story did not ring true. Fanshawe had stormed off to Harrogate the next day after the attack. He would have had no time to tell anyone about it, and even if he had, the trousers would surely never have been mentioned. Fanshawe was very upset about losing his dignity. Thornby must have inside knowledge.

Jacob laughed in his turn and said lightly, 'I suppose it was you, then, who upturned him. He did say it was a big, strong fella.' He had actually mentioned the red hair; Thornby must be the villain.

Pride struggled with prudence for a while in Thornby's face. 'Never tell that to PC Taylor, then. You could get me arrested with ought of that.' He was quite complacent.

'But what had he done to you, to earn a beating?' It seemed best to take this as a confession of guilt. Jacob drove rather more sedately, waiting for Thornby's reaction. They were leaving the main road now, taking the road to the moor.

'Nowt; I never knew him.' Thornby looked hard at Jacob. 'What's it to you, anyway?'

'Well, I was working for him at the time and it was me had to go and fish him out, so naturally I'm interested.' It was time to risk another shot in the dark. 'Must have been somebody's orders, most likely. Now, who would send you to thump Young Cecil?'

'You never know what you'll be asked to do by that Henry.' Thornby moved in his seat. 'They know I don't mind a bit of a scrap, see. Quite enjoy it.' He seemed to imply that a foreman could ask you to attack someone; a dangerous man, he must be, and Henry just as bad. Was it jealousy again – if it was Henry?

'I'd best be careful what I say to you, then. I'm all for a peace-

151

ful life.' Jacob shook his head and Silver went on clopping up the road. If Paterson had organized a bashing, that would not please Alice at all. It was not something she could tell Laura. What if the young miss was right, after all? From what Alice said, the young miss disliked her fiancé by instinct.

A few days later, Thornby rode up the drive to Birchwood Hall. 'Is Mr Burns about? I've got a note for him here, from Mr Paterson.' Jim Thornby knocked on the door as Adam was working in the office with Laura, over the final details of the spring plantings for the grounds. She had got her own way, and was allowed to finish off her plans, although her father had warned her about being alone with Adam. With luck, she would be able to come back next year and see the effects.

'That's me, thanks. Does he want a reply? Wait a moment, then.' Adam was aware that the big man's eyes flickered over Laura, before returning to his face.

'Er, yes please, sir. I'll take it back with me.' He wandered outside to wait by the door.

Adam looked over at Laura, frowning. 'He wants me to go up there tomorrow . . . apologies for the short notice, and all that. Wants advice on some sour land. I can go, as it happens, and the colonel has told me to make it a priority.'

When the man had gone, Laura sighed. 'Why should it be important to Papa? I wish I knew why he is so anxious to please Mr Paterson!' She was still reluctant to call him 'Bradley'.

Adam laughed; he had wondered the same thing. 'I will see him on the fourteenth, as well. I've been invited to your engagement party, Miss Laura. Now that's an honour for a wee Scot from the glens!' He pretended to polish up his shoes and smooth down his unruly copper hair.

Laura looked at him gloomily. She was hard to amuse, these days; all her fun and enthusiasm was slipping away as the date of the engagement drew nearer. 'Would you like to bring your . . . lady? I'm sure it could be arranged,' she said with an effort.

His lady. Of course, he had told them he had a lady in mind, to help Laura. It would not help at all to tell her that there was no lady; that Miss Laura herself was occupying more of Mr Burns's thoughts than was proper. 'No-o, thank you, Miss Grey.'

FOURTEEN

Riding through the Linley Grange gates the next day, Adam looked in vain for the first hint of spring. The sky was a little brighter, but the moorland was still wrapped in its winter sleep. Most of the Hall sheep were wintering on the lower slopes, the cattle were housed and the fields were silent, waiting for the return of the curlew to the moors.

There were no men in the yard and the first bull pen was empty; the animal that killed a man was gone, but Adam fancied that a gloom still hung over the place. Jacob had told him about the young lad's death. He would not like to work at Linley Grange, however progressive the owner might be.

Paterson appeared, his tall black horse led by Thornby. He mounted and they were off. 'I want to go round a few of the tenanted farms and there's not much time,' he said briefly. Then, with a brilliant smile, 'I am sorry to rush you, but your time is so valuable, and I would not want to waste it.' The landowner was impeccably dressed in highly polished riding boots, a well-fitting jacket and elegant moleskin breeches. Worn Scottish tweeds could not compete, Adam realized – but then, they did things differently in Scotland.

Riding quickly over the moor, they visited three farms on the lower land, and at each farm Paterson had suggestions and questions. The last farm was an intake from the moor. It was walled and fenced, but rather bare. The winds would sweep across the slopes and there was little shelter for stock. 'I would plant hawthorn hedges, with a few other species as well, like holly, but you'll be needing double fencing to protect the wee seedlings, or the sheep will doubtless eat them.' Adam sat still on his horse, thinking. 'A few clumps of trees could be planted in yon corner, too. Oak, ash and elm, for shade in the summer, with maybe a few birch on the slope.' Adam could see the little plantation in his mind's eye, creating a more sheltered and verdant place in a few years' time.

Paterson, looking very handsome on his big horse, seemed to share the vision. 'Future generations should thank me for improving the landscape. I agree with you, Burns, and that's what we will do.'

'Of course, this land was once covered with trees; that's why we have the peat bogs. So it should not be too hard to bring them back. I wonder why the landscape changed?' Adam looked over at Paterson. He would be able to tell Laura how interested her fiancé was in the improvement of estates; there might be some scope for his new wife there.

'The climate might have changed over thousands of years. But I suspect that once the human population grew, their sheep and goats ate the seedlings and gradually the moor grass took over. And now, let's go home.' Paterson set off at a gallop, with a sudden change of mood.

It was hard to keep up, if you were constantly watching for holes in the moorland turf, treacherous bogs and hidden stones, all of which could end your life too soon; not to mention the moor birds that flew up from under the horse's feet and threatened to make him shy. But it was a pity Laura could not see the black horse and rider, going like the wind, skimming across the moor, oblivious to the hidden dangers.

At the top of a rise with views down into the beginning of Wensleydale, Paterson reined in. 'You are evidently good at landscaping, Burns . . . perhaps too good?' His face was dark, as though he was brooding.

'I don't know what you mean, sir.' But Paterson was off like the wind again. It seemed best to follow more steadily, as Adam's horse was built for endurance rather than speed. Adam's mount, the colonel's Cleveland Bay, was heavier than Paterson's hunter, but it was a pleasant ride and it was good to be out on the moor instead of looking over accounts in the office. Eventually, Adam's horse caught up, and when they stopped Paterson seemed to be agitated.

Down there in the wide valley, the River Ure wound its way through farms and pastures in a peaceful landscape, but Paterson was far from peaceful. 'I have a few words to say to you, Burns.' What was wrong with the man? 'It has come to my notice that you have become rather too familiar with Miss Grey. As you are aware, we are to be formally engaged, tomorrow. This has been known for some time.' Paterson was breathing heavily.

Adam said nothing. What was there to say?

'You must know what I mean. Miss Grey is young, and easily impressed. You have encouraged her to spend time in the farm office and gardens. You have tried to influence her thinking, and I feel that you may even have set her against me!' He was shouting, and his fingers were clenched round the reins.

It was time to speak up. 'We have worked together on improvements to the estate, in which Miss Grey is interested. That's all. I have never tried to influence her in any way. She is a talented artist, and her father encouraged her in landscape design.' In the face of Paterson's fury, it was hard to keep calm, but Adam's conscience was clear. He, and particularly Alice, had rescued Laura out of a deep depression and had tried to reconcile her to the marriage.

Paterson turned in the saddle, his face a mask of fury. 'You have tried to ingratiate yourself with her – I know all about it! It's obvious to me. She is the heiress to a fine estate, as you see it, and you are a crofter's son, educated above your station in life. Always dangerous! You think it would be a good marriage for you, with an only child. And my poor Laura is too fine, too pure to see that you are a low schemer!'

Well, this was no time to lose his temper and live up to the copper hair. Laura would have to spend her life with this man, heaven help her. Adam looked down at the river again, calming himself. He would not make things more difficult for Laura, and neither would he be provoked to anger by these accusations. 'Mr Paterson, please understand that I have no designs upon Miss Grey. I work for her father, that's all.' The Scottish burr sounded more pronounced than usual. Who was this man, to insult Adam Burns?

The other man hardly heard him. 'And even yesterday when my groom brought you my note, Miss Grey was in the office with you. I have spoken to her father before about this. It seems to have had no effect. I warn you, Burns, that if I see you in Miss Grey's company again, you will have to answer for the consequences.' He looked dangerous, at that moment. What could the threat mean? What would he do? Of course, the portrait artist had been punched for touching Laura. 'You have plans to grab her fortune, and also, I am sure, her person. She is a beautiful young woman, and it would be easy for you to lure her into lonely places – the poor girl has no idea of the danger she is in! It must be stopped!' Paterson was shaking, his eyes glaring, as he turned his horse to the track.

Something should be said, although it was not likely to make any difference. 'Just a moment, sir. Perhaps you should realize that women these days are beginning to take an interest in a range of occupations. When they work with men on some enterprise such as estate management, they do so equally, as comrades. There is no question of an improper relationship. I have sisters, sir, and I have learned from them that women can enter the world of work, a man's world until now. Why should they not?'

'Low-bred ignorance! You speak of dairymaids!' Paterson's black horse wheeled, spattering Adam with mud.

Well, my sisters would be proud of me, Adam thought as he wiped his face. The man's mad; all that melodrama is wasted, off the stage. It would be laughable if Laura wasn't involved. But for her, it looked tragic. Such jealousy would follow her everywhere she went. She would never have a moment's peace, unless the man settled down once he had secured his bride. The farm tour was over, it might be as well to follow Paterson back to the farm and make his peace, since they would have to meet again at the party.

'Well, Burns, come in and have a bit to eat before you go,' Paterson said with another quick change of mood. As they walked into the house he added, 'Perhaps you think I am too intense, but you must understand that this marriage mean everything to me. Everything! You won't understand, unless one day you become obsessed!'

Well, it would have been good to leave, but Adam was hungry. 'Thank you, sir, something to eat would be welcome. But I must leave soon, to be home before dark.' Best not to get into an argument.

Soon they were sitting in front of a good fire with food and drink and Paterson was his usual self again. He talked well about his new estate in Jamaica and his plans for farm improvement there; Adam had to admit he had no experience of sugar cane. It was all very civilized, hard to equate with the outburst on the moor. Perhaps he had been indulged in his youth by rich parents, and had grown up to be entirely self-centred.

On the day of the engagement party, the sun shone from a blue sky for St Valentine's Day. Alice was baking bread when Mrs Dent came through into the kitchen. 'We've had a note from the Greys, asking whether you can help out at the Hall tonight, Alice. They will need more hands in the kitchen. We'll be at the dinner, so you won't need to cook for us.'

It was a pity that Laura was so unhappy; otherwise, the prospect of being at the Hall for the party, even to peel the potatoes, was quite a pleasant one. 'Yes, ma'am, I will be pleased to go.'

'Wear your black dress, Alice, and a white cap, of course. You may be asked to wait at table. Do you mind?'

'I was trained at the castle, Mrs Dent. It will be no trouble at all,' Alice reminded her.

'Jacob has gone to Ripon station with the trap, to pick up some urgent supplies; they were going to take days to come up the line to Masham. He could be needed as well. I'll tell him when he gets back, but I hope he's not too late.' Emily Dent looked at the kitchen clock. 'Do you know, I think he'll quite enjoy mixing with the other grooms. Apparently, they are short of outdoor staff at the Hall. A couple of men have been dismissed, so they asked for Jacob to help with the visiting horses and vehicles.'

Kneading the dough energetically, Alice thought about the Hall. Why would they get rid of staff? It might be a good idea to listen to the talk in the kitchen, and find out.

Jacob was tired of waiting for the train on Ripon station; it was over an hour late and there was only so much people watching you could do without feeling bored and cold. But there was no question of going home without the doctor's supplies; the practice depended on being ready for any emergency, or any ailment that might befall the folks of Masham. The practice, in fact, depended on Jacob.

Among the waiting, would-be passengers there were a few Masham folks, and one was a surprise: Henry Beal from Linley Grange, Mr Paterson's farm foreman, sitting on a suitcase and looking miserable and uncomfortable in his Sunday clothes. 'Henry! Going on holiday, lad? You don't look right happy about job!'

Henry groaned. 'Not holidays, Jacob. I'm off for good.'

'Let's sit out of wind on the bench yonder. I'm fair nithered myself and train won't be in for a while yet. Porter says there's trouble down the line.'

On the dreary station platform, Jacob and Henry looked

glumly down the tracks. 'Well, this is a surprise, although yon Jim Thornby told me you're aiming on a change.' Jacob waited, but Henry sat still without comment. 'Have you got a better place to go to?'

Henry looked across, his pale eyes rather wary. 'Nay, I'll go to see me sister for a week or two, and then have a look round down Doncaster way. I've had enough of Linley Grange, that's for sure.'

This was interesting. 'By gum, and I thought you were set for life. Jim says that Paterson's a good boss, and I know you've been there ever since he took over farm as a lad.'

Henry sighed. 'Aye, twenty year I've been at Linley Grange.' He said no more.

It would be good to get Henry to talk about Paterson; Alice badly needed some good news about him, but this did not look promising. They sat in silence for a while, and Jacob was just about to ask another question when Henry spoke again. 'His grandfather were a West Riding weaver, that were all. And yet he talks posh and rides the best horses, and owns all that land . . . it's just not right, to my way of thinking.'

'You mean Paterson. Why should it worry you, Henry? His family got into the wool trade, made some brass and then bought an estate.' Better not show too much interest. Henry had always been known for envy, in any case; this was how he often talked. 'He keeps a lot of folks in work.'

'I suppose it bothers me because our family went the other way; we went down in the world. My grandad had a good farm, but me father turned to drink and all was lost. So,' Henry smiled sourly, 'a man can't help thinking.'

'But you've known him for twenty years. You can't be leaving now, just because he's a nob, can you?' There was something deeper here; Henry had a frightened look about him.

'No, suppose not.' Henry shifted on the hard bench. 'To tell you the truth, Jake, I know too much. That's why I'm off.'

'Maybe – maybe you found out that he got Jim to . . . discourage Young Cecil? Dr Fanshawe?' Jacob spoke slowly, quietly. This might be the problem.

'Nay, that was nought. I knew about it, right enough, but it wasn't . . . that serious. Boss wanted to frighten him off. It seems he thought the little doctor was after his woman, that colonel's daughter. Leastways, that's what Jim Thornby said. Little doctor was at the Grange one day and was talking very familiar about her, boss was in a rage and stormed out to tell Jim. No, I suppose . . . it was a lot of things, all piled up.' Henry sighed deeply. 'You know how it is . . . one thing happens after another, and one day, it's too much. That's how it was with me.'

Another silence, and then Henry leaned forward. 'I knew about poor Maisie, for one thing. That was years ago, of course. She was in the family way after being noticed by young Mr Paterson, see. Nothing was said at the time, mind; she kept very quiet, but we all knew, like. They married her off right sharp to a young Wood from Ripon, and gave them a cottage. That lad Joseph was given a job when he left school. He was all right, just a lad, very keen. But he was never treated as Mr Paterson's son. And by now, nobody knows about it but me.'

'And the poor lad was killed.' Jacob waited again for a reaction.

Henry spoke so quietly that Jacob could hardly hear him. 'I'll never forget the sight, to my dying day. The poor lad lying there . . . and then his ma had words to say and next minute, she was certified. Locked up, insane, to shut her up.'

There was a strangled whistle as the long-awaited train finally pulled into Ripon station. 'I know over-much,' Henry said again heavily. He picked up his case and moved so as to be level with the third-class carriages on the train, at the tail end of the platform. He would be envious of the first-class, privileged people. 'And maybe you ought to know—'

A porter came up to Jacob. 'Parcels for Dr Dent of Masham, give us a hand, there, will you?' Together they hauled the boxes on to a barrow, and then Jacob raced down the platform until he saw Henry's pale, sad face at an open window. He held out his hand. 'Good luck, old lad. What else did you want to tell me?'

Henry leaned out and whispered hoarsely in Jacob's ear. 'I'll likely never see you again, mate. All the best, Jake, your Dad was good to me.' He turned away, but then looked back. The whistle blew and the train started to move, very slowly. 'You should know that it were no accident. He killed young Joseph in a fit of rage. He strangled the lad and then threw him in the bull pen, made it look like the bull got him. I'm scared of him, now. His temper's getting worse, I reckon.'

'Paterson?' The train gathered speed.

Henry raised his voice above the noise; he was half hidden in steam. 'Aye, him. Keep away from him, Jake.' It was a faint cry, almost like a wail.

Jacob plodded thoughtfully back to Masham with a trap full of parcels; now, he himself probably knew too much. The young miss had been right to feel that Paterson was not likely to make a good husband. Alice must know straight away; she must warn the Greys. But would she be believed? Nobody who spoke to Henry would doubt his word, but Henry was gone for good.

The big kitchen at Birchwood Hall was steamy, hot and very busy indeed. There was an underlying excitement that the engagement dinner was finally being prepared. Alice, with a large apron over her black dress, went quietly about her tasks; having worked at the castle, she was used to such scenes. She remembered the frenzy in the castle kitchens when royalty was expected.

The younger maids were ready to extract as much romance as possible from the evening and chattered happily about rings, dresses and weddings. Alice helped to top a dessert with whipped cream and nuts. 'We've got to put supper on for the grooms, next,' the cook told her, wiping her face with a floury arm. 'There'll be five or six, at least. Twenty-two to dinner and most of 'em driven here. It's a big night!'

'Ooh, which of the grooms do you like best?' The youngest

maid whispered to her senior.

'Most of them are old, or married!' The other girl sniffed. 'Who'd get excited over a parcel of horsemen?' The first carriage rumbled up the drive.

'I don't mind old Jacob, him with Dr Dent,' the parlourmaid said, with a mischievous look at Alice. 'He's too serious, but I reckon he's a decent enough lad.'

'Beats me why he never got married.' another girl chimed in.

The cook frowned severely. 'Never mind your gossip, get bread rolls out of the oven, Sadie. They'll be burned to a cinder, else.' When the grooms clattered in, Jacob was not with them. He hadn't been seen.

Mrs Grey descended to the kitchen, regal in purple velvet and pearls. 'Ah, Greenwood, there you are. You will have to dress my daughter's hair; she looks a perfect fright; why young girls cannot look tidy I will never know, and this on one of the most important days of her life—'

'Yes, ma'am.' Alice looked apologetically at the cook and went upstairs. Laura was sitting in a chair by the window in her bedroom, looking wistfully over the grounds. She wore a pretty pink and white gown, but she was near to tears. 'Oh, Alice, thank you for coming . . . Chandler can't do my hair.'

It was rather late to create a new hairstyle, but Alice did her best with curling tongs and ribbons. She was nearly finished when a maid knocked at the door. 'Miss Grey is wanted in the drawing-room,' said the maid, and whispered to Alice at the door, 'Jacob Fowler wants to see you. He says it's really urgent.'

Knowing her way round the big house by now, Alice let herself out by a side door. Jacob was in the stables as she expected, but the other grooms were in the house and the stalls were full of the rustle and stamp of horses. 'Lass, I've got to tell you this.' Jacob looked serious, and by the time he had finished reciting Henry's story Alice felt a deep dismay.

'I've got to see Laura . . . she must tell the colonel, right away.'

'There might be trouble.' Jacob warned with a set face. 'I'll hang about in case—'

Miss Grey was still in her bedroom, according to a maid, so Alice went heavily up the stairs. 'Miss Laura,' she began, but the old imperious miss forestalled her.

'I know quite well what I am supposed to do, there is no need to tell me, Alice,' she said frigidly. 'I will go down now.' Then she reverted to a friendlier tone. 'Oh, Alice! What can I do? All day I've tried to talk to Papa, but he's been shut in his study with papers and won't see me.' She bit her lip and turned away.

'If you tell him what I have just heard, it might make a difference, Miss Laura. I believe that Mr Paterson might be a murderer. He is certainly a most unpleasant person.' And she told Laura briefly what Jacob had found out, and watched the blue eyes widen in alarm. Alarm, but also the dawn of hope; she had been right to be afraid of Paterson.

Five minutes later, Laura was pounding on the study door. 'Papa! Papa! You must hear me!'

Alice stood beside her as the colonel came out, immaculate in evening dress. 'I wish you were not so theatrical, Laura,' he said stiffly, and brushed past them. 'Paterson is expected at any moment.' He stalked down the corridor, completely ignoring his daughter's cries.

'I must go – I don't know what to do.' Laura was white. 'But Alice, I am relieved. Somehow, I must get out of this engagement, and now I have a good reason. But I wish we had known all this before now!'

Alice went back to the kitchen and tried to concentrate on the work, but Jacob's news was so shocking that it was hard to think of anything else. Poor Young Cecil, set upon by Paterson's thug! Even worse, poor Joseph . . . presumably he had been killed in a fit of temper. Felix Mayo had got off lightly, with only a punch on the chin.

What would Laura do? There was a hum of conversation in the big drawing-room, and she must be in there by now. The poor lass would have to put on a brave face, greet the guests and go along with the whole occasion. Perhaps she would be able to tell her parents later, but how would she get through the evening?

All too soon, the sherry drinking was over and the guests trooped into the dining-room. Alice was putting bread rolls on the table and she saw Paterson, looking very handsome and self-satisfied, walking in with Laura. The girl looked afraid, and no wonder.

Dinner proceeded, and it was a lively party, judging by the volume of noise. Alice was asked to wait at table, having had more experience than most of the maids. The room shimmered; light from the many candles and lamps was reflected by the silver, the polished furniture and the shining silks and satin of the ladies' dresses. Dr Dent was there with Mrs Dent, and a few other people she knew. Paterson sat next to Laura, his arm frequently across the back of her chair.

The speeches were planned for after the main course and before dessert. Alice was in the room, standing unobtrusively at the door, when the colonel rose to his feet and started to speak. He praised Bradley Paterson as a fine man, a benefactor to the local community and a wonderful addition to his own family. 'We are here to celebrate their engagement, and I am sure that my daughter has a brilliant future before her.' He turned to look at his daughter, and Laura stood up. She was amazingly brave; Alice quailed for her.

'I would like to announce that I do not believe Mr Paterson to be the man my father thinks he is. I thought of waiting until tomorrow, but it would not be honest to proceed with this party, this engagement. I will not marry this man. He has harmed others—' She faltered and then saw Alice at the back of the room, and seemed to take courage again. 'Is it not so, Alice?'

Paterson was on his feet, his face a mask of fury. 'You are trying to humiliate me!' he shouted. 'I will not tolerate this treatment!'

'This is outrageous!' The colonel's face was purple as he, too, jumped to his feet, glaring at his daughter. Adam stood up and moved quietly so that he stood beside Laura.

There was a hush and Alice held her breath. Should she speak? It was unheard of for a servant to utter a word unless spoken to, especially when waiting at table, and especially at a formal dinner party. But poor Laura had the courage to speak up and she desperately needed support; she was asking for it. In the few seconds she had, Alice made up her mind. She spoke into the silence. There was no need to raise her voice. 'What about Joseph Wood? Were you responsible for him? Was his death an accident?'

FIFTEEN

'You bitch!' With a swift movement Paterson picked up a heavy silver bowl and hurled it across the room at Alice. It caught her on the side of the head and she fell to the floor. There was a sharp pain in her head and blood flowed from a cut, but she struggled up as Dr Dent moved towards her, full of concern.

Meanwhile, Adam moved in closer to Laura, obviously afraid for her. Paterson turned on him, slashing at him with a carving knife from the sideboard, aiming for Adam's face. But Laura hit his arm and the blow came down across Adam's hands, outstretched to fend him off. Adam moved in close, grabbed Paterson, knocked him down and firmly sat on him. From where Alice sat on the floor, the young Scotsman looked determined, and even happy.

Not without a struggle, the powerful and furious Paterson was immobilized by the younger men round the table. The colonel gave orders and he was marched off and locked in a storeroom, swearing and shouting. The dining-room was put to rights and the colonel apologized to his guests; the meal went on. The guests, shocked and pale, talked in whispers. A groom was quietly sent off by Dr Dent for the police.

'This is unthinkable! Unbelievable!' The colonel kept repeating, while Mrs Grey, ashen-faced, sat and stared in front of her.

Alice and Adam were both taken to the housekeeper's room, where Dr Dent bandaged Alice first. Soon afterwards, Jacob knocked and came in. 'Now, lass, I hear you stuck your neck out.

Is she much hurt, Doctor?' The look on his face was heart-warming: real concern, turning to relief when the doctor reassured him. 'I felt right bad, it was all my fault for telling you. I should have told doctor, and let him handle it.'

'I think you had better tell me now what you know,' the doctor said quietly. 'What was that about young Joseph? I was away when it happened, of course.' Adam, trying to hold a towel round his hands, looked up with interest.

'We were at the farm the day Joseph Wood died,' Alice explained, feeling her head gingerly. 'And I saw red marks on his neck, as if the lad had been throttled. He was supposed to have been killed by the bull, but afterwards I remembered those marks . . . and it fitted in with Henry Beal's story that Jacob heard today.'

Jacob quickly related his talk to Henry Beal, and threw in Jim Thornby's sorry story of the assault on Dr Fanshawe for good measure. 'Paterson's a right villain, Boss. Must be queer in the head, if you ask me.'

The doctor looked grim. 'Who would have thought it of him? He could be so charming! And so, Alice, you told Miss Grey, just a few minutes before the guests went in. But why did she not tell her father, and let him speak to the man, before the dinner? It was very public and, as it turned out, it was dangerous.'

"It could have been more dangerous, in private! Miss Grey did try, but she's tried before. It was no good talking to the colonel; his mind was made up.' It had been a tiring night and Alice sat back in her chair, trying to ease the tension. 'Do you think I could have a cup of tea?' Jacob scurried off to find the kitchen.

Dr Dent looked at Adam next. 'These gashes are quite deep; we must stop the bleeding. It was a heavy knife and brought down with force. Luckily, no bones appear to be broken, but your hands will take time to heal. No doubt Alice will recommend lavender water!' He applied a pad and held it firmly. 'Well, the man condemned himself by his reaction. If he had kept cool, most people would have believed his version of events.'

Adam smiled. 'Makes it easier, doesn't it? Although I was sorry that Alice was hurt.'

'I am recovering, thank you. But how is Miss Grey?'

'She is doing her duty, talking to the guests, since her mother is . . . not well. Miss Grey is a brave wee lassie.' Adam watched as Dr Dent swiftly bound his wounds. 'I am most relieved, I can tell you, Doctor. The other day, Paterson threatened me. I saw then that what I had thought was only a wee fault was real bad blood in the man. I wondered then whether he could kill some-one in a rage. That bull pen was a good way to cover up a murrrder, ye ken.' The drama seemed to have increased his Scottish accent. 'I was going to speak to the colonel, after the party. An engagement's no' the end of the world; Miss Grey could easily have broken it off, I thought. But perhaps the public display was a good thing – it convinced everybody in a few seconds!' For an injured man, Adam was very cheerful.

'I suppose no one would accuse a public benefactor, such a popular man.' Dr Dent looked thoughtful.

Alice looked up. 'One person did, but she was silenced. Joseph's mother told her story while I was there. But she's been certified, sent away where she can't tell anybody else.' Perhaps poor Mrs Wood might now be freed.

Laura came in to see the patients, her blue eyes full of concern, and the doctor reassured her. 'You were very quick,' he told her. 'Adam might have lost an eye, if you hadn't moved when you did.'

'It was dreadful, but I am so relieved!' A little colour had come back into Laura's face. 'But can you see Mama now, Dr Dent? Mama is having hysterics, and Papa looks very unwell.'

Laura woke early on the morning after the party. The shadow was there, as usual, but then a shaft of sunshine struck her face, and she remembered. She was free! Bradley Paterson was not going to claim her.

It was a pity that Mama and Papa had taken it so badly.

169

Perhaps it was because they were used to having their own way – especially Papa, who used to have his own regiment. She would have to be nice to them, and dutiful. After breakfast she would send a note to poor Alice, and see whether she was well enough to go for a walk with Hamish. Then, there were plans she would like to discuss with Adam. What a lovely day! There were drifts of snowdrops under the trees at the edge of the lawn. Alice had said it would soon be spring.

It was a cold February morning, but the sun was still bright as Laura went into the dining-room. 'It's a beautiful day! Good morning, Papa.' She helped herself to toast and coffee. There was silence. Papa was sitting at the table with his head in his hands, his breakfast untouched. 'Never mind, Papa, it was embarrassing I know, but it was for the best.' Laura put a light hand on his shoulder. 'I wish I could have warned you. I thought of leaving it until the next day, but I couldn't . . . keep up the pretence.'

The colonel raised a haggard face and looked at his daughter with red-rimmed eyes. 'You don't understand, Laura. You don't understand, at all.'

This was upsetting. 'Where is Mama?'

'Your mother is prostrated; Chandler is with her. And I must say that she blames you; your outburst could not have been more badly timed.'

Well, the maid could look after her until breakfast was over and by then she might have simmered down. Laura attacked her toast. 'What's wrong, Papa? Surely, it's not that bad, about Mr Paterson? It was just as well to find out before I was married to him.' Papa looked dreadful, yellow and ill. It couldn't be the drink; very little had been drunk at the party. 'Is it the digestion again? Shall I call Dr Dent?'

'Things could not be worse. Two policemen took Paterson off to the cells. I planned to bail him out, this morning.' The colonel sighed deeply. 'He behaved badly, of course, but hitting servants is not the end of the world. We saw far worse in India, in the heat. Yes, I know they were slightly injured,' he waved a hand to stop his daughter's indignant protest, 'but it was nothing that a few guineas wouldn't put right. We could say that he had drunk too much wine—'

Laura couldn't believe it. 'So, you will try to cover it up?'

'That is what I thought. The other accusations were probably just servants' tales; no wonder he was upset. Servants can be very malicious, Laura, and often, untruthful. You are too trusting in this regard. But Paterson persuaded the constables not to put the handcuffs on him; said he was a gentleman, and would come quietly. Halfway across the square, he knocked them both down. He took a horse from in front of the Bruce Arms and galloped off. This was not a good move, on his part.'

'Oh, goodness!' Laura thought quickly. He would probably go overseas; he had talked about buying an estate in Jamaica. It would be important to find out the truth about young Wood, so that if Paterson ever appeared again, criminal charges would be waiting for him. Otherwise, Papa might welcome him back.

With an effort, the colonel stood up. 'See me in my study, as soon as you have eaten, Laura.' He left the room.

Something must be wrong, but whatever it was, it couldn't be as bad as the engagement would have been. It was horrible to think about Paterson and her narrow escape; the marriage had been planned for April. But now that was over, and whatever Papa said, she was NEVER going to marry Paterson. Anything else could be faced and overcome. After a cup of coffee Laura crossed the hall to the study to find out what the problem could be.

Colonel Grey was turning over papers on his desk. 'Sit down, Laura,' he said without looking up. There was silence again, broken only by the crackle of the fire. Eventually her father shook his head. 'This is very difficult for me. But you will have to know, sooner or later. Your marriage to Paterson, Laura, was essential if we were to continue to live here. We are ruined, girl, financially. And that man was my only hope.'

So that was why he had insisted, why he had been so cruel. Even when Paterson was being taken away, Papa had muttered about 'some mistake' and was going to make excuses for him. He could not believe the truth. 'Ruined? What do you mean, Papa?' It was frightening.

'I mean that Paterson was going to help us financially.' The colonel paused, almost unable to speak. 'We agreed that he would take the deeds of the Hall, the whole estate, in return for a loan. In time I might redeem them, if my shares paid dividends. We could stay here, and no one would know.' He bowed his head.

'Has something happened suddenly?' Why had she not picked up some hint of disaster, some idea of what was going on?

'My affairs have been going badly for some time, I'm afraid. I suppose we paid too much for the Hall, but I always wanted to live in Yorkshire . . . but that's beside the point. I hired Adam Burns to run the estate as a business, so that we could get some income from it. But that will take time.' The colonel looked old and tired.

'But of course, Papa! Adam will help us to do that!' It seemed important to Laura that she should sound cheerful, and it was easy for her – Paterson was gone.

Her father fiddled with pens on his desk. 'To improve the estate, we've spent money. And I have lost money in companies that were supposed to pay dividends, but didn't . . . Paterson recommended them, as a matter of fact.'

Well, Papa was bound to trust a future son-in-law's advice; the man was successful, rich himself and made no secret of it. But the investments had gone wrong. Had he done that on purpose, to get the Greys in his power?

'I didn't pay much attention to the accounts, you see, until it was too late, and of course Burns didn't know the state of my finances. He has looked after the farms quite well. I can see the mistake, now. But after last night, well, it was our last chance. We'll have to sell Birchwood Hall. I may have to go back to India.'

It was impossible not to feel sorry for him, even after his harsh treatment. 'Let me help, Papa. I'm old enough to be of some use. I think we should look at all the assets, decide whether some could be sold . . . and I think Adam might be a great help; he could organize things.' Adam had explained to her about assets.

That was the wrong thing to say; Colonel Grey was horrified. 'We cannot tell the servants! No one must know of this! What are you thinking of, girl?'

It was time to be patient. 'Adam Burns isn't exactly a servant, Papa. He has been to university and has, well, wide experience of estate management. We'll need expert advice, and here he is. We can use his knowledge.' Laura looked her father in the eye. 'But we will have to tell him the truth.'

It was obviously not going to help if Miss Grey burst into tears and retired to her bedroom, her usual reaction to trouble. Why not try to influence events? To keep the Hall and the estate and work with Adam, that was the aim. It was good to know what you wanted to do, at last. 'If we sold some of the farms, we might be able to keep the Hall and the home farm. Let's plan for that, Papa.' She tried to smile brightly.

Amazingly, her father had heard her and appeared to be thinking. 'I will certainly need professional advice, and Burns is paid to run the estate.' He broke off as the door flew open and his wife erupted into the room. The colonel sank down in his chair. Mrs Grey was in black, with a pale face, and her mouth was already open when her husband cut in first. 'Now, Lavinia, don't make a scene, please. I have told Laura of our problems and she is very brave.'

Laura's mother snorted. 'Laura! It's her fault that we are in this horrible situation. If the girl had married Bradley in the first place and behaved as a dutiful young girl should, this would never have happened; he was very upset, he's been waiting all this time, devoted to Laura, no wonder he was difficult, with servants accusing him; my own father used to throw things at servants when he was in a rage and that Greenwood woman is probably no better

173

than she ought to be; why we encourage such people I do not know, and now we are ruined because of the delay, and—'

'Mother, you don't mean it. You can't really be sorry that I am not to be married to that man. He is dangerous!' It felt strange to be speaking quietly to Mama as an adult, but her attitude was shocking. Paterson's good looks and wealth had blinded her to his real character.

Mrs Grey had not finished. 'You would do better to submit to your elders, Laura; how else will you please a husband, and I suppose you still expect to be married, rather than grow into a sour old maid; but now there is no fortune, how we are to arrange to marry you off I really cannot think.' Mama subsided into a chair and fanned herself. 'You are a very selfish girl, Laura. You never consider your father and me.' Finally the high voice stopped, and the silence was a blessing.

There were things that had to be said. 'Dr Dent employs Alice and he vouches for her honesty and so do I, having got to know her quite well. She is a very decent woman, Mama. We have to believe what she tells us. You may not have heard the full story. Last night, Jacob Fowler, the doctor's groom, came back from Ripon and told Alice that he was sure Bradley Paterson had treated his servants very badly indeed, over a long period. I spoke to Jacob myself, and Mr Burns also knew some of the truth.'

'Servants will say anything, Laura; they are not to be believed.' Mrs Grey was loudly scornful. 'I must say that you seem bent on associating with the lower orders; it is not wise to treat them as equals, believe me, it leads to all sorts of trouble; Burns is a worry to me, he presumes—'

This time, the colonel intervened. 'Lavinia, you must remember that Burns was injured last night and helped to overpower Paterson. There could have been more bloodshed, if he had not acted quickly. He has a cool head in a crisis – he would make a good soldier.'

Well, from Papa, this was high praise.

'I have been considering the matter,' the colonel continued, who five minutes before had been horrified at the idea, 'and I think that he would be able to help us. Burns is employed by me; he is no doubt of humble origin, but he has a degree in agriculture and he knows about the new methods. I intend to take his advice, for the time being at least. But,' he looked sternly at his wife, 'some of the other servants will have to go.'

Laura looked at her parents, both bound by nineteenth-century thinking in the rigid class structure of the British in India. What would they say if they knew of Adam's ideas on modern women taking up careers? 'Don't worry, Mama. Papa and I will work it out!'

This seemed to startle both parents; Mrs Grey stared at them both with faded blue eyes. 'What if we have no money? Oh, dear, Roderick! I have no experience of this kind of thing, at all.' She began to weep.

'Please, Lavinia! I could go back to India, I suppose, as a district officer, or a professional hunter, taking Europeans on tiger shoots.' The Colonel sighed. 'But I am getting rather old for that type of thing.'

Mrs Grey sat up straight. 'Back to India?' she hooted. 'I should think not, indeed! When I consider what I put up with on the plains . . . and now you are making my life a misery again! I hope you realize how very unhappy I am, how humiliated I was last night, when the dinner party was such a disaster. I don't know how my nerves will survive—'

What a relief; there was a light tap on the door. Laura opened it and Adam stood there, fresh-faced and smiling, and very welcome. She looked at his bandages. 'Yes, ma'am, I am going to survive; I have it on the best authority.'

It seemed best to lead Mama away to the sewing-room, and then go back to the study. 'Do we need you, Laura?' Papa said on her return, not understanding how she had changed. He looked at her over the top of his reading glasses, expecting her to scurry obediently away. Only a few weeks ago, Laura would have meekly withdrawn; but this was a new life, full of interesting possibilities.

It would not do to upset Papa too much. Laura said humbly, 'I would like to learn about managing business. And I'd like to help, in some way.' Adam smiled his encouragement.

'And how are your hands, my poor fellow? It was a sorry business last night, indeed it was, and now I wish to talk to you about the estate. I will not beat about the bush. There is at present . . . um . . . a cash shortfall. We need to make the estate profitable, possibly sell some land to finance the improvements. We are not talking about planting new gardens, Laura, but about increasing farm yields. What do you think, Burns?' The colonel sat back, handing over the problem to the younger man. He had not mentioned Paterson and the reason for the sudden crisis.

Adam considered, in his quiet way. 'It depends on the urgency, sir. Are we to consider . . . er . . . short-term or long-term profits?'

Colonel Grey looked blank.

'How would you plan for either, Mr Burns?' Laura asked.

'Long term, we can do several things. Increase production, keep more stock, sell shooting rights – the pheasants, of course – and grow more timber on the poorer land. We could grow more corn, for example, on the lower farms, but we would need more horses to work the land and perhaps a few more labourers.'

Roderick Grey looked glum and Laura thought that it sounded expensive. 'And short term?'

Adam frowned. 'I would not advise increasing the farm rents, although some landowners use it as a solution.' He spoke as though 'cash shortfalls' were common. 'It makes for dissatisfied tenants, obviously. We want them to farm well.' He looked at them both. 'Do ye mind the new plantation? In twenty years, there will be some very good timber to sell. In the short term, we'd need to sell the land itself.'

The colonel stood up with his back to the fire. 'Burns, I am afraid we need to consider what can be done immediately. We've spent money on the estate – surely it will yield some profit?'

'Only if it's put up for sale, sir,' said Adam bluntly.

Papa rang for coffee, and Laura wondered how it would feel if you couldn't ring a bell and have a servant appear. 'How does the system work at present? You are often working on accounts, Mr Burns.'

Adam waited until the order for coffee had been given. 'Well, the farm produce – that's the corn, fat lambs, beef – pays for the workers, with a wee bit profit. We keep all the hay for winter feed.' He looked at Laura. 'Shall I go on?' She nodded. 'Our dairy is small; as you know, it produces milk, butter and so on for the Hall, but has no surplus for sale. The gardens are the same, just producing for the house, although I suppose we could sell a wee surplus, but it wouldna be very significant.' He paused, thinking. 'Farm rents pay the estate expenses, fencing, tree planting, farm repairs, but there isn't enough left to keep the hall going. I always assumed that there was no problem, ye ken.' He picked up a pencil, but the bandages made writing difficult.

'But can't we change the system, now that we need to? Make a profit to support the Hall?' It seemed to Laura that the whole estate was being run to keep the people on it in work.

'There's another wee problem.' Adam put down the pencil. 'The weather. A couple of years ago, it would be before you were here, they had a disastrous summer. The rain spoiled both the hay and corn harvest, so there was no food for the stock in winter. And no surplus to sell. I dinna want to be dramatic, but it could happen again. You can't count on the corn until it's sold.'

Laura looked out of the window, where clouds were now moving over the sun. 'This winter's been mild, Alice says. But what if we get snow now?'

Adam nodded. 'That's just it. The sheep are lambing and if we get drifting snow as we did once before Christmas, the shepherds will work hard to save them, but we will lose some sheep. That's farming for you, sir. Perhaps you should have invested in coal mining or railways.'

Laura looked at her father, slumped and dejected. 'It sounds as though I should earn my own living. Perhaps I could teach art at a school? Or . . . I would really like to learn about garden design—'

177

She had made things worse; the colonel was horrified. 'Ridiculous girl! You will no doubt marry well, Laura. I have no fears for your future.'

Adam stood up to go. He said slowly, 'There is one way it might be done. If an investor bought the estate, you might lease it back and stay here. Perhaps even buy it back, in time. Good farm management should pay for the lease. And the owner might put in some capital, plant trees, that sort of thing.'

That had been the plan with Paterson. 'Please leave me out of it,' said Laura with feeling.

'In the short term, you could sell Wrenswood. It's not really part of the estate and it wouldn't be missed. If you put it on the market right away, with spring coming, it might sell quickly. That would keep everything going as it is now, for a while, until we can make . . . other arrangements.' Adam looked down at his bandaged hands. 'I really came to see you, sir, to ask for a few days' leave. I would like to visit my family in Scotland. I can't write at the moment, to do accounts . . . I could be back in a week or two, travelling by train.'

The colonel looked reluctant. 'Very well, Burns, but don't stay away too long. When you come back, we must do an evaluation of the whole estate, as a matter of some urgency.'

'Yes, sir, that will be the first thing to do, and Miss Grey can help us with it.'

When Adam had gone, there was silence for a while. The colonel looked over to his map of the estate, covering one wall. 'I don't suppose you know, Laura, where Wrenswood is? I am not familiar with it, I'm afraid.'

'Of course, Papa.' Laura went to the map and pointed out a group of fields outlined in red, about three miles from the main estate. 'I remember it because of the pretty name. Mr Burns talked about planting trees there, once.' Papa hadn't taken very much interest in the land, until now.

SIXTEEN

The day had come at last; Alice was free to go home. The Dents' maid was back, full of apologies, it was nearly spring, and the lavender girl needed to work with her herbs again.

'Please tell me what present we can buy you,' Emily Dent said firmly on Alice's last day at the doctor's. 'We are grateful to you for staying on so long.' It felt rather like being a treasured lady's maid, rather than the maid of all work she had become, although they had given her the title of housekeeper while Mrs Dent was away.

'Thank you, but I've been well paid – and also, I've had free treatment!' Alice laughed and fingered the scar on her head. Two weeks later, she could still feel the wound inflicted by Paterson on the night of the party, and she sometimes had bad dreams about him. She looked at Mrs Dent and realized that the doctor's wife, as always, was quite determined. "Well, I would be very grateful for some lavender oil, when doctor makes up another order for the chemist. I use it myself, and sell it in little bottles on the stall.'

'I thought you grew your own lavender? A lavender girl shouldn't need to buy it! But of course, that's an easy thing to do. An order will go in next week.'

Alice smiled her thanks. 'My lavender bushes are still quite small. I suppose Masham is a bit too cool for them,' she confessed. 'And of course I haven't a still; you need to distil the oil. But lavender is so popular! I sell mint and sage and so on, of course, and they're easier to grow.' But lavender was the most popular. Her pretty muslin bags of dried flowers, for scenting drawers and linen cupboards, were usually sold as soon as they appeared on the stall.

Alice was relieved to be going back to her cottage and the cat, and to be able to give more help to Ruby in the dairy. Ruby, however, was keen to keep on with the market stall. 'I've sold a lot of cheese and butter that way. Let's keep it going between us, shall we?'

It seemed to Jacob Fowler that nothing ever went right. Just as he had got used to Alice's company, and after all they had gone through together, she was going off again, back to her own house. True, he could visit her on the market stall which was only a few yards from the Dent's gate, but there would be no more cups of tea in the kitchen, no more private talks. You wouldn't really be able talk at the stall, with Alice serving customers and half of Masham looking on, busily forming their own conclusions. Alice was a sensible lass, good to talk to, but not on market day.

There was no question at all of visiting Alice's little cottage; that would put the cat among the pigeons for sure, and ruin her reputation as a good-living single woman. Convention was a damn nuisance, you couldn't help thinking.

The winter was nearly over. Alice had been a grand help, that night in the snow; the good weather was coming, but everything seemed flat. It was hard to understand. There wasn't much to be said about it, least of all to Alice. She saw him as a dyed-in-the-wool, miserable old bachelor. Well, he was, wasn't he? Maybe a bit young for it at thirty-two, but well on the way. Not much of a friend for anybody, especially a female.

'I suppose you'll have a good cry when you get home, and then settle down and black lead the kitchen stove,' he offered as a parting shot on the day Alice left.

'Naturally. Of course I'll sob myself to sleep, now that I'm leaving you,' she flashed back tartly. Then she softened a little. 'Keep smiling, Fowler. It suits you.'

After Alice had been gone for a week, Jacob felt worse than ever. He really missed the woman. He'd better find some extra work to do on a Saturday, to keep his mind occupied. He usually had a few hours to spare on Saturdays, unless some unlucky female decided to give birth and the doctor was sent for in a hurry. It might be an idea to offer to help Gabriel Turner; there was that young horse Brownie to finish breaking in and somebody would need to ride it out a few times, to get it used to being handled. Of course Alice might be there, she was often at her sister's, but it wouldn't be the same as sitting in the kitchen at the Dents'. Consorting, as Young Cecil had called it, had turned out to be quite enjoyable. He should have done more of it while he had the chance.

What would another man do, in his shoes? Jacob thought about it as he worked in the stable yard, which was strangely quiet now that Alice was not about. A bright young bloke would offer to walk out with her, but Jacob Fowler could not bring himself to ask. He imagined the scene; Alice might laugh at him, or even worse, feel sorry for him.

A really foolhardy man might even ask her to marry him, so that they could live happily ever after . . . what a thought, with her bonny face at the breakfast table every morning! But Alice was happy on her own, he was sure. She was so pleased when Greenwood turned out not to be her husband, and she'd said how much she liked to be single. It was hopeless, so there was no point in thinking about it. Jacob had been burned once, and swore that it would never happen again.

A strong smell of lavender in the Turner's farm kitchen lifted Jacob's heart when he visited the next Saturday morning, It was a scent of summer, and of Alice, the lavender girl. Of course she was there, bending over Gabriel Turner and looking serious, while her sister Ruby hovered uneasily.

'Good day, Jacob, I'll be with you in a minute.' Gabriel looked up briefly. 'Sit yourself down. I burned my hand on a lamp, while I was trying to find summat in the cellar . . . that feels better already, Alice.'

Alice looked prettier than Jacob remembered, in a blue dress instead of the housekeeper's black or grey she had worn at the Dents', bonny even though she was frowning over the burn. 'Hold still now, Gabriel, while I put a pin in the bandage; I don't want to stick you in the arm . . . that's better. Remember next time, lavender oil's good on a burn, heals it up without a scar.' She relaxed a little and looked across at Jacob, who felt he was staring at her. 'Come to take the horse out, Fowler? Take care. I don't want to have to patch you up as well.'

'I should just about be able to stick on its back, by now,' Jacob growled in the old way, but Alice only laughed.

'If you've a mind to ride over the common, you could call in at the Thorpe blacksmith for me,' Gabriel suggested. 'He's making us a set of harrows and I'd like to know when they're to be ready.'

'If you are going that far, you need a bite of bread and cheese before you start,' Ruby said firmly, and a crusty loaf appeared on the table.

'Nay—' Jacob began, but he was pushed down into a chair by Alice and the kettle was put on to boil. And in spite of his impatience to be off, the horseman found himself enjoying a talk round the Turners' kitchen table. 'Have you found a tenant for Ellershaw yet?' he asked casually, as the talk turned to farming and the prospects for the summer.

Ruby sighed and Gabriel smiled rather grimly through his beard. 'It's a long story, lad, but the short answer is – not yet. We thought we had let it, and of course we've been improving it all winter—'

'We digged the drains, Pa, didn't we?' Bobby demanded eagerly, always there when farming was discussed.

'But, as I was saying,' Gabriel continued with a reproving look at his son, 'it's not let. The fellow we had in mind turned out to be a mucky tyke, with no idea of how to go on. One look at his own place was enough, so we turned him down.'

'It would make a grand farm for you one day, Bobby,' Jacob suggested to the little lad, who grinned from ear to ear.

'I was about to say the same to you, Jacob.' Gabriel looked serious. 'You're of good farming stock. I know you'll have a bob or two behind you. Why not get into a place of your own, while you're still young enough?'

Jacob was aware of four pairs of eyes watching him round the table. Had this idea been discussed before? 'Who, me? I'm just the doctor's man, you know that. Doctor can't manage without me.' Scheming had been going on, Jacob suddenly realized.

'If you're worried about Dr Dent, we've an idea about that. You remember young Will Sanderson from Oak Bank? He's looking for a place with horses, and a better lad you couldn't wish to find. If you was to train him up, why then, Dr Dent would hardly miss you, Jacob.' Ruby smiled at him, her argument complete.

'Right. You've worked it all out, I can see. Thanks for letting me know.' Jacob decided not to protest too much. This new idea needed thinking about. 'Meanwhile, there's work to be done,' he said in his most repressive way. 'Let's get saddled up.' He winked at Alice as he went out, and she gave him a smile that went with him all the way over the common to Thorpe.

The wind was freshening as Jacob set out; wind was not good for a young horse with no experience. Branches moving in the wind, a piece of paper blowing across the track could cause a young animal to bolt in fear. This horse was used to the saddle, but had not been ridden very often because Gabriel was nervous with unbroken horses and had left it to Jacob. 'Had a bad fall, years ago,' he had explained. Gabriel was over forty and already stiffening up a little, as a result of years of hard work on the farm. He did not want another injury.

Neither did Jacob want trouble, so he decided to take it easy; he would walk Brownie gently over the common, maybe trot a

Ann Cliff

little up the rise, then steady away down to the beck and up again steeply into Thorpe village, where the blacksmith lived beside the green.

The harrows were ready for collection, Jacob was told, and Gabriel could pick them up any time he took the cart over to Thorpe. 'Yon's a handy young colt,' the smith said approvingly as Jacob's mount stood waiting quietly.

'Ay, he's good for a young 'un, Brownie.' Jacob looked up at him. 'He just needs more work. Gabriel's going to put him in the trap, and ride him, once we can trust him to behave.'

'What's the news round your way?' the smith asked as Jacob swung up lightly into the saddle.

'Why, I thought you'd know everything. Folks always come to a forge for the news. They stand round your fire for hours, on a cold day.'

The smith agreed. 'Some days I can hardly shift for 'em. But I was wondering if it's true that Mr Paterson's dead? Yon Bradley Paterson from Linley Grange?'

'I've heard nowt of that,' Jacob admitted. Alice would be very interested, if it were true. 'What happened to him, do you know?' He turned the horse's head for home and it pricked up its ears.

'Nobody seems to know for sure, but most of folks that work there have been turned off, and house shut up. Agent said it's to be sold.' The man shrugged powerful shoulders. 'A funny business, if you ask me. I saw him just a few weeks ago – fit as a fiddle, he was then.'

'Ah well, there's no knowing, with gentry,' Jacob offered as he gathered his reins and dug his heels in gently. He was not going to tell anybody what he knew about Paterson. The man could have spread the rumour of his own death; it would have suited him to disappear.

The wind had shifted to the west and squally rain blew over the common. Jacob turned up his collar and plodded on, getting colder as the rain seeped into his jacket. The horse tossed his

184

head restlessly. 'Steady, lad, a bit of rain won't hurt you,' Jacob told him. It would be good to get Brownie back into his stable, and maybe Ruby would offer a warm drink before he went home to do the evening chores in the doctor's stables.

From the crest of the ridge, the spire of Masham church stood out down below in its patchwork of fields and woods, lit by a pale ray of sunshine as the squall moved on across the river. Jacob urged the horse on gently and it responded well, but then things went wrong. A sheep rushed out from behind a gorse bush under Brownie's feet and he reared suddenly, but Jacob hung on. Scared, the horse swung in a circle and at that moment the wind blew an old bag across the common, straight towards them. It was too much for the young horse; he swerved off the road, cantered a little and then bucked. Jacob was thrown over the horse's head and into the bracken. He saw greenery rushing towards him, then felt a sharp crack and everything went black.

The dusk was deepening as Alice gathered up her gardening tools rather wearily, after a satisfying afternoon's work among the plants. Her garden gate clicked and there was Ruby on the path, looking serious. 'We're a mite worried about Jacob. He should be back from Thorpe by now,' she said. Ruby was wearing her milking apron and boots; she was on the way to the dairy. 'Horse came back without him, so Gabriel's off to look for the lad. I do hope we find him before dark.'

'Well, I'd better go with him; you've got to milk the cows,' Alice said with a sinking heart. If the horse had come back, Jacob must be lying injured somewhere. 'Will Gabriel take the trap?'

'Nay, he thought to follow Brownie's tracks, if he can. Thanks lass, I'm sorry to put it on you, but it would be a great help. It might take two of you to help him home.'

Alice put on a warm cloak before leaving; should she take a lantern? Eventually she decided against it and went to meet Gabriel, who was standing in the lane. 'At least we know which road he took,' Gabriel said, his eyes on the soft ground, where

185

the horse's prints were clearly visible. It might not be so easy on the hard ground of the common. And if the horse had left the road, Jacob could be anywhere, on hundreds of acres of sheep grazing and scrub.

There were clouds scudding across the sky and the wind was still high, but the rain held off. Trying not to fear the worst, Alice walked quietly beside the farmer, thinking her own thoughts. It was strange to realize only now how fond she was of Jacob. She had missed his company for the last two weeks, which had surprised her. They had come a long way from the old hostility. But their friendship, if you could call it that, had crept up on her. She had been so pleased to get rid of Greenwood that she had hardly realized how hard Jacob had worked to uncover the truth. Had she thanked him enough; did he realize that she really appreciated it?

Only a mile out of town, they found what they were looking for. Gabriel spotted the faint tracks where they left the road; the horse must have bolted. A little farther and he saw a boot sticking out of a clump of bracken. 'Here he is.'

Her heart thumping, Alice bent down. Jacob was lying very still; still and cold. She put a hand on his chest. 'I can't feel him breathing.' There was a stone near his head and blood, drying now, trickling down the side of his head.

Gabriel tried to rouse Jacob, but he was inert. 'He's very wet; that's why he's so cold. I hope to goodness he'll come round. I'll go back and fetch trap, if you stay with him, Alice. Try to get him warm.'

Was Jacob dead? Alice felt a dreadful chill creep over her. The world without Jacob would be a cold, unfriendly place.

Dusk crept over the moor and the wind felt chill, but at least there was no frost. Alice covered the still, damp body of Jacob with part of her cloak. How could she warm him? Gently, she lay down beside him and took him in her arms, then pulled the cloak round them both. 'I know it's taking a liberty, Fowler,' she said quietly, in case he could hear her. 'But you'll have to put up with it.' At first she felt his chill go right to her bones, but soon she warmed up again and gradually Jacob's body against hers seemed a little less cold. If only he were not hurt too badly.

Alice was very careful, in case some of his bones were broken, but the groom had no obvious injuries apart from the cut on his head. Time passed, and they grew warmer. Thank goodness, Alice thought, she had been working hard in the garden and had walked up the hill; her body was warm with exercise. Then she felt a faint movement of his chest. The lad was breathing!

With the last of the light, she looked into his face and then realized that the grey eyes were open, and looking at her. 'Consorting again, Alice?' he whispered hoarsely, but did not try to move away. In any case, he was being held too closely.

'This is just a medical treatment; ask Dr Dent,' Alice said. 'My body heat is passing to you; they do it to save people lost in the snow. I am staying here, unless you object, until Gabriel gets back with the trap. Now, how do you feel, Fowler?'

'It feels like heaven to me. I don't object, lass, far from it. Lying in the bracken on the common is an old country pastime, they tell me.' There was the ghost of a chuckle and then a gasp of pain. 'Were you worried? I suppose Brownie came home all right? Gabriel will kill me, if he's missing. Ouch, that hurt—' he had tried to put his arms round her.

'You could have broken ribs. Yes, Brownie is safe. We were very worried, Jacob. I was worried that I would have nobody to be rude to.' Alice shifted her position slightly and felt Jacob's arms slide more tightly round her. He was much warmer now. He probably did not need her warmth to survive; but she would not move, just in case. She relaxed a little, sighing with relief. Jacob was going to live; the worry was over.

'Can I try being medical? My word, my head hurts. Come here, lass.' And Jacob kissed Alice. Miserable, grumpy old Jacob kissed her very gently and hesitantly. 'My, I've missed you, my girl, since you went home.'

'Jacob, I have missed you, too.' Alice felt ridiculously happy.

187

Far in the distance, they heard a horse approaching. Alice lifted her head as it came near; there was none of the creaking sounds made by the trap. 'It's not Gabriel. My goodness, it looks like . . . Paterson. Why would he—?' The horse went on steadily up the hill and over the common. It was hard to be sure.

Jacob drew her down again. 'Never mind him, he's supposed to be dead. Before Gabriel comes, I want to tell you a few things, while I've got you nice and close. No, I'm not much hurt, I don't think,' he said, seeing her look of concern. 'I am a coward, I suppose, but it takes a runaway horse to get me to realize that I don't have to flinch, every time you come near me.' Again, a quiet laugh. 'I've been daft, Alice. I want to get closer to you – but I couldn't find a way to get started, somehow. I'm too shy, as I once told you.'

'Well, now you have started, my lad, you can forget about being shy and give me another kiss.' He couldn't have too many bruises; Jacob was holding her tightly now.

'You're such a bonny lass—' Jacob began, and then they heard the trap approaching. 'Shall we come back here, one warm summer's day? When we're walking out together?'

Alice laughed. 'I can't think of anything better.' The injured man reluctantly moved away from Alice and staggered to his feet. Then reality set in; how could Jacob change from being a woman hater? 'You need to see doctor, Fowler. By morning when your head clears, you might change your mind, so I'll wait to be asked, another day,' Alice said cautiously; this happiness was too good to last, surely.

Jacob did not agree. 'Nay, lass, I've been thinking about this for months. Only problem was, I didn't dare tell you about it.' When Gabriel shone his lantern on them, Jacob was leaning feebly against Alice as she supported his tottering steps.' I'm right enough, thank you, Gabriel. Should never have let Brownie get away. I won't let one get away again.'

SEVENTEEN

'That is quite good, Laura. You may have some little talent.' The colonel had paused in his walk in the grounds. Evidently trying to encourage her, he was staring at the efforts of the artist, who sat at the front of the Hall with her chair on the gravel.

'Thank you, Papa. Do you think I could go into business, offering to paint your friends' houses? Flattering likenesses, of course.' Laura was determined to keep her father smiling; she made light of their problems by suggesting various ingenious ways to earn money

Things were difficult, but they were slightly easier now that Mama had gone off to visit her relatives in the south of England. Mama had been tragic, voluble, but she had no useful ideas about what they might do. Mrs Grey was naturally very worried about the future, having been looked after by servants all her life; she could not imagine a life without servants. Laura had sympathized as often as was necessary. One day she mentioned her mother's family and Mrs Grey was soon persuaded that it was her duty to pay them a visit. It would take her mind off their trouble, while giving the colonel a little peace. She wanted to take Laura with her, but agreed to let her stay behind to keep Papa company. So the carriage took Mrs Grey to catch the London train, and the house settled down with what seemed like a sigh of relief.

'I am almost reconciled to the thought of India,' Mrs Grey had confessed before she left. 'Labour is cheap, and servants know their place. I am not strong, you know, and all this is very bad for my nerves! But nobody realizes how ill I am; I am not sure whether I can stand a change in circumstances.'

Papa did not complain, but he was inclined to be gloomy. Laura tried, sometimes successfully, to cheer him; a daily walk was prescribed for his health, and to please her he paced solemnly round the shrubbery or through the park.

The colonel had mellowed a little since the Paterson affair. Laura had to forgive him, now that he was so sad, for nearly ruining her own life by insisting on the marriage. She tried to see his point of view. He had thought he was doing his best for her future, and he believed Bradley Paterson to be a man of high principles, even to the point of taking his advice on investments. He had never seen the darker side of the man, but few people had; her own aversion had been pure instinct.

Now that they were about to lose it, how lovely the Hall looked, how precious! It was suddenly important to capture the atmosphere of the old stone house in a painting. The mellow sandstone of the front was nearly covered by ivy. The windows were long and pointed at the top, with stone sills, and the roof melted into the landscape, hoary with moss. When she was old, Laura would be able to look at the picture and remember the happy days at Birchwood Hall; although it was almost impossible to imagine oneself as old.

March had brought the usual carpet of daffodils, and slightly warmer weather; Laura thought she might attempt a painting of the Highland cattle when the house was finished. Adam would like that. But Adam had not yet come back from Scotland.

'Burns is away a long time. He is probably looking for another job,' the colonel observed and Laura started. Could he read her thoughts? 'Of course, I can't blame him. Poor men have to look out for themselves, and his place here could soon be gone.'

Laura looked across at her father. 'But he said he'd come back. I'm sure he will.' True, it was three weeks since they had seen him, but there had been a letter to apologize for the delay. It was very vague, and didn't say when they could expect him, or what he was up to. It could, Laura thought, have something to do with his lady. There seemed to be no lady friend at Masham, so presumably she was waiting for him in Scotland.

'Well, he'll need to make his own way here,' the colonel said briskly. 'We can't send a man to meet his train if we don't know what his movements are.' Papa still liked to plan things on the lines of a military exercise; he did not like vagueness, and until now Adam had been precise enough to please him.

By the end of the afternoon, the painting of the Hall was almost finished. The building was now down in line and wash, since Laura had decided that architecture needed lines rather than brush strokes. The day was bright and as she worked she could hear small birds in the bushes, busy making their nests.

Absorbed in her work, Laura hardly noticed when the birds fell silent. A shadow crossed the paper and she looked up into Adam's smiling face. The young manager looked taller than she remembered, and somehow more handsome. His smile had a hint of excitement in it. Then she saw Dr Dent behind him and stood up to greet them both as the lady of the house, since her mother was away.

'The doctor kindly brought me up from Ripon. I'm sorry I have been away so long. How are you, Miss Grey?' Adam no longer wore bandages.

'Miss Laura's health is remarkably good.' Dr Dent spoke firmly. He was evidently not going to allow her to slide back into invalidism.

'Your recipe, Doctor. Fresh air and exercise, as I tell Papa,' Laura said dutifully, leading the way to the house. It was shaming to think now of the petulant young lady she had been last summer, but then there had been the shadow hanging over her.

The next morning, Adam was out in the grounds as Laura and her father took their morning walk. 'Do you want to talk business now, sir? The farm is in good order, as far as I can see. The

191

foreman has looked after everything very well.'

The older man sighed, but he led the way to the study. 'Ring for coffee, Laura. Nearly time for tiffin. And I suppose you should join us, since you are so determined to be a modern young woman.' This raised a smile from Adam, which he tried to conceal by drawing up a chair for Miss Grey.

Adam appeared to have planned this meeting. First of all, he wanted to know whether the colonel had an inventory of the estate as he bought it. But it seemed that there was only a map and the list of assets that Adam kept in the farm office.

'Of course, we have spent money on the place since then. We will have to draw up a new list, in any case. I suggest that you are the man to do it, Burns. You will have a good idea of the value of things.' The colonel sighed. 'I do hope we don't have to sell up entirely!' His pale eyes were anxious.

'In order to follow the proper procedure, you or one of your staff should come with me, sir.' Adam looked the picture of inno-cence. 'To guard against fraud, it is usual for two people to conduct an inventory.' What did he mean? The manager turned to Laura. 'The buyer will want to bring the value down, of course, and the seller to get the best price he can. Since it's possi-ble that I could know the buyer, you could imagine that I might have been bribed to leave things out, or undervalue them. In theory, of course.'

Papa did not seem to like this idea. 'Don't know enough about it, I'm afraid. Only been round the whole place once or twice. But young Laura is capable of counting horses and sheep and that kind of thing, and she can check on prices. Will you keep an eye on him, Laura? Not that I don't trust him, but we must do the right thing.' He leaned back as coffee was brought in, happy that there was a procedure to follow.

Alice's brother-in-law was a farmer; he could tell her the price of livestock and so on. Laura sat up straight. 'I can certainly count heads and write down what Adam says. I think I can get current values, from newspapers and farmers. Alice could help, if you like.' Just in case he still objected to her being alone with Adam.

Colonel Grey looked alarmed. 'Don't tell anyone at all why we are doing it, that's all.'

Adam looked pleased. 'We need to do this right away, sir. You see, I might have found a buyer for the estate.'

This was happening too quickly. Why was the manager so cheerful about losing his job? 'Do you mean that we might have to leave quite soon, Adam – Mr Burns? Will the buyer want to live here himself?' And if that happened, where on earth could they go? Laura felt suddenly afraid.

'The prospective buyer was the reason for my delay. This person agreed to travel with me from Scotland to view the property. But no, she's got a nice wee place of her own; she just wants to invest some money in land.' Adam was evidently not at all afraid of what might happen next; he spoke calmly, as if to reassure the Greys.

'She? Are we talking about selling to a woman?' The colonel looked horrified.

'You didna want to sell to a farming man, sir, who would take it out of your hands. I think we can come to a satisfactory arrangement. But she's a sharp old body and she will want to know all about everything. That is why we have to go through the entire place, very carefully – and she might want to send her own valuer. We haven't got much time.'

The next few days were a blur of activity as Laura followed Adam, writing to his dictation and checking numbers. They did not go so far as to count hand tools, but all the implements, down to chaff cutters and corn binders, were carefully itemized. The assistant learned a great deal about the running of the estate, and the improvements that Adam had already put in place. The spring corn was shooting green spears through the brown earth, lambs were jumping and playing in the pastures and the tenants looked forward to the summer, not at all alarmed by a valuation. The estate workers and tenants were all told of the valuation – they could hardly miss it – but not the reason for it. They accepted Laura's presence as a little unusual, but quite welcome. 'It's grand to see a young lady take an interest in stock and land,' one tenant told her.

'You see, Miss Laura? Young ladies can be involved, these days. The novelty soon wears off,' Adam said quietly.

Information about the prospective buyer was very sparse; Adam didn't seem to want to talk about her. 'She has put up at the Spa Hotel in Ripon and she's taking the waters,' he said with a wry smile. 'Ripon spa is not so fashionable as Harrogate, mind, but she won't worry about that. Ripon is quieter and cheaper, and the water tastes just as bad.'

Why would a woman wealthy enough to think of buying a few thousand acres of Yorkshire worry about the cost of staying in Harrogate? But then she was Scottish and perhaps they were different.

Laura enjoyed the work. It was good to be out on the land in her boots, with clipboard and pencil, with Adam, who was an ideal workmate. He clarified things that puzzled her and he worked logically and steadily, taking one farm at a time and classifying assets under separate headings. One day when Laura began to tire, Adam took her to one of the farmhouses for lunch. It was fun to sit in a farm kitchen, eating fat rascals, the rich Dales scones. 'We never had anything like this in India,' she admitted.

The farmer's wife, Mrs Slater, laughed. 'You're a Yorkshire lass, miss. They tell me your pa came from York. You should learn how to cook rascals, and Yorkshire pudding and such.'

Adam grinned at Laura across the table. 'I agree. Everybody should learn to cook. Miss Grey would probably be good at it. And of course, you'll make a better wifie in the end.'

After the meal Laura lingered in the kitchen to thank Mrs Slater and Adam went out. Going to join him in the farm stables, she overheard a snatch of conversation that made her blush.

Mr Slater was putting their horse into the trap for Adam and laughing as he said, 'I know what you're up to, Mr Burns. You're after that bonny lass. She'd make you a grand wife, and you'd get the estate! Now, am I right?'

Adam laughed, totally at ease. 'How did you guess?' How familiar these northern people were! Laura wondered what Adam thought of the remark. A few weeks ago she had been the heiress to the estate. But Adam knew that the estate was gone – and that changed everything. Papa didn't suspect Adam of designs on Laura, now that they had no money, and he didn't seem to mind them working together – or perhaps that was because mama was away. But it was nice to think that she could value his company – friendship, almost – for itself.

They visited another farm in the afternoon and jogged back to the Hall in the trap as dusk was falling, after a solid day's work. Laura watched the pattern of fields and woods as they passed; the whole landscape was bathed in evening light and the hedges were green with bursting buds. It would be good to live here for ever. The flies and the dust of India sometimes came into Laura's dreams, the beggars and the poverty . . . she did not want to go back to India, ever again. This was the world she wanted to live in, as it was now, with plenty of occupation and good company. But would it be possible?

Adam was driving with Laura beside him and as they went into a green tunnel where trees overhung the lane, he smiled. 'I would like to thank you for your help with all this, Miss Laura. Your work is making the job much easier—' At that moment the horse shied slightly as a shot rang out, and a few pellets spattered the woodwork of the trap. 'Head down!' Adam pulled her down with him. There was another loud bang and another spray of pellets spattered on the leaves overhead.

'Two barrels, we should be safe now. Some idiot shooting rabbits, I expect.' Adam sat up cautiously and raised his head. 'Watch out, you there with the gun! You could kill someone, shooting on to a road!' He shook the reins and the horse trotted briskly through the gloom and out into the light again. 'Some people have no idea of safety. I shall speak to whoever owns that bit of woodland. You're not hurt, are you, Miss Laura? I'd go after him, but I don't like to leave you with the horse.'

Laura swallowed and sat up, adjusting her hat. 'A little shocked, that's all. Papa won't be happy about the splinters in the woodwork!' The varnished, glossy side of the trap had been hit in several places. A cold feeling crept up her spine as she said, 'Adam, you don't think it was deliberate, do you?'

The manager looked even more serious as he urged on the horse to go faster. 'But who would want to? Oh my, I suppose you're thinking of Paterson.'

'Well, I don't want to be too dramatic, but we have no idea where he's gone. I had hoped he would go abroad, but – we don't know.' Laura hesitated. 'He was so very possessive, he frightened me. He was completely obsessed with his own plans, determined to have his own way. He might be planning to kill either of us . . . you, or me, for standing in his way.'

The young man turned the horse into the Hall park through the big gateposts and they looked over to where the Highland cattle were munching their evening hay, red in the setting sun. 'I will speak to the police about this,' he said quite formally. 'And I had better tell the colonel. I hope that someone will know that Paterson has left the country.'

In the stable yard Adam handed Laura down from the trap and a groom came out to take the horse. They went into the farm office with their papers and Laura decided it was time to change the subject. 'We'll be off again tomorrow, I take it? There are three farms left to inspect, I believe.'

Adam looked thoughtful. 'Well, we could go to Ox Close, it's near enough to walk over and we could avoid the public road. I don't want to put you in danger, Miss Laura.'

'I am not going to hide away, Adam,' Laura said firmly. 'I was warned about the dacoits in India, but it didn't stop me from riding my pony. The most dangerous thing for me would have been marriage, and that possibility is over, thank goodness!' She managed a laugh.

'I wouldn't forget about marriage entirely, if I were you. It's quite possible you might please your mama and find a rich husband after all. I think the Yorkshire folk have a saying – don't marry for munny, but luv where munny is!' Adam's attempt at a Yorkshire accent was comical. 'Of course, you will need someone who owns an estate and will allow you to design gardens and plant trees. With the right man, you could take an active part in running it. Don't forget to ask your suitors for their opinion on rightful occupations for females, and that kind of thing. You need to know whether they would be embarrassed by an intelligent wife.'

'That's a very commercial suggestion, Mr Burns, and I do not approve of it. Money should not matter; people should marry purely for personal reasons.' But of course, it was true that there was the problem of money. Laura turned to go up to the house.

After locking the office door for the night, Adam fell into step beside Laura. 'I will walk with you to the house; it's nearly dark. So, I take it that if a penniless wee laddie, like me just for instance, were to ask for Miss Grey's hand in marriage, on the grounds of purely personal reasons, there would be no objection in theory? Is that so?' His tone was light and he was laughing gently.

Laura said nothing and looked away. What did he mean?

Adam persisted. 'That you'd come to live with me in a wee but and ben in Scotland, and bathe in the loch and all? In theory, of course?'

It wasn't comfortable to joke about marriage with Adam Burns. 'You already have a lady in mind; you said so! And . . . what's a but and ben, anyway?'

They were passing the kitchen garden and Adam was looking round carefully, even while they talked. 'It refers to a two-roomed cottage,' he said easily. 'The but is the outside room, the kitchen. The ben is the room on the inside. That's the sort of wee house we live in, up north. I was just taking your argument to its logical conclusion, mind. Love in a cottage is very well, but you have to live on something.'

Laura paused and looked at the manager in the light from the long windows. 'Well, if you're giving me good advice, Adam Burns, perhaps I should give you some. A young man like you, well-educated and intelligent, should be able to find a like-minded young lady to share his life.' She paused.

'And?'

'And you should be getting to know some rich woman with land, so that you could set up with your own estate. Don't waste your time flirting with me, Adam, even if it's just to take my mind off the gunshots. You should remember which side your bread is buttered on, as they say in Yorkshire.' Laura found she was breathing quickly and felt faintly ruffled, as she put her hand on the handle of the side door.

'Sorry, Miss Grey.' Adam was still standing there, looking at Laura contritely. 'Forgive me if I've spoken out of turn. No doubt you'll be sensitive about your altered circumstances. But take heart, Laura. If all goes well, you will be able to stay on here at the Hall.'

Laura opened the door and then turned to him again. 'And what about you? Will you still have a job here, when – if – the new owner takes over?' It wouldn't be the same without Adam.

'Och, lassie, it'll depend on whether she likes my bonny blue eyes.' Adam suddenly stopped laughing. 'May I come in for a moment? I think I should tell your father about the shotgun incident.'

Laura walked thoughtfully up the big staircase to her room. What if – what if the new owner turned out to be Adam's lady friend? He might be hatching a deep plot to get hold of the estate for himself in this way. It was not pleasant to imagine that in time, Adam might marry the owner and . . . Laura would lose his company for good. But of course, he had been talking about marriage in his facetious way to take her mind off the danger, the possibility that they had been deliberately shot at. Adam was quite devious, sometimes.

'Come to the study, Burns.' Colonel Grey stalked down the corridor ahead of the manager. 'Inventory going well, eh?' To Adam's surprise, he pulled a bottle of whisky and two glasses out of a cabinet. 'Have a drink? I assume you prefer a single malt.'

'Thank you, sir, I'll take just a wee dram.' It seemed that he was now socially acceptable, but perhaps it was because Mrs Grey was away. When the drinks were poured Adam quietly told the colonel what had happened on the ride home. 'And so, sir, I think we must alert the police and try to find out where Paterson has gone. It might have been nothing but a careless farmer's son out after rabbits, who forgot himself so far as to shoot across a public road. But just in case ... I did spend some time with Paterson, sir, as you know. And I believe that he might think of reprisals, after what happened. Miss Grey could be in danger, although I don't want to alarm you, or her either.'

'Did you mention Paterson to my daughter?' The colonel looked stern.

Adam put down his crystal glass carefully. 'As a matter of fact, it was she who suggested him. But she was brave ... she said the dacoits had never frightened her.'

Colonel Grey smiled faintly. 'British Army families are not easily frightened.' He sat in silence for a while, looking into the fire. 'I have been thinking of visiting my brother in York this spring. I will go at the end of the week, and take Laura with me.' He looked at Adam. 'This is not a case of running away, you understand. But if the man is mad he should be caught and locked up. I will use all the influence I can. Meanwhile, Burns, you will continue with the inventory as planned, but you will ensure that Miss Laura is in no possible danger. Is that understood?'

'Yes, sir.' Adam wondered whether he should be standing to attention.

*

Laura was quite pleased at the prospect of going to York, but she wanted to see Alice first. The two had spent only one day together since the night of the party and since the news of financial trouble, Laura had not liked to incur even the small expense represented by Alice. And also, she knew that the herb garden was busy in spring, and that Alice would have little time to spare. Eventually she sent a servant to see Alice on her market stall, with a note for the lavender girl. 'Come when you can,' it said, and late that afternoon Alice walked up the drive and asked for Laura.

That day's inventory had been a short one and Laura was walking Hamish down the drive, so they met in the middle. 'See how pleased he is? Hamish misses you!' Laura cried. 'I must say you are looking very well, Alice!'

Alice had a worried frown when she heard Laura's tale of the shooting. 'Goodness, I should have told you. One night – we were on the common, Jacob Fowler had an accident – I thought I saw Paterson riding over towards Thorpe. But then Jacob had heard a rumour that he was dead.'

'My father is trying to find out. I must go with him to York, Alice, but I wanted to see you first. Has your wound healed? And how will you manage, now that you've left Dr Dent's?' A few months ago, Laura would not have taken any interest in a servant's life, but now she saw them as people and she was fond of Alice. It was a pity that they couldn't afford to employ her at the Hall.

'Thank you, Miss Laura, I am managing quite well. The herbs keep me busy. I won't worry about another place until next winter.'

EIGHTEEN

A warm spring evening in York, with a breeze coming up from the river, was just the setting for Laura's holiday and she felt quite excited. Papa had suddenly wanted to see his brother, but it was clear he hated the idea of selling his home, and hoped that the sordid financial details would all be sorted out in his absence. He also hoped that the criminal Paterson would be apprehended soon, preferably while Laura was away from Masham.

'You have seen very little of city life, my girl,' her father realized as they made their way to the theatre. 'You were a baby when we went to India.' He sighed. 'Sometimes I miss the old life with the regiment . . . don't you?'

Laura looked down at her pretty dress. 'Not now, Papa. I love Yorkshire, and it is exciting to be going to the theatre.' Her hair was put up in a sophisticated way and she felt much older than the girl who had left India last year.

Her Uncle and Aunt Grey smiled at her enthusiasm. 'It's only Shakespeare, not a modern play,' her aunt reminded them. 'But I do hope you enjoy it.'

Although York was so enticing, Laura was sorry to be missing the business discussions at home, where Adam would be busy trying to impress the potential buyer. She was curious about the Scottish lady, who might be a person after her own heart, interested in planning and looking at livestock, and all the things that Adam knew so much about . . . as long as she wasn't too attractive or seductive.

Looking round the Theatre Royal with its red plush seats, Laura realized how countrified life was in Masham. She had never seen so many well-dressed people since she had been to a regimental ball as a shy seventeen-year-old. York was the northern capital, Papa said, an important city, and the people at the theatre looked like leaders of society. It was quite unlikely that they would meet anyone they knew, but it was good to feel that they fitted in quite well, Papa looking distinguished in evening dress, although he still had a worried frown.

The play was *A Midsummer Night's Dream* and the orchestra was already playing Mendelssohn's enchanting music. The curtain rose and the lights, the costumes and the set were all enthralling. This was a play Laura had read at school, but now, acted by professionals, it came to life for the first time.

At the first interval Laura found it hard to adjust again to the real world and to talk to her relations. They went for a walk, for the colonel to stretch his legs, and Laura was aware that he was looking over the crowds as if searching for someone. All too soon, she found out who it was.

The Greys were going back to their seats when Laura was accosted by a dumpy figure. 'My dear Miss Grey! How delightful, how very pleasant to see you! How do you do?' It was the high-pitched voice of Dr Fanshawe. He took her hand in his moist one and squeezed it, while Laura tried to smile. What was Young Cecil doing here?

'A little bird told me you might attend the theatah tonight,' Dr Fanshawe beamed, his chins wobbling over the high, starched collar. 'And I am delighted that we meet again! Do you believe in Fate, Miss Grey?' He rubbed his hands and did not wait for an answer. 'How is your dear mother? Is she here tonight? I do not see her, but I see the colonel!' He bowed fussily and Laura thought how much an eighteenth-century wig would suit his style. 'Delighted to meet the uncle of dear Miss Grey, sir,' he said as he was introduced.

Colonel Grey's frown disappeared and he smiled happily at

Fanshawe. 'Good evening, Doctor, good to see you,' he said in his military way. 'I gather you are prospering, here in York?' Fanshawe was launching into a long account of his prosperity when the bell rang and people began to settle down for the next act. With a wave, the doctor went back to his own seat.

'Nice to have seen you, Doctor,' Laura said firmly in the past tense. She would try to avoid him for the rest of the evening.

'Good man, Fanshawe,' Papa said with enthusiasm as they sat down. 'He's the young surgeon I was telling you about,' he said to his brother. 'Very able, plenty of money. And he seems to be interested in young Laura.'

Laura's heart sank. Surely they would not try to marry her off again so soon? And not to that pompous little man? Perhaps Papa had been in touch with him, told him they were coming to York . . . oh, dear.

'Could do worse, could do worse,' Laura's uncle said in a non-committal way that made Laura feel that he, at least, could see Cecil's lack of attractive features. Trying to concentrate on the play, Laura was in a turmoil. It wasn't his lack of good looks, or height; it was just that Cecil was pompous, cold and heartless. She knew, too, a little of how he had treated his servants in Masham. She had heard his disparagement of Dr Dent and the practice. Fanshawe was not a pleasant person.

Dr Fanshawe bounced back at the second interval, so sure of his welcome that Laura's coolness had no effect. The colonel manoeuvred Laura to stand next to him and she was compelled to listen to his story of success. 'I have purchased a superior prac-tice in a very good area of York,' he announced, standing far too close to Laura and with his hand on her arm. He looked at her keenly. 'Wealthy patients, very good social class – on the Mount, you know. Just west of the city. There are several retired Indian Army officers there, and so forth.' He patted her arm. 'Do you know the area at all?'

From what she had seen, York was very flat, with no mounts to speak of. 'I'm afraid I don't know the city very well, but I think it will suit you, Dr Fanshawe. Papa says there are some very important people here,' Laura murmured quite truthfully. They could all tell each other stories of 'when I was in India'.

Cecil moved closer and Laura tried to step back. 'I think I can say that my position is favourable. And now, I think of marrying.' He looked at her meaningfully.

'Really? I hope you'll be very happy, Doctor,' Laura said with a bright smile. 'Do we know the lady? One of our acquaintance in India, perhaps?'

'Now, now, Miss Laura, you are a tease.' Cecil was horribly arch. He hesitated. 'I really should not talk about the future at this stage, of course. But it has come to my notice that you are . . . ah . . . free from your engagement. A happy circumstance, I do believe. And so I . . . that is . . . I hope to visit your father before long. But I have said too much; my heart has ruled my head. I will leave you now, my dear. And I hope to see you again, quite soon.' Another pat on her arm, and he oozed away into the crowd, quite oblivious to Laura's reaction. Cecil must be either extremely confident and sure of his attractions, or perhaps he thought that if the colonel willed it, Laura must marry him.

As the carriage rolled them back to her uncle's house after the performance, Laura leaned back on the cushions and watched the passing lights of York reflected in the river. She felt deflated. The theatre had been a wonderful experience, but Cecil had spoiled it for her. Marriage to Dr Fanshawe! Laura felt sick at the thought that her father was scheming once again to organize his daughter's life.

'Are you tired, Laura?' Papa smiled kindly, but he was not to be trusted. 'Young Fanshawe had a lot to say to you. He seems to be doing well, and we know he's a good surgeon.' He looked over to the seats opposite, but their relations were both snoring gently. 'Now this is entirely for your own good, my girl. You should consider your future carefully. Your mother and I want to see you married to a successful man who can look after you, and of course Fanshawe is only a few years older than you are, well, about eight or ten, but that is not very much. You may need to get rid of romantic, girlish notions. Fanshawe is not handsome, to be sure, but he is very solid. A sound man.' He was sounding rather like her mother. 'We are not able to leave you a fortune, Laura, and so it is most important for you to marry well.'

'Yes, Papa,' Laura murmured, and closed her eyes. Colonel Grey was not a man to argue with. But she was not going to marry Cecil.

Brushing her hair before bed, Laura tried not to think of Fanshawe. There was something missing in York, in spite of the novelty. The truth was that York was flat without Adam Burns. Adam had a wonderful zest for life; he was a source of excitement. The thought of his dancing blue eyes and copper curls made her smile. Adam was modest, but very capable. He considered other people and could even sympathize with women and their restricted lives.

The contrast between Adam and the fussy little doctor was extreme. Cecil was so full of self-importance that he hardly noticed – really noticed – anyone else. He needed a wife, and Laura was there to hand. He probably expected her to be grateful for his attentions. What a pity, Laura sighed, that life did not work out as it should. A crofter's son was not quite the thing, of course. She must not think of Adam.

Forty miles away on the Hall estate, Adam would have spent the day driving, showing off the farms and plantations, the fields and woods of home. After the rain, the crops looked well; everything was at its spring best. Last spring she had hardly appreciated it, but Alice had persuaded her out into the fresh air . . . and then Laura had worked with Adam. An odd little pang shot through her. How she missed him! He would have so enjoyed the evening at the theatre. Adam enjoyed everything. Marriage to Adam would be heaven . . . but then, he seemed to look forward to living in a two-roomed cottage in Scotland. Not that one cared what other people thought, but the sheer discomfort . . . it would never do.

When they returned from York, Mama was still away and there was no news of Paterson. Papa wanted to settle their affairs before Mama came back, so he sent for Adam immediately. The manager came in with a cheerful look, but he started off in a rather formal way.

'Glad to see you back, sir, and Miss Grey. Now, you may prefer to have an independent valuation before the price is settled. As I mentioned, because the buyer is known to me, there may be bias, or seem to be.' He paused. 'Apart from that, Lady Forbes has had a preliminary inspection and she's interested in buying the entire estate, at what I believe is a good price, and will agree to lease it back to you. We can pay the rent from the estate income. We will need a legal agreement drawn up, of course, and she is happy for that to be done by your solicitor in consultation with hers.'

'She will buy? Ask the dear lady to luncheon!' Colonel Grey could not sit still, but paced about the study. 'Lady Forbes? Is she the widow of that clever fellow who invented a lot of fishing flies?'

'She is, sir, and she will be pleased to talk to you about them. If you'll excuse me, I will take the trap down to Ripon to collect her.' He turned to Laura in his considerate way. 'Is it convenient to provide lunch today? I believe she likes simple food, soup, something like that would be just right. But we can leave it for another day—'

'Of course we can provide a meal, Mr Burns, and I hope you will join us,' Laura said in best housekeeper style.

'Thank you.' Adam winked at Laura, and was gone. She hurried off to find Cook. A rich widow! Perhaps she was a pretty one. No doubt Adam would marry her, and then – Laura's thoughts stopped abruptly. Perhaps Adam was a schemer, after all. What could he have been up to, those weeks in Scotland?

About two hours later, the trap rolled up the drive. Laura and Papa went out to meet it and Lady Forbes was tenderly handed down. What a relief! The new owner of the Hall was old; Lady

Forbes was aged and birdlike, small and sprightly, but walking with a stick. Her bright eyes seemed to miss nothing. 'So this is Miss Grey. Your daughter is a pretty girl, Colonel. Make the most of your youth, young woman. May we take a turn in the gardens? My joints are stiff, after the journey.'

The party proceeded at a stately pace past flowerbeds and greenhouses, Lady Forbes leaning on Adam's arm. She seemed to be fond of him, but Laura could see that she liked to order him about. He accepted this gracefully, laughing and joking with her. Getting well in with the new owner, no doubt, so that he could keep his job. Laura lingered behind in the hothouse, enjoying the warmth and the scent of growing things in the moist air. Adam could show off the place without her help, she decided, and look after his future at the same time.

Lance Drake, the head gardener, peered out from behind a vine and grinned at her, his weatherbeaten face creasing into wrinkles. 'Good day, miss. Glad to see you home. So Mr Burns has brought his granny on a visit again!' The servants were not to be told of the impending sale of the estate, so naturally they would wonder at the old lady's keen interest.

Laura laughed. 'I don't think so. That is Lady Forbes, she's coming to lunch today.'

'Aye. Wants to see into everything, she's right interested in what lad's . . . er . . . Mr Burns is doing. She's his granny, all right. We heard him call her "Grandmother dear", when she came last week. So I must be right!' Mr Drake smiled again. 'Said she thought kitchen garden was grand.'

Laura's thoughts were whirling as she followed the others down to the lake. If this were true, what about the poor crofter father, the dairymaid sisters? She could not actually remember Adam talking about their humble circumstances. He had been teasing her, of course, about the 'wee but and ben'. Adam had always been reticent about his family, in fact.

The next day Adam asked Laura to redraw the map of the estate so that the latest improvements could be included, such as a new plantation of beeches. Alone with him in the farm office, she felt a sudden urge to confront him with his duplicity. 'You should have told my father that the buyer is a relative of yours.' The words came out more severely than she intended, but Laura looked Adam straight in the eye. 'Or you could have told me. I think that you and I have worked together long enough to be honest with each other.' She leaned back from the table. 'Why are you so secretive, Adam?'

The young man laughed, but he looked uncomfortable. 'I have organized a second valuation, if that worries you. I told you before that we need another opinion. But she will pay a good price and I believe your father will be happy.'

He had missed the point; he didn't care how she felt. 'Adam, it's not the money, at all! I trust you to look after Papa's interests; you always do. But it's the thought that you have been . . . almost deceiving us. Letting us think that your family was poor. There was talk of your father being a poor crofter, or a weaver. If Lady Forbes is your grandmother, then your family is wealthy.' Laura turned away to hide a tear. 'We . . . I didn't know the real Adam Burns. You pretended to be someone else.'

The manager put down his files and extended his hands to Laura. 'Come for a walk across the park. I think one of the Highland cows has a wee calf.' His voice was warm, affectionate.

They walked in silence through the farmyard, under a misty sunshine. When they were out of earshot of the farm men, Adam looked at Laura. 'I am sorry, you know, Laura. I can see how it looks to you. But to tell you the truth, I have never mentioned my family because I want to stand on my own two feet.'

'What do you mean?' They came to the park gate and leaned on it.

'Well, the family sort of dominated me, in Scotland. You should know how that feels! My father has a couple of big estates and I am Grandmother's heir. In Ayrshire, I can't move for family. And what was worse, some of them were wanting to marry me off to this or that young lass . . . yes, it happens to men as well, you know! So I planned to make a success of my work here and to be judged on my own achievements, or lack of them, rather than on five hundred years of ancestors. And eventually, to make my own choice of a wife.'

He had probably made his choice already. He said he had a lady in mind. Laura swallowed. 'I see. You wanted to be plain Adam, and get on with your life in your own way. I can understand, now.' But it was still deception.

Adam's smile was relieved. 'I thought you would. Dr Dent knows my family, of course. He's been fishing with my father in Scotland. He got me the job with the colonel . . . hey, there's the wee Highlander!' A delightful little creature bounded past, ginger and furry, closely followed by the anxious mother. 'We had better stay at this side of the gate; she might be over-protective. Cows can be aggressive when they have small calves. You can't blame them, it's a survival instinct. But don't go anywhere near the herd with Hamish.'

Entranced, Laura watched the new calf for several minutes, and then sat on a fallen tree. Adam sat down beside her. The sun was shining more strongly as it climbed towards noon. The heavy scent of bluebells saturated the air and their colour glowed with brilliance in the dappled shade of the birch trees.

Very gently, Adam took Laura's hand. 'I knew how you felt about Paterson, and being expected to conform . . . so, Miss Grey, I politely request your permission,' – he rolled his Scottish 'r's – 'to ask your father for your hand in marriage. He may now appreciate that I can manage to support you.'

Laura's heart beat faster than ever before as Adam leaned over and kissed her. Then he laughed, and the moment was spoiled. 'It is the best outcome for you financially, after all. People must be sensible about money.' It struck a jarring note on the edge of a bluebell wood, in what should have been a romantic moment.

'Adam, I have had too much advice about money and I am not impressed. I would be a fortune hunter if I married you now, to save the family from poverty. I will never try to snare a rich husband! I despise such things!' Laura felt herself getting angry and she twisted her bonnet in her hands.

The cold-hearted monster only laughed at that; he seemed to be enjoying himself. 'Remember, your Papa and Mama will probably give us their blessing.'

It was time to be cool and rational. 'Papa and Mama will be quite happy if they can lease back the estate. I do not wish to be part of the arrangement, thank you. I am not a commodity, Adam. And in any case,' Laura stood up to go, 'I intend to go to the college you told me of, where ladies learn gardening and design.'

Surprisingly, Adam agreed. 'I'm sure you would enjoy that. I will find out more about it.' He rose from the log and gave Laura his hand. 'I promise not to talk about marriage any more, Laura, since it offends you.' His smile was as open and sunny as ever.

Well, that was a relief; they walked back to the Hall, talking about farming. But wait a minute . . . as she went into the house Laura stood still. Adam had asked her to marry him. Not some lady he had in mind, but Laura Grey. How surprising!

It was hard to get Adam out of her mind. His dancing blue eyes came between Laura and the book she was reading several times that evening. Thinking back, it was the money aspect that had offended her. It was true that Adam's wealth was convenient, but it was not romantic. Laura had never been in love before, and now she knew what it felt like, she wanted a romantic relationship, nothing to do with money. It would be too convenient to marry the heir to the Hall; her family would be so pleased, but he had seemed to give up very easily. Had Adam proposed marriage just to ease his conscience, so that he could marry elsewhere? Perhaps that was the truth behind it all; but Laura felt as though her heart might be broken.

Alice had told her that the best cure for troubled spirits was walking, so Laura walked. Over the next few days, she and Hamish the terrier traversed most of the paths about the estate, although she was careful to keep clear of the Highland cows, now that they had started to calve.

The trip to York and the subsequent events had pushed Bradley Paterson to the back of her mind, but Laura was still deeply uneasy about him and she knew that Adam was worried, too. There was a shadow hanging over them both. 'I can't understand why the police haven't caught up with him by now. Surely they can find out where he is?' she asked Adam one day, when she noticed him looking to each side as he drove down the road. They were going to view progress on the new house.

'From what I can tell, the Masham police didn't report him at the time. The colonel told them it was a case of unfortunate behaviour after the man had drunk too much wine, and so, as he was gentry and well known, they decided to overlook the incident. But later, the workers at the farm reported him missing. Then, it was found that he had moved most of his money overseas and left instructions for the estate to be sold, with the proceeds to be forwarded to a Swiss bank. I heard that while you were in York.'

'So you think he's left the country? I do hope so!'

Adam frowned. 'Until we have proof, we can't be sure we've seen the last of Paterson.'

Laura decided to keep to walks on their own land, and to be careful to get home before dusk. Surely she should be safe on the Birchwood Hall estate? But she was unprepared, when trouble came one sunny day. She was walking along at the edge of a wood, when strong arms seized her from behind and a cloth was thrown over her head. Before she had time to think, she was bundled into what seemed to be a cart. There were creaking sounds and a strong smell of horses.

'Got you at last, Laura!' It was Paterson's deep voice. 'Tie her hands, Thornby.' When that was done the cloth was taken from her head and before she could move, Paterson pulled her into his arms and crushed her against him.

Where was the dog? But Hamish had vanished into the wood,

chasing a rabbit, some minutes before. 'Hamish, Hamish! Come here, boy!' Laura called as loudly as she could, before a hand was clamped over her mouth. If only the dog would come back, to distract him! Hamish had seemed to enjoy biting Paterson.

'Get on, quick as you can,' Paterson ordered and the cart began to move off, driven by the grinning red-haired groom. Laura was pulled down behind some sacks of corn; she would never be seen, even if a keeper came along. Paterson was wearing a cloth cap and workman's clothes; he looked like a carter. If anyone was looking for him, this must be a perfect disguise. No one would recognize the elegant landowner in the dress of a workman.

He held her in a close embrace. 'I have had several weeks to think about what to do,' Paterson said quite quietly. 'At first I wanted to kill you, and that upstart manager too. Yes, I took a shot at you; it was the only chance I got.' He took his hand away from her mouth, because Laura was doing her best to bite him.

It would be dangerous to panic. It might be good to keep him talking, in the hope that Hamish would come back, although the little dog could do nothing against two men. There was not much chance of anyone from the estate coming by. 'But you have given so much to charity, and looked after your workers; how can you be so cruel?' Laura twisted her head to look up at him and she could see the cruel lines in the handsome face.

'Laura, when will you understand? I am obsessed with you, woman! I can think of nothing else! But now the way forward is clear. I am going to take you away with me, Laura, willing or unwilling. We are going to Jamaica, to be married there. And I intend to lock you up until you see sense. You will be mine, or one day, you will probably die. I am not prepared to give you up to anyone else. The choice is yours, my darling.'

NINETEEN

Laura's mouth was dry with fear; this was her worst nightmare, suddenly realized. She had been so foolish. She should have known better than to imagine that he would quietly give up and go away. His single-minded urgency had always frightened her; why had she taken such a risk? Paterson was smiling now with triumph. But she must not panic, she must try to find a way out.

They were clopping through the park now, down to the back entrance, no doubt looking like an innocent farm cart, going about estate business. Laura sat up cautiously and peered above the sacks, but there was no one in sight. She fiddled with the ropes round her wrists, but they were so tight that they cut into her. If she got the chance to run away, she wouldn't get far with her hands tied.

'So you do kill people,' she said quietly, between parched lips. 'Alice was right.'

Paterson looked older and much rougher than she remembered him, in farm clothes and with stubble on his chin. He frowned at her then and shook his head. 'Accidents have happened, I admit, but I've never killed anyone in cold blood. I could not kill you, Laura, unless I lost my temper. Unfortunately I can be violent; it's something I can't help. And that might happen one day, if you continue to resist me.' There was something abnormal about his matter-of-fact tone. 'So – it will be dangerous to resist, sweetheart. I mean it.' The dark eyes were almost pleading. 'Just give in, Laura, give up . . . you will be very happy, I know … meanwhile, I suppose you will have to be drugged, for the journey. It will calm you down, in case you try to escape.' He smiled. 'I have thought it all out, most carefully. Thornby will travel with us as my man, and between us I think we can handle you, Miss Laura.'

How foolish she had been, to walk on her own so far from the house! Laura thought of jumping from the cart, but they would only pick her up again. It had high sides and with her hands still tied, she was bound to hurt herself.

'But when this is discovered, when they find I am missing, they will come after you, of course. And they will lock you up for the rest of your life. Please see reason … you can't take some-one away against their will!' They probably would catch him in the end, but it could be too late to save her. Laura was staring at him, willing him to be rational. She felt like screaming, but that might make him violent.

'I've burned my boats here already, Laura, although nothing has been proved against me as yet. Too many people would like to see Bradley Paterson brought down!' There was a wild look in his eyes that she had not seen before. 'I think of going eventually to some country where British law cannot follow.'

'You want to be on the run for the rest of your life? Surely, if you stay here you have such a good reputation that you can live down the last few months. Take me home now, Bradley, and you can start again. Let's go to the house and talk to my father. He will help you.' Laura felt herself shaking.

'Laura, you are mine – all mine. No one else shall have you! Mine in life … or in death.'

Now she was sure he was mad.

'Hamish! Oh, Hamish!' Back from rabbiting, Hamish had arrived on the scene; realizing that Laura was in the cart, he bounced up and down at the side, trying to jump in. Thornby hit out with his whip and the dog howled. Just at that moment, the Highland cattle were crossing the road with their calves. The dog's howls upset them and the cows turned and came towards the vehicle, tossing their horns, the long hair streaming in the wind. They were a fearsome sight.

Thornby did the wrong thing; he lashed out with the whip at the leading cow and, enraged, she bellowed, pawed the ground and came on. Another cow hit the side of the cart with her ferocious horns and the horse reared in fright. Jim Thornby had been standing up to use the whip and he lost his balance, falling into the road. But now he was between one of the cows and her calf; she charged at him. He rolled over and Paterson jumped down to help him, grabbing the whip and swearing at the cattle. The cows backed off a little.

The big carthorse was terrified by now. It reared again and the harness broke; it turned and galloped off down the drive towards the farm, away from the cattle. One of the cows pushed the shafts with her horns and tipped up the cart; Laura was able to slide out and then looked round in terror for Paterson, but he had been trampled by the horse in its panic. Both men lay still on the road.

Laura's danger now was from the enraged cows, but Hamish was drawing them off, running away so that they would chase him. To the dog, it was all a game. It had happened so quickly that it was like a dream. Laura slipped through a fence into the wood, which was difficult with bound wrists, and after a few minutes Hamish joined her. The cows could not reach them now.

Weak with relief, Laura bent down to the little dog and he licked her face. 'Come on, boy,' she whispered. 'Keep quiet, don't bark.' They hurried quickly into the trees, out of sight of the road. They would not catch her now; she was determined to escape. She stopped and listened, but there was only the sound of bellowing cattle.

Laura and the dog were halfway home when Adam appeared with two farm workers, having caught the runaway horse. She stepped out of the trees and Adam was horrified. 'I had no idea you were down here!' He cut through the ropes with a pocket knife and rubbed her wrists gently to get the circulation back. They could still hear the cows roaring in the park, thoroughly unsettled; even the calves were joining in.

'Adam, I am so glad you are here!' Now that it was over, Laura felt her head spinning and she almost fell. When he heard the story, Adam sent on the workers with sticks, warning them to be careful of the cows, and walked back to the house supporting Laura, who was trembling, weak with relief. 'He was going to take me to Jamaica!' she whispered. 'Do be careful, Adam, he's dangerous. He looked to be injured, but I didn't wait to find out. They were both lying there.' she shuddered.

'Don't worry, Laura, we'll go back with plenty of men, and I'd better send for the doctor. But we certainly won't let him get away this time. We need to know just where he is.'

Later in the day, a sombre Dr Dent presented himself at the Hall to see Laura and her father. 'Mr Paterson and the man, Thornby, were taken to hospital, of course,' he reported. 'But I am afraid that Mr Paterson died – he was dead when he arrived; I think the horse had kicked his head.' He paused. 'It's a sad end for him, but I suppose it's a relief, in a way. I think by what I hear that his madness was getting worse.'

Laura's mother came home a few days later, and was happy to find that her clever husband had arranged all their affairs to her satisfaction. But even better, the colonel had discovered that Adam Burns was a rich young man with land of his own in Scotland, and that Lady Forbes was his grandmother. It was all too delightful, and Laura's head ached with all the good advice.

'How very satisfactory! There will be no changes to speak of, and the servants need know nothing. I am sure it will be quite easy; I am much relieved in my mind.'

'But Papa wanted me to marry Dr Fanshawe,' Laura pointed out demurely.

'Nonsense, child.' Mrs Grey's bosom heaved with anticipation. 'Such a handsome young man, Mr Burns, and so polite and well-mannered! I always knew he was a superior type of person, and he seems to like you, Laura; you must do your best to attract him; it would be a brilliant marriage for you, and you can then settle down and produce some grandchildren for Papa and me; it's about time you thought seriously about your future; your Papa says that he may already have a bride in mind, but however it should not be too late.'

Laura decided to ignore this advice. Her mother's attitude to Adam was now even more embarrassing. In any case, she was not going to be in love, at least not for years and years. Adam Burns was not romantic enough, as it turned out. His matter-of-fact, casual proposal had been a disappointment, he thought like an accountant, but Laura would not fade away with grief. Instead, she would go to the college in Berkshire and study landscaping, and become a no-nonsense bluestocking, as Papa called clever women.

Worse than the lack of romance was the deception. It had been devious of Adam to pretend to be the son of a crofter. Laura had imagined the struggle on the hillside, the scrimping to send the boy to university, but it had not been like that at all. She would forget about Adam and keep herself busy until it was time to go to Berkshire.

The colonel took his family out on several visits to the neighbours; evidently he could face them, now that he knew the Greys were staying at the Hall. Laura took a notebook with her and much to her mother's dismay, she sketched details of the gardens they visited. Taking tea on the lawn with Mama had never been a favourite occupation of Laura's, chatting languidly about how to help the poor. But now the visits held a great deal of interest and there was always something to learn.

'Laura dear, come back and sit down,' her mother wailed. 'It is not polite to go off like that, peering here and there and analysing people's gardens and talking to their servants, it is most unladylike.' But the owners often asked her to come again, and offered plant cuttings.

Coming back to the Hall full of enthusiasm after one of these visits, Laura had to talk to Adam about what she had seen. Mama complained about Laura talking to funny old men about gardening, but Adam understood. She wanted to make their lake more picturesque. 'I think a little summer house, built of wood, might be pretty, at the point where the lake bends round into the woods. What do you think?'

They were in the farm office, and Adam stood up and went to the wall map of the estate. 'Nice idea, but we can't get over there, the undergrowth is too thick. I wonder . . . could we go by boat?' He grinned at Laura. 'Would you risk your life in a rowing boat?'

There was an old boat by the lake and Mr Drake was persuaded to haul it up and varnish it. Laura thought that boating might be pleasant, and once the summer house was built it could be visited by boat. It would be good to invite some of the younger neighbours, those interested in landscapes, and give them tea in the summerhouse.

Rain held up any outdoor activity for over a week, but it cleared eventually and Adam told Laura one Saturday morning that the boat was ready, if she would like to inspect the summer-house site. She was determined to be practical; boats were not particularly romantic, she would take stout boots, a notebook and a pencil. 'And of course, any improvements like this will increase the value of the estate,' she pointed out to Adam, to prove that she too could talk like an accountant. 'No, Hamish, you can't come along. You might upset the boat.' There was a mysterious string trailing from the stem and a rope at the front end; there must be much to learn about boating. The smallest boat Laura had travelled on was the ship back from India.

Laura brought a wicker picnic basket from the kitchen and Adam stowed it carefully under the seat. He was obviously used to this. 'We lived in boats, when I was a wee laddie, on various lochs in Scotland,' he admitted, taking the oars.

Laura sat back on the cushions and watched the familiar landscape glide past. 'The gardens look very different from the water, and the park looks larger from here.' She could just see the Highland cattle in the distance; the colonel had wanted to get rid of them after the catastrophe, but Laura had argued that they were not normally dangerous, and should be kept, but perhaps fenced off from the road through the park. After all, they had helped to save her from Paterson. She still felt cold when she thought of her narrow escape from Jamaica.

The sun was quite hot and there was very little breeze; the lake was mirror-like except where ripples from the oars disturbed the surface. Spring blossoms peeped out here and there from the woods.

Adam stopped rowing. 'I rather think this has been done before . . . see that grouping of trees and the way the lake winds in and out? It's been planned very carefully to be seen from the water, although it looks so natural. But that must have been many years ago, and a summerhouse will certainly add to the effect.'

He rowed on and the creak of the oars hardly disturbed the peace of the day. Birds flew among the trees and a thrush sang sweetly as they moved slowly past. 'It is very beautiful,' Laura admitted. 'We'll probably see more birds and animals than we would if we were walking through the wood.'

'Is there anywhere you would rather be?' Adam beamed as he looked around. 'I wouldn't be anywhere else in the world – rowing over a lake with a beautiful woman and a packed lunch!'

'Yes, it's a good thing we brought lunch,' agreed Laura, doggedly practical.

Adam kept fairly close to the shore; soon they were passing the bluebell wood and the heavy scent floated out to them over the water from the flowers, shimmering under the trees. 'A lovely colour . . . almost the colour of your eyes,' Adam said, unexpectedly for such a commercially minded person. On the next section the vegetation was thinner and Adam suggested that they should tie up the boat and explore on foot.

The morning went by quickly; Laura was absorbed in sketching and planning. They embarked again and Adam rowed quietly up one of the inlets and into the shade of some overhanging willows that leaned out over the water, the gnarled trunks showing their great age. Laura looked at the basket. 'Time for lunch, do you think?'

Adam put the oars up and said deliberately, 'In a moment. Let's just listen, for a minute or two.'

They sat quiet, the boat rocking gently, and Laura felt herself relax. Alice, too had appreciated the value of sitting still, listening to nature. There were rustlings of creatures in the wood, but most of the birds were now silent. A brood of swans sailed across the water, swimming behind their stately parents in a dutiful line, round the corner and out of sight. For the first time since her escape, she felt totally at peace.

Adam moved slightly. 'Is this just a little romantic, do you think?'

Laura looked at him, surprised. 'But you are not romantic, Adam. You are a . . . realist.' He was laughing at her again, thinking she had foolish notions.

The young man sighed. 'I knew I'd said the wrong things to you, the other day in the wood; I can be too flippant. Laura, can we start again?'

'I don't know what you mean, Adam. Don't spoil a lovely day, I don't want to quarrel, it's so peaceful here. I feel happy.'

Adam Burns looked contrite. 'Quarrelling was far from my mind . . . I love you, Laura. I want to spend the rest of my life with you, even though it will please your parents so much! There I go again. On this perfect day, and in this lovely place, I ask you most seriously, forgetting about family, money or land – just think about you and me – do you love me, Laura? Have I any hope?' He had never before looked so earnest.

It was time to be honest. 'Yes, Adam, I do! But—' Laura felt herself blushing as Adam leaned over and took her hand.

'That is all that matters, in the end. No buts, Laura; everything else can be worked out. We can do so many wonderful things together! I'd love to take you to Scotland . . . please marry me!'

'Yes, Adam, I will marry you. Oh!' Laura gave a little cry as the boat rocked dangerously. Adam was moving over to sit beside her and soon his arm was round her waist. She had never been so happy before, still at peace, even though her heart was beating quickly.

At length Adam withdrew his arm and carefully he pulled on the string at the back of the boat. A bottle came bobbing to the surface. 'Champagne, my dearest, to celebrate our special day.'

Laura opened the basket and found that it held two glasses. 'You planned this!' she accused him.

'I admit it. I wanted to get you away, just for a little while, from the Hall and its problems.' He poured two glasses and they toasted each other; the golden bubbles were perfect for the occasion. 'I have loved you for a long time, Laura, ever since we started working together. But at first there was Paterson; the marriage was arranged and I could do nothing about it. Once Paterson was gone, and after I put my foot in it by talking about money, well, I thought you might need time to adjust, to enjoy your freedom. But when I found you after your escape from Paterson, I realized that I couldn't wait any longer.' His eyes were full of love as they looked into hers. 'Laura, we'll have a wonderful life together! Now, where are the chicken sandwiches?'

On the same day as Adam rowed Laura over the lake, a Saturday outing of a different kind was taking place in Masham. Alice was surprised to be called from her herb stall, but Ruby said she could manage the stall alone. 'Jacob needs a hand, love. He's at our place with a horse.'

It was rather a strange request, but Alice hurried over the square and down the lane to the farm. Gabriel's cart was out in the yard and Jacob was there, backing a horse into the shafts.

Not Brownie, she noted thankfully, but an older and wiser horse that Gabriel drove. The farmer was nowhere to be seen. 'Gone to Fearby with a load of turnips,' Jacob said briefly. 'He asked me to go over to Ellershaw for him, and Ruby thought you might like to come. There's gooseberries to pick in the garden there, and they need a woman's hand.'

'You seem to spend a lot of Saturdays helping Gabriel,' Alice observed. Since the night of his accident, Jacob had been friendly, relaxed enough, but nothing more. She was quite happy to leave things as they were; it was pleasant to have a friend, after all. His normal shyness had probably come back, and he had not invited her to 'walk out' with him.

'Now, lass, have you got a basket for the berries? Ruby's packed us some scones and such, as we'll not be back until night. You might need a shawl for the ride back.' Jacob turned to smile at Alice and she thought how organized he was, how practical.

In a few minutes Alice was ready. 'Right, Fowler. Have you got a map? You might lose your way, else.' They had teased him about needing to be rescued from the common.

Jacob laughed and shook the reins, and they clattered out of the yard. The cart had two comfortable seats at the front and, perched up there, Alice could see more of the countryside than usual. 'There's a dozen sheep at Ellershaw that Gabriel wants fetching down to Masham, and we'll have to round them up. They tell me you're good with sheep, Alice.' His eyes were on the road ahead.

'Well, I'll do my best, but I can't run as fast as a dog.' The cart moved on through the golden morning, up the steep road past the castle wall that Alice had walked so often, and out onto the moorland, where the little farms were scattered, the houses huddled into sheltering banks. Ellershaw was one of those little holdings, more sheltered than most and with a band of woodland to the windward side.

'I thought Gabriel would have found a tenant before now,' Alice remarked as they turned into the farm lane. 'It's a neat little place.' Jacob nodded, but said nothing.

The sheep were confined in a small paddock near the house, a lovely sunny spot with a small beck running through it. They were quiet crossbred animals and they would be easy enough to load. Alice looked round the little paddock. 'We could have our bite to eat here, if you like.'

'Aye.' Jacob was quiet; he seemed preoccupied. 'But if we go into the kitchen we can boil a kettle for a cup of tea, lass.'

In the freshly whitewashed kitchen, Jacob lit the fire while Alice looked round. 'I hardly like to come in here . . . it looks as though someone lives here. Has Gabriel found a tenant, then? He never said anything to me about it.' There were red geraniums on the window sill; the big deal table was scrubbed white, and on the dresser was a gleaming set of willow-pattern plates. 'We shouldn't be here, Jacob! It's someone else's house!'

'Sit down; here's your cup of tea. And promise not to laugh at me, lass.' Jacob stood with his back to the fire, looking down at her. 'The truth is, I am the new tenant of Ellershaw. Hundred and fifty acres, with some good meadows on bottom land. I've agreed to take it, as long as . . . as long as. . . .' he faltered and looked grim.

'As long as what? This is a surprise, Fowler. You're a dark horse!' Alice kept her tone light, but she felt hurt that nobody had told her. It was a big step for Jacob to take, and she thought he could have talked it over. She took a sip of tea. Well, it was his business, after all, his and Gabriel's.

Jacob was still looking at Alice intently. 'As long as you'll be here, Alice. I want you to share it with me, we can do it together. The little garth where the sheep are will be perfect for growing lavender . . . I asked Mr Burns about it.' Jacob had blushed a deep red. 'About what sort of soil that lavender likes, and that . . . oh heck, lass, I can't seem to . . . I'm too shy . . . but shall we get wed?'

There was only one thing to do. Alice went round the table and put her arms round the poor embarrassed man, holding him

223

close as she had that night on the common.

'You always said you were very happy to be single, so I thought—' Jacob whispered.

Alice looked up into his face and smiled. 'I am not laughing, Jacob, but I might cry with happiness. Do you love me, Fowler?'

'Aye, little lavender girl. I'll love you for ever. There's nobody like you, in the whole world.' Then Jacob gave Alice a very bold kiss.

I a 5/11